Praise for *Red Dagger*

"A brilliant writer, Dan Wooding, who has authored over 40 books, has written a wonderful, compelling, evangelistic novel about Middle East terrorism. I highly recommend it."
   - Dr. Ted Baehr, Founder and Publisher of Movieguide® and chairman of the Christian Film & Television Commission®

"Dan Wooding's latest book, *Red Dagger*, is a gripping novel about terror, betrayal and redemption. Much of it is set in Gaza, but also features a Northern Ireland terrorist and an American journalist who, after moving to London, finds himself spending too much time in a bar called 'The Stab in the Back' with other drunken hacks. The conclusion of the book has a most dramatic twist that held my attention right to the very end. I enthusiastically endorse *Red Dagger*, which is written by one of the world's most traveled journalists."
   - Pat Boone, entertainer

"Terrorism is a dangerous subject both in reality and in fiction. To bring Christianity in as a major part of the plot is potentially even more dangerous, but Dan Wooding portrays all his characters as both very real and very believable in this novel that literally sets off at a tremendous pace from the very first page. I found myself thinking very visually whilst reading it and that's the secret of any good novel."
   - Rick Wakeman, world-class keyboard player and composer

SOME BOOKS BY DAN WOODING

Junkies Are People Too
Stresspoint
I Thought Terry Dene Was Dead
Exit the Devil (with Trevor Dearing)
Train of Terror (with Mini Loman)
Rick Wakeman, the Caped Crusader
King Squealer (with Maurice O'Mahoney)
Farewell Leicester Square (with Henry Hollis)
Uganda Holocaust (with Ray Barnett)
Miracles in Sin City (with Howard Cooper)
God's Smuggler to China (with Brother David and Sara Bruce)
Prophets of Revolution (with Peter Asael Gonzales)
Brother Andrew
Guerrilla for Christ (with Salu Daka Ndebele)
Million Dollar Promise (with Duane Logsdon)
Twenty-Six Lead Soldiers
Secret Missions
Singing in the Dark (with Barry Taylor)
Lost For Words (with Stuart Mill)
Let There Be Light (with Roger Oakland)
Rock Priest (with David Pierce)
He Intends Victory
Only Believe (with Hannu Haukka)
A Light to India (with Lillian Doerksen)
Blind Faith (with Anne Wooding)
Never Say Never
From Tabloid to Truth
God's Ambassadors in Japan

RED DAGGER

A NOVEL

by

Dan Wooding

Tanswell Books
California, USA

Red Dagger
First published in 2010 by
Tanswell Books
PO Box 609
Lake Forest, CA 92609-0609
USA

© Dan Wooding 2010
Phone: +1 (949) 380-1558
Email: danjuma1@aol.com
Website: www.assistnews.net

ISBN: 978-0-578-05653-1

This book is a work of fiction. Names, characters, places and
incidents are the product of the author's imagination and are used
fictitiously. Any resemblance to actual events, locales or persons,
living or dead, is purely coincidental.

Acknowledgements

I wish to express my thanks to the following people who played a wonderful role in helping me complete this book: Dr. Ted Baehr, Andrew Wooding (my son), Michael Ireland, Jeremy Reynalds.

Contents

1
Happy Birthday, Pastor Spy

The date was Friday, February 26, 1993 and in New York City, a truck bomb parked below the North Tower of the World Trade Center went off, killing six and injuring over a thousand.

Although this was good news for many of her colleagues, it was far from the thoughts of Reem Rudeniah who impatiently drummed her fingers on the side wall of the impromptu cell on the second floor of a seedy flat in a dingy apartment building in Gaza City. At 25 years of age, her tall statuette figure, long black shiny hair wrapped in a keffiah, piercing brown eyes, and a shawal dress with the slogan, "WE SHALL RETURN" embroidered on it, made her a figure that could turn any man's eye - all except the bumbling Palestinian jailer.

The bearded man, who knew her reputation for violence, clumsily inserted the oversize key in the door.

"Hurry up, you imbecile," she snapped coldly, her patience already on edge as she stood behind the squat ugly man with a panting animal face and piggish eyes.

The door creaked open and Reem peered in to get her first look at the man she was to "crack." In the half-light of the drab green room, she could barely make out the form of an elderly man sitting on a filthy floor; his left arm handcuffed to a radiator. As she got closer, Reem saw he had close-shaven white hair, and a face lined and haggard.

"Happy birthday, Pastor Spy," she called out cheerfully, a false warmness masking her real intention. "Guard, bring in the birthday cake."

As the order left her tight lips, the uncouth guard appeared at the doorway bearing a cake all aglow. There were seven lit candles, each one marking ten years of this man's traumatic life. The candles were already melting and the wax was dripping onto the cake.

"Blow them out, Pastor, and make a wish," suggested Reem, as the jailer laid the cake down on a small wooden table at the side of the bed. The candlelight flickered, casting eerie shadows around the cell. She could just make out a rat scurrying out of the light and disappearing down a hole in the wall.

"You mean, like your people have tried to snuff out my life and all those I have met since being here," responded the American, as he shifted his weight on the floor and brushed aside a cockroach.

"Blow them out yourself!" There was a savage bite to his voice.

Reem Rudeniah effectively controlled her temper and smiled sweetly. Taking a deep breath she blew them out, extinguishing the remaining light in the cell. She edged her way through the ominous darkness to the wall and flicked the switch, lighting up the bare bulb in the room.

Reem Rudeniah was in Gaza on a special mission. She had been in Damascus with a group of terrorists who had devised a plan called "Operation Red Dagger" which, if it succeeded, would wipe out some of the world's leaders in one stroke and see Islam become the dominant world power.

After the relative success of various Jihadist attacks around the world, the group who also called themselves "Red Dagger" had decided that now they needed an even more daring plan to finalize their take-over of the world.

The formidable Reem Rudeniah, born Reem Salameh, was to be a key player in the dangerous game, and the plotters all knew she was up to it. She had been summoned to Damascus to meet with the man who had become her step-father. When she arrived at the dirty hotel building at 4:00 P.M. that afternoon, she felt she was wasting time as she was supposed to be in Prague on a very special assignment - to change history!

"This is ridiculous," she muttered to herself.

It was difficult to tolerate the demands of superiors when they interfered with her objective of arranging the calculated wipeout of world leaders such as American President Lincoln Patrick, British Prime Minister Anthony Steele and German Chancellor Gertrud Schmeling.

* * * * *

As Reem walked down the grimy green corridor of the run-down building, lined with frayed red carpet, past the armed guards packed in like a subway station at rush hour, the dank, musty smell overwhelmed her, bringing back vivid memories of her mother and father looking desperately at her in their last moments, as they faced eternity at the hands of a group of "Red Dagger" killers, of which she was a part.

Desperately trying to shake the haunting remembrance from her mind, Reem reached the room where they were to meet and rapped on the door.

"Come," the deep baritone voice said from inside. Ibrahim Rudeniah stood up as Reem walked through the door and strode over to her. "Good to see you daughter. Please sit down."

Ibrahim had been her teacher in "Middle East Peace Studies" at the Gaza University and now he had adopted her to be his own daughter.

"Daughter, we have a problem which we are hoping you can help us with," said Rudeniah, lighting up a cigarette and drawing deeply on it. Reem allowed her eyes to sweep the room. She noted that the furniture was dark, heavy, and highly lacquered. The upholstery was plush, but somber.

"The reason I have brought you back here is that we have captured from his 'home in Jerusalem, an American pastor who refuses to admit he is an American spy," continued Rudeniah. "We managed to spring him from his church, which we know is his 'spy' headquarters and now the world assumes that he is dead. But he is too valuable to kill at the moment as we believe he has been spying on us and we need to know what he has discovered. I understand today is his birthday...give him our regards."

The "Red Dagger" leader wore a hard, phlegmatic expression as he continued. "He is our hostage now and we want to make sure we get some powerful information from him before we 'sell' him to the highest bidder," he explained.

Reem was handed a brown manila file to study. It read, BECKETT, JOSEPH. She took the well-thumbed dossier and began ploughing through the ocean of papers that had been compiled over the years. It told how this Baptist pastor had come to Jerusalem to take over a church there, but had been a constant visitor to Gaza and the West Bank to supposedly meet with Baptist leaders.

"He is definitely a spy, but refuses to admit it!" concluded the writer of the dossier. "He has a mania of grandeur. He says he is a pastor, but we know that is just a front!"

* * * * *

Back in Gaza, Reem sighed and asked herself, "Why, oh why, wouldn't this man just confess to his 'sins' and then go free?"

She pulled up a crudely made wooden chair and tried to smile in a friendly fashion, something that was not easy for her.

"Joseph," she began softly, "I can call you Joseph, can't I? My name is Reem and I am your friend. I have come to help you."

The old pastor sat motionless.

"How would you like to return to the States?" she said. Reem gazed at the man's impassive face for any sign of a positive reaction. "That was your wish, wasn't it, when I blew out the candles?"

Beckett stared straight ahead as if thinking of something else. He had received the same offer many times since his kidnapping.

"Joseph, I know you would like to spend the final days of your life with your family back home in America," said Reem softly, moving closer to Beckett's face. "Just tell me what information the Americans wanted you to get and you will be home before the week is out."

Beckett remained silent, so she pressed on. "We know you were working for the CIA. All you have to do is admit your guilt and we can return you to your home in Wisconsin."

Beckett smiled wryly.

"Why do you smile?" Reem demanded angrily, her temper by now burning on a short fuse. "Don't you know that I can decide whether you live or die?"

"You can kill my body, but you will never kill my soul," retorted Beckett. "We both know you will never let me go, because your colleagues have already announced to the world that I am dead. How then could you produce me after all this time? What would you say in explanation?"

13

Beckett pondered a thought that had just struck him. "You may have declared me dead, but my corpse just won't lie still."

Joseph Beckett was a living rebuke to all those who had come in touch with him. He had suffered tremendously at the hands of his captors, but would not show hatred or cry out for mercy from his torturers.

"Mr. Beckett, your file says that you were sent to Jerusalem by the American 'warmongers' to discover the leaders of our group so then we could be wiped out," said Reem with a conspiratorial air. "Is that true?"

With infinite patience, the pastor responded. "You people cannot understand that a person would do something purely for the good of others," he stated. "I am a Christian and the Bible says in John 15, verse 13, '*Greater love has no one than this; that he lay down his life for his friends.*' The Jews were my friends. That's why I did it!"

Reem was playing a deadly game of chess with this man and was aware that she was losing each move. She found her voice, and her temper, rising as he continued.

"All you people care about is yourselves and spreading your ridiculous message of hate," said Beckett, leaping to his feet and pointing a quivering finger at her. "I don't see that you and yours are any better than the Nazis we fought against in World War II. You hate Jews, just like they did, and you also hate the God of the Bible!

"I came to Jerusalem with a message of God's Love for God's chosen people," he continued. "Surely, even you can understand that. I was trying to do good, but I don't think the word is in your vocabulary. You exterminate people like me. Still you may destroy my body, but you will never destroy my soul!"

Reem was by now tight-lipped with agitation as she vainly tried to control her temper. Finally, it erupted. "Beckett," she spluttered, "you are a stupid old man. All you have to do is to confirm our information, and you won't."

"I have no information to give," the American responded curtly. "But I want to ask you a question."

She looked blankly at him.

"I want to know if you are human or not; if you actually feel the pain and suffering that you, and your kind, dole out to people. Or, have you been programmed so much that you are now just a robot? What brought you to do such a terrible kind of work? What drives you and those like you to cause pain and death with such relish?"

"I do it for my religion; the religion that will soon rule the world," she responded smugly. "You see us as terrorists, but your country was founded by terrorists. Didn't your founding fathers take up arms? You wouldn't have America if these men had not fought against the British, your oppressors at the time. We are doing just the same here in Palestine. We are fighting for our freedom against the Zionist oppressors and all those who support them, including your country."

Reem smiled, feeling that she had scored a knockout punch, but Beckett wasn't finished yet.

"I agree that our country was born out of revolution, but we fought against soldiers, not innocent men, women and children like you do," he said. "You send off your suicide bombers who use their bodies as weapons and don't care who they kill. So many of your people dream of suicide, but don't you know that suicide is regarded as an 'unforgivable sin' in Islam. You, and your kind, are just puppets with evil men and women behind you pulling the strings. I think those pulling your strings are very evil indeed!

"Don't you realize that the more you people kill others, the more the light within you is being extinguished until you all become completely dark?"

Beckett paused briefly then allowed a huge smile to crease his line-worn face. "Well, at least you have done something that our Lord spoke about."

Reem looked puzzled, so the pastor explained. "Jesus said, '*I was in prison, and you visited me.*' Thank you for visiting me!"

Reem winced and decided she could get no further with the stubborn old man. She felt the need of an urgent drink, so she signaled the guard to let her out.

"Goodnight, Mr. Beckett, I'll be back," she said as she beat a hasty retreat, leaving the guard to slam the heavy door behind her.

"Think about what we have discussed, Ms. Persecutor," were the parting words of the pastor. "Think deeply!"

Beckett's words had hit Reem like a shower of ice. She tried to shake off the impact that Joseph Beckett had had on her. He was not the first person she had interviewed who was not cowed by her threats. Each time she went head-to-head with a Christian leader, they had showed no fear at all. There were periods when she was overwhelmed by their bravery...until she was again overwhelmed by her deep-seated hatred for all Christians and Jews whom she called "misguided people."

Some years before her encounter with Beckett, Reem had watched with morbid fascination as electrodes were attached to a Palestinian pastor's head and then the electricity was turned on. She was involved by now in an advanced study of the macabre and once had boasted to a colleague, "Give me one night with a man and I will have him confessing that he is King of England." But this Palestinian pastor would not confess to anything.

"Admit you have made a mistake," hissed Reem as the man began to shudder with the excruciating pain that was jolting through his brain.

"Never...."

"Turn up the voltage," she ordered, determined to win this battle.

The man, watching through the glass in the next room, did just as he was ordered, and the Christian shuddered again.

"Will you give in?" she yelled, her voice peppered with uncontrollable anger.

The man gazed pleadingly into her eyes, but refused to submit.

"You can kill me," he shouted through swollen lips, "but all that will mean is that you will have one more martyr for Christ in Palestine."

"You will die," said Reem, "but not until you have suffered." She turned to the man, and barked, "Put him on the rack."

The believer was unplugged from the electrodes and then taken to another room, stripped and strapped onto a table. Then more electrodes were attached to his extremities. Soon, electricity was forced into his body, but he refused to cry out for the torture to stop. The power was lowered and then upped, but he would not betray what he believed.

"All right, I want full power," exploded Reem as she began to froth like a rabid dog. Even as she spoke, the man cried out, "Father, into thy hands I commend my spirit." His face was by now an ashen gray, his lips faintly blue.

The guard proceeded to throw a lever and press two black buttons, and the first 2,400-volt surge of current tore through the man's 5-ft 4 ins, 126-lb. frame. His lips moved and his lids fluttered open but only the whites showed. By now his eyes were rolled up in their sockets. Two minutes later the power stopped and he stopped shuddering. His body went still...deathly still.

Reem strode over to the corpse and cackled into his ear, "Hello, hello. Is there anybody in there?" She turned to her fellow torturer, held up her hands and declared, "Stupid man. Take him away and put him out with the rest of the garbage."

Even as she spoke, the image of her parents rose involuntarily into her mind to haunt her. "Reem, how did you become like this?" her mother seemed to be saying. "You've let us all down, but worse still, you turned against the Lord and betrayed all of us."

* * * * *

Reem left the Gaza building after her confrontation with Joseph Beckett and pulled her coat that now covered her shawal tightly around her shoulders to try to combat the dismal Middle Eastern evening chill that was coursing through her body. It did little to stop the cold. Had her blood, she pondered, finally turned to ice? It seemed that it had.

2
The Picture on the Wall

Salman Salameh's eyes flamed with anger. "Reem, take down that picture of Kareema Jabir from your wall," he yelled at his young daughter. He had walked into her bedroom in their cramped apartment located in the modest district of Shati, near Gaza City's shabby beachfront, where the streets were strewn with trash.

She had just come inside to escape the putrid smell of festering garbage, dead animals and burning trash which hung over the area, the result of the latest strike by civil servants demanding that the local government pay them their long-overdue salaries.

"You know I ordered you not to put it up. That woman is a terrorist and you know that we Christians do not believe in what she did."

He was not only angry with his daughter displaying the photograph of this woman, which made her the symbol of Palestinian resistance and female power, but what made his flesh creep was the way she held the gun in her fragile hands, the shiny hair wrapped in a keffiah, the delicate elfish face, and he especially hated the ring that was resting on her third finger. She had made it from the pin of the first grenade she used in training and had wrapped it around a bullet.

Jabir had been involved in a highjacking of a plane full of Israelis and had become a "pin-up" for many of the children of

Gaza. Reem had heard so many stories about this woman that she had bought her picture and put it on the wall of her tiny bedroom.

The fourteen-year-old girl gazed pleadingly at her father, who was wearing his gray bus driver's outfit. "But, Papa, all the other kids in my class have the picture. What's wrong with me having it as well?"

Salman looked sadly at his only daughter. "I know you long to be accepted by the others, but this is a matter of conscience. This woman is a terrorist and is no role model to you."

With that he ripped the picture from the wall and tore it into little pieces.

The next morning, he accompanied his daughter to the gates of the primary school and there he saw a street vendor selling the same picture of Jabir.

"Is this where you bought the picture?" he asked his daughter

Near to tears, she nodded.

He then turned his anger onto the vendor. "You ought to be ashamed of yourself," he hissed. "These kids are wasting their money on a picture of a woman who has brought shame on our people."

The vendor wasn't having this and retorted, "She has brought no shame on our people. She is a hero to the cause of Palestinian freedom."

With that, Reem, tears welling up in her eyes, ran into the school and her father watched her as if she was slipping away from all he had taught her.

* * * * *

Troubles for the Salameh family were nothing new. Being Christians in the Gaza Strip, the most densely populated area in the world, with more than 1.2 million people, mainly Muslims, packed into this small area, was very difficult.

Salman Salameh ran a small house-church out of their cramped two-bedroom apartment and was determined that he would try to live for Christ in this dangerously unfriendly environment.

"I must teach Reem, and the children of my congregation, in the ways of the Lord," he told his wife after taking down the picture. "I will never deviate from this."

His actions were the beginning of his ongoing private war with one of the local Jihadist groups whose young gunmen controlled much of the trash-strewn area where they lived.

During a service in their home, a group of men wearing ski-masks and carrying automatic rifles had, on one occasion, smashed down the door with axes and interrupted the worship service. They had grabbed Bibles out of the hands of the dozen or so people gathered there, removing them for a book burning to be held later that night.

Taking one of the Bibles in his hand, the head man tore page after page from it. "If your God exists, why doesn't He stop me from doing this?" he yelled sarcastically at Salman as the thin papers of the torn Bible fluttered to the floor and Salman's wife Rafa broke into uncontrollable sobs.

Salman Salameh stood erect and told the man, "Be careful, sir, for God is not mocked!"

Shortly afterwards, Mr. Salameh went to his bedroom and brought out his Bible from a secret compartment and opened it at Proverbs 22, verse 6, and began reading aloud, "*Train up a child in the way he should go and when he is old, he will not depart from it.*"

He pointed out the verse to his daughter, and said, "Reem, we find our happiness in God, not in pictures of terrorists. We must not betray what we believe...whatever the cost."

The "cost," as they would soon discover, would be severe.

* * * * *

Reem was walking to school when a car suddenly overtook her and three gunmen jumped out, grabbed her and pushed her roughly into the back seat.

"Go!" yelled one of the men as the car sped off with Reem shaking uncontrollably in her seat.

"Where are you taking me?" she cried out as tears fell down her cheeks.

"Shut up. You'll soon find out!" said one of the two burly men seated either side of her.

One of them put a scarf around her eyes and after a few minutes, the car screeched to a halt. She was bundled out of the vehicle and taken up a stairway to a room where she was to be held.

"Your father is stupid and pig-headed!" the man screamed. "He believes in old wives' tales."

Reem shivered with fright as she was roughly pushed into a chair. She could smell the acrid smoke of her captors as they lit up cigarettes and began talking amongst themselves.

Eventually, the scarf was removed and she blinked at the sight of three men all wearing masks who sat around the room.

Feeling miserable and hungry, Reem sat perched precariously on a chair as Wael Mashaal, a man in his early twenties, who appeared to be the leader of the gang, stubbed out his cigarette in an ashtray already overflowing with half-smoked butts. Her feet had, by now, become as cold as gravestones.

"Well, we have heard that you are spreading your Christian beliefs at school. So we picked up so you can learn the truth," he began. "And the first lesson you will learn is that you will do what I tell you to do." He fixed the shivering girl with a look that chilled her to the bone as she saw his thin eyes through his mask.

He handed her a copy of the Koran and told her she had to read it. "But first you have to be punished," he said.

"For what?"

"For being a member of an illegal church!"

He took Reem by the arm and guided her down the corridor to a bedroom.

"Now, I want you to take part in a special experiment," he said as he opened up the door and roughly pushed the girl into the darkened room.

"I want you to ask your God to provide light and food and let's see what happens."

With that, the door was shut and Reem was left alone in the small room and a surge of claustrophobic panic rose up in her. The girl screwed up her eyes to try to see what was in the room, but it was pitch black. Even though her eyes brought nothing to her brain, her ears locked onto the sound of something scampering across the floor.

"It's a rat," she screamed with short uneven breathing.

An avalanche of terror engulfed her as she groped her way around the cell and discovered there was a bare mattress that reeked of mildew in the far corner. Reem's young body trembled as she lay down on it and curled up into a fetus-like position and began to sob.

"God," she shouted through salty tears, "If You exist, please help me!" Even as she spoke, she felt her words come bouncing back from the ceiling. Her heart was once again racing in terror. God had seemed so real two years before when she had knelt by her bedside with her parents and asked Jesus Christ to become her

Savior and Lord. But now, she thought, He had disappeared, or maybe He hadn't been "real" in the first place.

Hunger now gnawed at her inside. She asked God to provide her with food, but none came. It could have been hours - or days - when Reem finally heard footsteps echoing hollowly outside the door and it was opened. She peered to see the figure of the man standing there, the light from his cigarette burning into the darkness.

"Reem, my dear," he said in a heavy expressionless voice, switching on a torch that focused on her face, "are you all right?"

A solitary tear trickled down Reem's wasted cheeks, then another. Her eyes were dark-circled and tear-streaked as she shuddered and gasped.

"Didn't your God give you light or food then?" he sneered as his voice changed.

"Nooo...."

"Well, why don't you ask our great Islamic leader, Abdel Yassin, to give it to you, instead? I'll give you five minutes to make your request and then I'll be back and see what happens."

Reem's muscles were cramped and she shivered uncontrollably as the door shut tight and terrifying blackness again surrounded her. What could she lose by doing that? At the top of her voice, she shouted, "Abdel Yassin, please give me light." As the words left her lips, a light suddenly came on in the cell. The man, who was waiting outside the door, had turned on the switch in the corridor.

"Okay, Abdel Yassin, I am very hungry, please give me something to eat." She spoke in a slow, halting whisper that struggled for breath.

The door swung open again and the smiling man reappeared, bearing a bowl of hot soup. "Here you are, Reem," he said glibly, holding out the food. "Didn't I tell you that your God doesn't exist? It is only our great leader who can take care of you. If you remember that, you and I will get on just fine."

Reem hungrily lifted a spoon that had been provided and began to slurp up the soup to mollify her rumbling stomach. She sank her teeth into the crisp hunk of brown bread with it. As she did, the man slid onto the bed beside her.

"Reem, you must know by now, that all this Christian nonsense is just that - nonsense! These people are nothing more than subversives who fight against all that we believe in.

"Christians," he continued, wagging a finger at her to emphasize his point, "are lazy parasites that won't work, but want to sit around all day singing their stupid hymns and reading the Bible. They are against the cause of Palestine and even have a Jew as their leader. Face up to it, Reem, your parents are our enemies."

In her confusion, Reem did begin to question the existence of God. After all, when the teachers at school had explained how "illogical" it was to believe in God, it seemed to make sense. Or did it? She was confused, but it just was not worth making an issue of it. Survival was the name of this game!

"Reem, you are a bright girl and you will discover that if you become a model Palestinian freedom-fighter, your life will be fulfilled, and you will become a leader in our society," the man told her, flicking ash into the nearby ash-tray.

He then surprised her with his next comment.

"Reem, there is no need to be nervous," he said, smiling thinly. "I am going to let you go home. But, only on one condition; that you help us."

Reem stared blankly at the man. "What do mean? Help you? How can I do that?" she asked in puzzlement.

Mashaal leaned forward and signaled for the girl to do the same.

"I'll give you some advice for free," he said, a contemptuous shine in his eyes. "We are going to drive the Israelis into the sea and when you grow up, you can be part of the wonderful struggle to free our people. But we must be vigilant against our enemies within. Your parents are enemies. They are undermining all that we do in our great effort and we cannot allow them to continue with what they are doing.

"Reem, we want you to play a game of charades for us," he continued in a deceptively soft voice. "Go home and pretend to be a good Christian, but keep an eye out for any illegal meetings in your home and, if they do occur, I want you to report them to the police. This is a very important mission I am giving you." The man had by now swiftly changed his expression and tone, like a chameleon.

"You see, my girl, knowledge is power!"

Reem blinked. She would certainly like to be home again, but how could she betray her mother and father? "Reem, you have the choice of doing this or we will have to capture you again" he added, taking another deep drag on his cigarette and allowing it to settle in his lungs.

What could she say? "All right, I'll go home," she said in a faint voice after a long moment of awkward silence. "I'll do what you ask."

A wry smile came to his mouth. "Reem, you have made a good decision. Now remember, whatever you might think, just keep your tongue behind your teeth and your mouth shut tight."

* * * * *

Rafa Salameh shed tears of joy when she opened the door and saw Reem standing there. The car bearing her had already headed off into the chaos that is Gaza City. With glistening eyes, she ran forward and swept her daughter into her arms.

"My girl, let me look at you," she said hoarsely. "What happened? Where have you been?" Before Reem could answer, she pulled her through the front door. Rafa whispered, "Praise God. He has brought you back to us." Reem looked at her mother sharply and noticed that she seemed to have become much thinner. The sprinkling of gray hairs had grown more noticeable, making her hair nearer to silver than black.

Reem tried to smile, but found it difficult, knowing that she was now only home to spy on her parents. When her father came in shortly after visiting a sick member of his flock in the hospital, his face lit up like a beacon.

"Reem," he smiled. "God has heard our prayers. We asked Him to bring you back to us." Her father took off his overcoat and scarf and went over to hug his daughter. "The timing couldn't be better," he enthused. "We are having a special prayer and praise meeting here tonight. Now we have a lot to praise God for."

3
The Metamorphosis of Reem Salameh

The rotund and bearded figure of Ibrahim Rudeniah stood admiring his large - by Gaza standards - home. He had acquired the cash to pay for it from wealthy Palestinians in the Gaza Strip by collecting "protection" money in his neighborhood and he enforced it by not refraining from hurting those who refused to pay up. His abode was the ultimate symbol of privilege in Palestinian society and Reem, who stood proudly beside him, knew he deserved it. Low-paid workers were putting the final touches to his private home.

"Be careful with that," Rudeniah yelled at the men maneuvering an antique hall mirror through the front door. "Remember, you will have to pay if you break it."

More workers arrived with a pair of bronze candelabra that he had brought back from New York where he had embarked in a successful "fund raising" trip to help finance his "humanitarian" work in Gaza and the "occupied" West Bank. He beamed with pride, as the place was now looking habitable. After all, he had worked for many years to be able to enjoy these few special privileges.

Little did the American donors realize that the money was actually going to buy weapons for the recently formed "Red Dagger" terrorist group of which he was a co-founder.

"Reem, what do you think of it?" he asked the sixteen-year-old dark-haired young lady at his side as they stood enjoying the fresh air.

"I think it's wonderful," she breathed with excitement. "You have certainly worked hard for this."

Rudeniah slipped his arm around his recently-adopted daughter's shoulder. "Reem," he said pinching the girl's chin, "you are all my wife and I have ever dreamed of. You have made us very proud."

Reem, who was wearing a keffiah (shawl), fringed with wool in the Palestinian colors of red, green, black and white, which she felt was the model a terrorist in training should wear for her new family.

"I'm proud of you, too," said the girl. "You have done so much for me since you adopted me."

Her stepfather was an upright, model Palestinian citizen. To her, he was wise and omniscient. Reem laughed happily and embraced him.

She knew that her new father had become rich "fighting for the cause" while teenagers like her, were blowing themselves up as "martyrs." Still, she had a good home to live in and a "father" who made her feel quite special.

That night, as she lay in her comfortable bed, Reem allowed her mind to slip back over the past few years. She felt no regret at what had happened. After all, her real parents were subversives to the "cause," having in a nonsensical belief in Jesus Christ, instead of accepting the reality of the present struggle to free her people. They deserved all they had gotten. The philosophy of the "Red Dagger" faction was now beginning to control her mind and actions.

The morning after Reem had returned home from her kidnapping, she had told her parents that she wanted to go for a walk. She had sat through the interminable "prayer and praise meeting" the night before as they shouted prayers of thanks to God for her safe return.

As Reem left the house, she shouted to her mother, "I'll be back soon."

She walked a few blocks, unaware of the donkey carts. There she met a group of friends who were attending the Gaza University. They stood at the side of the road as the traffic was snarled by a parade of cars and taxis blaring their horns exuberantly behind a bridal car.

Wafa, a girl to whom she had become close to, smiled and said, "Reem, I'm never going to get married. My dream is to become a martyr in Israel. I've already begun my training."

"What about you?"

Reem felt her face flush. "I don't think so. I value my life too much."

Wafa seemed surprised. "Well, can you at least join us for a coffee?"

She nodded and soon they were seated at a table in the packed coffee shop. Over some dark, bitter black coffee, they began discussing their latest plans to attack a nearby Jewish settlement.

After a few minutes, Wafa said to Reem, "Why don't you join us tonight? We want to give the settlers the fright of their lives. We've got the weapons and we've found a hole in the fence that we can slip through."

Reem wasn't sure, but still it did sound exciting. "Okay, I'll come, but just as an observer," she said.

Coffee by now was fuelling the conversation and as soon as the sun had gone down on that February day, the group filed out of the coffee shop and went to the home of one of the young men.

There they picked up their AK-47s and mortars and a launcher. They climbed into a black sedan parked outside and headed towards the fence where they were to enter the settlement. Just outside the fence, one of the men set up his launcher and began firing the mortars into the settlement.

"Okay, let's go," he shouted and the group began climbing through the fence and running towards the settlement. Reem tried to keep up with them and suddenly she heard automatic fire coming in their direction.

After about 100 yards, Reem heard her friend Wafa shout, "Get down." With that Wafa fell to the ground grasping her weapon.

Reem felt her heart pounding as she too found herself lying face down with the others who were breathing heavily.

When Reem looked up, she could just make out the darkened figures of a group of Jewish settlers heading towards them. This was the signal for the Palestinians to start firing. Reem heard a scream, then another, as two of the settlers had been hit. Then she heard a cry from Wafa, who had taken a series of bullets in her arm. She was now unconscious and so Reem grabbed her and dragged her back towards the fence. When she pulled her through the hole there, she took off her scarf and tied it tightly around the wounds as a tourniquet.

The others were now also out of the settlement area. They carried Wafa to the car and drove at great speed towards the nearest hospital.

As they carried her into the Emergency Room, Reem saw her friend blink and then look at her. "Reem, carry on my work for freedom for our people...." With that she closed her eyes – for the last time.

When she got home that night, her father was beside himself with worry.

"Where have you been?" he yelled at her. "I have been worried sick about you."

"I've just been with my friends at the coffee shop," she replied. "Nothing more than that!"

Despite the horror of that evening, Reem became more and more intrigued with these young people who seemed willing to die for a cause they believed in. It seemed so much more challenging than the stultifying Christianity that felt her parents practiced.

* * * * *

Reem spent more and more time with these new friends, but had no idea where this was all leading. One night, while in the coffee shop, one of the men said that they wanted to "teach" her parents a lesson - no more than that.

"Will you take us to your home and introduce us?" he said as he munched on pita bread stuffed with hummus.

She nodded, thinking it might be fun to see her father and mother being humiliated.

"Are they going to be in tonight?" he asked.

"They are and they will be having another of their meetings in the house," she replied.

"Good," he said. "You can join us if you wish and we will teach them a lesson they will never forget."

Reem felt that they were just going to frighten them, so was quite relaxed when, a few hours later, just as the sun was going down, she left the coffee shop where they had spent some time, and rendezvoused with them just around the corner from the crowded alley where their apartment block was located.

She froze when she saw that the men all carried automatic weapons and had put their ski-masks back on.

They banged on the front door of the Salameh's apartment. As her father opened up, Reem pointed an accusing finger at him and said, "This is the man who has been holding illegal meetings here."

Her father's face clouded with disbelief. "Reem, what are you saying? You cannot betray your parents." His voice trembled with ill-disguised emotion.

"I am not betraying you," she said. "I am doing you a favor. You will thank me when you realize what nonsense you have believed in for all of these years."

One of the men roughly seized Salman, while the other rushed inside to take hold of Rafa, who had been sitting close to her short-wave radio listening to an Arabic Gospel teaching program over the airwaves from a western station.

Her heart pounding, Reem watched in horror as one of the men took aim at the head of her father and let go a hail of bullets. He fell to the floor with blood pouring from the many gaping wounds.

"No, no more," she screamed, but by now it was too late. She couldn't stop one of the other men as he pumped bullets into the body of her mother who died instantly.

Tears streamed down her face onto her father as the men ransacked the apartment and took with them Bibles, hymnals and the short-wave radio as proof that the couple had been running an illegal church. Of course, they could have attended one of the few legal churches in the Gaza Strip, but they had decided that they didn't need spies checking everything that occurred in their services.

She consoled herself with the thought that she was free at last from what she considered to be their mind-numbing influence on her life. She had done her duty and knew she would be well rewarded for it.

* * * * *

"Reem, you have served the cause well," said Ibrahim Rudeniah, the following day. The killers had taken her to their sparse home and when she had awoken after a night full of nightmares on a couch in the living room, she rubbed the sleep from her eyes as the large figure of Rudeniah began to speak.

"I have a nice surprise for you," he continued. "My wife and I have never had any children of our own, so I'd like you to become our adopted daughter."

He paused as she tried to take in what he was saying.

"You can come and live with us and then I've got some wonderful training in mind for you – in Syria."

Reem didn't know at the time, that Ibrahim Rudeniah not only wanted her as his daughter, but could see down the road that she could be a powerful figure in the "Red Dagger" Palestinian freedom movement.

The adoption papers were quickly processed and her metamorphosis into the cold, calculating Reem Rudeniah had begun. She had decided to take their last name as hers.

The family enjoyed having their precocious young daughter around them and began looking for ways to advance her education. The first step that Ibrahim Rudeniah took was to enroll Reem in the Gaza University, close to the seashore and advertized that it was there to "serve the urgent education needs of about one million people living in Gaza Strip." He played his own role in this by teaching there.

It wasn't long before Reem discovered that university student movements there were hothouses for future suicide bombers and that a portion of the funds collected by its "charitable societies" for the needy were channeled to the families of "martyrs," prisoners and those wanted by Israel. Some of the funds trickled down to the operational-terrorist wing and provided employment for high-ranking operatives on one of the terrorist groups in its "charitable societies" and other institutions.

The professors in her course in Palestinian history spent much of their time outlining the reasons why head knowledge was not enough – but the students needed to play an active role in "driving the Jews into the sea."

Most of the "clubs" were designed to "encourage" the students to join one of the militant groups based in Gaza and also go for further training in countries like Lebanon and Syria.

They also learned how to sing "intifada songs," including one urging them to "kill Zionists wherever they are."

It was part of a culture of hatred, where many where being taught how to become "walking bombs."

More than 80 percent of the 1.3 million people in the Gaza Strip live below the poverty line, with an unemployment rate of 50 per cent, and so these disenfranchised young people were easy pickings to join the various terrorist groups operating there.

* * * * *

"Death to America! Death to Israel!" The chant, that was begun by the instructor at the Ayn Tzahab terrorist training camp in Syria, was soon taken up by the 40 "students" - including Reem Salameh – as they sat in their barrack-like classroom.

Then the instructor led them in shouting out "moqawama!" (resistance) followed by, "If it takes a thousand martyrs, we will kill the Zionists wherever they are, in the name of God!"

The camp was supported by Iran and used for operational training for Palestinian terrorists including Hamas and the Palestinian Islamic Jihad. Reem was to become the first to represent the new group, "Red Dagger."

Soon she was immersed in the production of improvised explosives and rockets and the use of mobile shoulder-launched surface-to-air missiles for targeting non-combat aircraft.

The training also included manufacturing explosive devices and explosive belts, intelligence collection, training in kidnapping, and instruction in preparing and carrying out terrorist attacks against military and civilian targets. Reem, along with the others, learned to fire Uzis and M-16s, throw grenades, and prepare and detonate explosives. It was now time for her to put her training into action!

It was all very intense for Reem and the others until one day a man from Northern Ireland called Randy Burke arrived to give some lectures on the armed struggle in his country. Reem immediately liked the man, who was a pleasant change from the intense men who had been training them. His smile and Ulster brogue made her listen intensely to the history lesson he was giving.

"I salute you in your battle for freedom for your people," he began. "We Irish have had a tradition of armed resistance to the British military and the political occupation of our country. Our struggle has gone on for many years.

"The Easter Rising of 1916 was the defining event in the history of republicanism in my country. Many of us regard the 'Proclamation of the Republic' issued then as the founding document of the Irish Republican Army (IRA), of which I am a part. It declared an independent Republic and pledged republicans to 'equal rights and equal opportunities' for all the Irish people."

He added that "The Easter Rising" was crushed after a week and sixteen of its leaders were executed by the British government.

"It was then that the British decided on a plan to partition Ireland and in 1918 my people saw the threat of conscription being imposed. By an overwhelming majority in the General Election of that year the Irish people voted for the Sinn Féin party which sought to establish an Irish Republic.

"But it was not until well into 1919 that a widespread and effective guerrilla campaign began. Once again this occurred after the British government had spurned an opportunity to recognize the democratically expressed wishes of the Irish people.

"The response from the British government was to ban all these republican institutions and declare war on the new Irish democracy.

"This period saw international revulsion at the campaign waged by British crown forces in Ireland. Three mayors of Irish cities, all members of the IRA, were killed by the British; martial law was declared through nearly half of the country. Streets, shops and factories in many towns were burnt to the ground; there were executions in prisons and torture in internment camps. In response, the IRA waged an increasingly effective guerrilla campaign against the crack troops of the British - the Auxiliaries and Black and Tans."

Burke said that the guerrilla tactics used at this time - notably those of Tom Barry's Flying Column in Cork - later became textbook examples of this type of warfare. The popular Irish struggle, both in its civil and military side, inspired future anti-colonial struggles throughout the world.

"In the Civil War which followed, the Irish Republican Army held out for the complete independence of Ireland from Britain and for a United Ireland. Their former comrades who formed the army of the new Free State (26 Counties) opposed them in a savage campaign which witnessed all the tragedy common to every civil war."

He explained that in May 1923 the Civil War ended with the IRA order to its volunteers to dump arms. Then throughout the

1920s the IRA reorganized and played a key role in the election of the first government of the Fianna Fáil party - which had emerged from the IRA - under Eamon de Valera in 1932.

"In 1949, in response to the British government's Ireland Act, which reinforced partition, all parties in the Irish parliament declared their unanimous opposition to partition. The same year the IRA issued an Order which forbade military action against the forces of the 26-County state. The early 1950s saw an anti-partition campaign conducted by Irish governments and supported by all parties in parliament. Its ineffectiveness in the face of the British government's indifference contributed to the renewal of the IRA.

"My earlier colleagues in the IRA carried out raids for arms in the Six Counties of Northern Ireland and in Britain. This was in preparation for an armed campaign which was conducted between 1956 and 1962 mainly in the border regions."

Burke said: "After the border campaign ended, the leadership of the IRA decided that support should be given to campaigns to highlight the status of second-class citizenship for nationalists in the Six Counties."

Reem was growing impatient with the history lesson and asked Burke if he would move forward to the emergence of the Civil Rights Movement in the mid-1960s.

"Good question," he said. "This was to transform the political situation. My people demanded basic rights - to jobs, housing, voting – and this threw Northern Ireland into a state of crisis. Our peaceful demand for civil rights was met with violence from the forces of the sectarian state."

She listened intently as he told her that in Belfast and Derry in 1969, nationalist districts were attacked by the state police, the Royal Ulster Constabulary (RUC), and by unionist mobs. The demand for defense made by nationalist communities could not be met initially by the IRA because, through the 1960s, the leadership had abandoned planning and preparation for a future armed campaign. As a military organization the IRA had been run down.

"So what happened then?" she asked.

"Well in 1969 this caused a split in the IRA and eventually we formed the Provisional Wing of the IRA of which I am a member. We are continuing our armed struggle although many of our former members have given up. Like you, we have an aim – of a United Ireland – and you wish to have your freedom from your oppressors, so let's work together to see our aims come true!"

Reem led the applause and afterwards went up to Randy Burke and shook his hand warmly. "I like what you had to say," she said. "Let's keep in touch."

With that, they exchanged contact information and Reem let others in the group talk with the Irishman.

* * * * *

Ibrahim Rudeniah beamed as he handed a forged American passport to his adopted daughter. "Reem, I want you to lead an all-female brigade into Netanya to kill as many Israelis as you can," he said. "I will have a boat ready for you tomorrow evening and you will sail it up the coast to Netanya. There is a shopping mall there and you can stage your attack when the most number of people are there."

Reem's heart began to beat faster than she could ever remember. At last she could serve the cause!

That evening, the four other women joined her at the home and they pored over maps of the coastline and of the coastal city they were to attack. They also checked their weapons.

Ibrahim sat with them and beamed as one of the women, Darine

Abu Idris, told the group that she planned to blow herself up at the start of the attack on the shopping mall.

"You are a true hero," he told her. "And your family will be well rewarded for your sacrifice."

Less than 24 hours later, the women were driven by Ibrahim to the beach where a boat was waiting for them. Darine checked her bomb belt and smiled as the others loaded their weapons and bombs onto the vessel.

The captain was an expert on navigating the Mediterranean waters down the Israeli coast and after few hours of sailing in the darkness, he spotted the lights of Netanya and began heading in.

They managed to quickly run ashore, all dressed in Western clothing and they carried their weapons of war in shopping bags. The sun was just coming up over the horizon as they found a park where they could wait for the shoppers to appear.

Reem consulted her map and, at about 10:00 AM, she told the group that it was time to head towards the mall. She gave each one a different route to take and told them that they should rendezvous at the entrance in 30 minutes.

After a slow walk, Reem arrived at what she hoped would be the killing fields. As shoppers began entering the mall, she instructed Darine to walk into the shopping center and detonate herself. With that, the young women began walking briskly into the mall, hit the detonator, and a huge explosion followed.

Screams followed as bodies of dying mothers clasping their dead children and men who were blown to pieces littered the floor.

Reem then gave the order to begin shooting with their M-16s and as the deadly fire poured from their weapons, scores more lay dead. It was total mayhem.

In the confusion, Reem and the others dropped their weapons and calmly walked away from the scene. They headed back to the sea-shore where their waiting boat took them quickly along the coast to Gaza – and a hero's welcome from the leader of "Red Dagger."

Ibrahim had been in radio contact during the return trip and embraced them on the beach. As he did, Reem smiled in a frightening way. She hadn't used the American passport, but she knew it would come in useful in the days ahead.

The metamorphosis of Reem Salameh - Christian - to Reem Rudeniah - cruel killer - was complete.

4
The Stab in the Back

The Stab in the Back pub in New Fetter Lane, London, was filling up with British hacks, who were taking time out from inventing their expense reports and writing up stories about the misdeeds and misfortunes of the high, mighty, mediocre and detestable. The remnants of Britain's newspaper village - many had already moved out of the area to new offices in east London's docklands - was awash in booze and Arch Bishop was also about to drown in the river of alcohol.

His hands shook helplessly at that midday hour as he held a glass of gin-and-tonic by its stem and quickly tossed the colorless, fizzing liquid down his throat. His throat blessed him for the relief it brought, and his meaty, typewriter hands showed their gratitude by ceasing to shake.

Feeling a little better, he hooked his legs around the barstool, took a deep drag on his cigarette and allowed, with satisfaction, the warm smoke to reach snugly down into the dark recesses of his lungs. Then he slowly exhaled, watching the smoke as it snaked upward toward the grubby ceiling.

"Another 'g & t,'" he signaled to George, the large, curly-haired bartender who so enjoyed overhearing all the scandal about British life revealed by the many journalists who packed this off-Fleet Street pub. The hacks flocked there, eager to impart or catch up with the latest scandals...and also tell not a few lies.

Just then a slender arm entwined itself around his neck and a voice, full of upper crust inflection, whispered in his ear, "If you're buying, daahling, I'll have a sherry."

With that, Lady Philda "Fida" Tintagel, the Queen's second cousin, drew up a stool to the long bar and perched herself on it. She leaned over and affectionately rubbed his right hand.

"How's my 'archbishop' then?" she chirped in a bubbly, effervescent way, tapping the top of her tongue around her mouth.

"Don't do that," Bishop said testily, not able to disguise the annoyance in his deep voice, overlaid with its Brooklyn accent. "You know it makes me mad when you do that, Fida." Suddenly, he stopped speaking in mid-sentence and his eyes rolled back in their sockets, leaving only the bottom of the pupils showing. After some ten seconds or so, his eyelids flickered, momentarily and his mind quickly snapped back to the present. Groping momentarily for a lost train of thought, he growled, "...and stop calling me by that silly clerical name." With that he slammed down his fist on the bar for emphasis. The lines on his face - which looked as if it had been hewn from pure Italian marble - became even more taut than usual.

Fida looked at him quizzically.

"Why did you suddenly stop talking just then?" she asked. "You've been doing that a lot lately. Are you all right?"

"Of course I'm all right, you silly woman." He lowered his steely gray eyes toward his toothy, fresh-faced companion, as if burdened by what he saw. Bishop did not recall stopping in midstream, but he guessed it must have been another of his petit mal epileptic seizures, which were coming thick and fast these days. He fixed his eyes on Fida as her face appeared to strangely dissolve into that of a leering witch. When would she realize that he did not fancy her one little bit? Why couldn't she understand that the more she offered herself, the more she repelled him? She could never compare with his ex-wife Gloria who, in a few hours, would soon be pacing down the Avenue of the Americas to the Manhattan television studio where she brought New York the "Award-winning Mid-Day News." Her glorious image remained with him, vivid, alive, etched into his mind.

Just then, he was distracted from his thoughts when a news flash came on the pub's TV screen. The American looked up and caught the report that "some 20 Israelis have been killed in a suicide bomb attack in the seaside town of Netanya in Israel."

The man on the screen went on to say, "An all-female group of Palestinian terrorists began shooting at the Israelis in a mall after one of them blew herself up. The IDF is now searching for the killers."

"Those Palestinians are crazy," he muttered under his breath. "They are worse than the IRA."

* * * * *

It had been a frustrating day for both Bishop and his faithful lens girl. At 5:00 A.M., Bishop had been jerked from a disturbing nightmare - in which he felt he was falling down a dark, bottomless shaft - by a phone call from Al Farr, his crusty editor in New York who was well known for his short fuse and gruff manner. The shrill ringing had started him up to a sitting position that made his bed creak. He tried to brace himself against the headboard to offset the sudden dizziness.

"Bishop!" barked the voice over the trans-Atlantic line from the noisy office of the New York Tribune. "Get yourself out of bed and get to Heathrow Airport pronto. We understand that the Prime

Minister is flying out of there this morning on his way to Prague, for what was meant to be a secret meeting with that Czech leader. What's his name? Husdack, I think it is. Anyway, find out what's going on...."

With that, the line went dead. "Farr," thought Bishop, "has all the charm of a Pit-Bull."

"Stupid man," he spat, still groggy and perspiring from the nightmarish dream. For a moment he stared vacantly at the phone. "Doesn't Farr know that Steele always flies out of Northolt, not Heathrow? Well, it's his problem it if he's not at Heathrow." Arch Bishop fluttered his eyelids urgently, trying to rid himself of the numbing hangover that throbbed in his brain. For a long, bleary, second, he looked at the phone as if it was something nauseating, and then he replaced it on its cradle.

Switching to automatic pilot, he allowed his early-morning radar to guide him through his tiny barracks-like Barbican flat, a stiff twenty-minute walk from Fleet Street, and staggered toward the bathroom. Fortunately, he had little furniture to navigate around as aesthetics had a low priority in his life at this time. When Bishop reached the sink, he tossed cold water over his unshaven face. He had a splitting headache and his mouth tasted like the bottom of a birdcage. He was soaking in sweat and his damp hair looked like an unwrung mop. Trying to focus his visibly hung-over eyes, he squinted despairingly into the mirror. Despite his eyes being red raw, his head weighing a ton, and his pallor being tombstone gray, he was grateful for one thing - he was still alive...just!

Swaying uncertainly from an unrecalled number of "g & t's" the previous night, he began dialing Fida's number. As he did he was attacked by an all-too-frequent bout of the shakes.

"Yesssss," said the sleep-blurred voice at the other end. "Who is this?"

"It's Bishop, you aristocratic nerd." His hands continued to shake. "New York's had a tip-off that Maggie Thatcher is trying to flee the country in search of the Holy Grail."

"Do you realize what time it is?" Fida mumbled, her voice hoarse, husky and unbelieving. "It's taken me hours to get off to sleep and now you call to tell me this twaddle." Like Queen Victoria, her long-dead distant relative, Lady "Fida" Tintagel was not amused.

"Look, you stupid woman," - his nostrils flared as he spat out the words - "I called to tell you to forget your beauty sleep and grab your cameras and meet me at Heathrow Terminal Three in thirty minutes."

With that, he hung up, picked up his rumpled suit from the place on the floor where he had dropped it the night before, and climbed into it in preparation for the drive to the airport.

Bishop's tour of duty in London as the New York Tribune's correspondent had taken a heavy toll on his body, soul and spirit. He had arrived, two years before, in high spirits to cover "The British Beat." Now all he felt was a dead, heavy weight inside him; a never-ending melancholia. His view of the British Isles before this had been colored with images of pomp, circumstance and quaint thatched cottages. But London's contemptible hack writers had changed that image for him.

The journalists who inhabited Fleet Street - dubbed "The Street of Shame" in the iconoclastic columns of Private Eye magazine - were quite a shock for Arch Bishop. He expected those who wrote news for the most literate nation on earth, to be giants with the pen. After all, weren't they following in the footsteps of William Shakespeare, H.G. Wells and Edgar Wallace? It did not take long, however, to discover that most of them, especially those that congregated in the smoky atmosphere of The Stab in the Back, were far from that.

In fact, they appeared to Arch Bishop to be mental Lilliputians with an insatiable urge to destroy all that was once great in their own country; a greatness that had once enabled their leaders to rule one-fourth of the world. These hacks were, in his jaundiced eyes, little more than town criers publicly proclaiming the misdeeds and misfortunes of others. "But what of their - my - misdeeds?" he pondered. "Who judges us?"

Berkeley Percival, a photographer who worked for one of the vicious gossip columns so popular with the British, had put the Fleet Street view to the pub's pet Yank, one day.

"You love the newspapers here, yet you hate them," said this guru with midday Scotch on his breath. "You want to get out and do something worthwhile, but what else could you do? The expenses are good and the comradeship, well, sometimes that can be good, too." Pointing around the "Stab" at the huddles of hacks and hackettes, he added: "Most of them are wracked by disillusionment and booze."

Bishop had looked at Percival and asked him if he, too, was "wracked by disillusionment and booze".

The photographer shrugged in a non-committal way. "I think I'd better go and have another drink, Archie boy. Tomorrow's another day." With that he ordered Scotch-on-the-rocks.

* * * * *

Bishop parked his green Renault in the multi-story parking lot at Heathrow, and walked across the street into Terminal Three. As he did, he noticed a turbaned Sikh shuffling with little enthusiasm around the building, his motorized polisher feebly grinding into the dirt of thousands of travelers and swishing it into smaller particles of dirt. The man, Bishop felt, was not really there. His thoughts were back in his beloved Punjab.

A few airline ground staff had already begun drifting in for another day of dealing with another ungrateful horde of travelers, all anxious to be on their way around the world.

Bishop made his way to Lockharts, a small news agency that covered London Airport mainly for the British yellow press. Its staff was briefed to look out for tidbits on movie and rock stars that were departing or arriving.

"You won't find Steele leaving from here," said Charles Craddock, the tired-eyed young reporter who was coming to the end of an overnight shift. As he drained the last dregs of cold coffee from his Styrofoam cup, he added, "Now if you want to know the dirt on Rod Stewart - who is his latest - I can give you an exclusive."

Bishop suppressed a sigh, but could not prevent his lip from curling up into a sneer.

"My paper isn't into that sort of trash," he hissed as his face reddened with contempt.

"Why not?" retorted Craddock. "It sells!"

Just then, a flustered Fida staggered into the office with a couple of Canons dangling awkwardly by shoulder straps around her slim neck.

"You could have told me where to meet you," she yelled petulantly at Bishop. "I've been checking out all the men's restrooms thinking you were being sick again."

Bishop marveled at how someone with so much breeding could be so crude. It seemed as if she felt she had to outdo even the most foul-mouthed news reporter in the street to be accepted as one of the gang.

"Look, kiddo, you found me, didn't you? Isn't that enough?"

"Well, what's this rubbish about the Holy Grail and the Man of Steele?"

"Well, sweetie, we obviously won't find either of them here with this creep." Ill-disguised sarcasm dripped from Arch Bishop's voice. The click-clack of Craddock's typewriter drowned out the insult for the ambitious young news-hound. He was now enthralled in knocking out a story that aging Hollywood star, Burt Richards, had been seen boarding a Pan Am flight to Los Angeles with the wife of a British racehorse owner from Newmarket. The hastily developed "snatch" picture of the clandestine pair lay curling up on his desk as he bashed out the story for an early edition of the London Evening Star.

Bishop grabbed Fida's arm and began dragging her into the terminal. Muted announcements were now being relayed on echoing loudspeakers as Nigerians in their colorful flowing robes mingled with swarthy, chain-smoking Arabs resplendent in their headgear.

"Steele always leaves on these kind of trips by military aircraft from Northolt, so why does Farr think he's leaving from here this time? Stupid idiot...."

An exasperated Fida suddenly stopped dead.

"Look, you creep," she said, her face coloring with anger. "It's enough for me to put up with your constant insults. At least you could tell me what's going on. You never tell me the full story - yet you expect me to take the right pictures. I don't think it's fair..."

"You're not paid to think, sweetheart!"

With that Fida took a swipe at her embittered colleague. He ducked quickly, and then headed out for the multi-level parking lot.

"Just follow me. We're going to Northolt."

* * * * *

As Bishop's Renault screeched to a halt outside the terminal building at Northolt, a knot of hacks were swinging their arms and trying to protect themselves against the northeasterly wind that ripped through the little military airport on the west side of London. A line had already formed at the large, enclosed, red pay phone. Through the pearl-gray early morning gloom and through hung-over eyes, the reporters looked to Bishop like grotesque ghosts awaiting the crash of dawn.

"What's happening, guys?" he shouted through his window, blowing smoke into the frozen morning air that quickly merged with a drifting membrane of fog.

"Steele's decided to become a communist," responded George Lloyd, the ever-cynical correspondent for The Guardian, his breath popping in the cold.

"He's just left to pledge allegiance to the Czechs in Prague and tell them that his government will right the Russians if they try and come back."

"Why are you Brits always so 'helpful?'" With that Bishop wound up his window, parked the car, and joined the freezing scribes as the wind viciously slapped their faces and their feet became like blocks of ice as they stood on a sidewalk clad in early December frost.

Fida, who had tried to keep up with his erratic driving, was quickly out of her Mini-car and at his side, ready to snap anything that moved.

"Any sign of the Holy Grail?" she asked, trying to humor her frustrated colleague, hoping maybe, by the end of the day, he would at least try to be pleasant to her.

Bishop ignored her remark and began mingling with the

reporters, hoping that someone would tell him what on earth was going on.

"It seems that, with the general election coming up, Steele's trying to be a little more friendly towards other countries," said John Johnson-Jones, a BBC TV "mannequin" who, as usual, did not have a strand out of place on his heavily lacquered hair.

"He's flown off to Prague to have a meeting with the Czech Prime Minister. It's to discuss Britain's attitude toward the further deployment of your Yankee missiles in our fair land," he exulted.

"Did he say anything before he left?"

"He sure did," chirped in Bert Jones, the BBC camera operator, full of rough, cockney humor.

"He said to, 'Cool Britannia...'"

* * * * *

A strange, almost reverential hush, came over the drinkers in the "Stab" as the large figure of an American dressed in a well-tailored, pin-striped suit, complete with matching dotted red and white tie, entered this place of "sin." It was now "lunchtime-o-booze" time and half-told stories remained half-told as every eye turned to examine this alien intruder who had dared to enter this not-so-holy sanctuary of the press.

Bishop, who had cobbled up a "think piece" for New York on Steele's "surprise visit to Czechoslovakia," before heading for the Stab, recognized him immediately as evangelist William Franklin, a spell-binding southern preacher who had taken his fiery brand of gospel shows to some of the largest arenas in the United States. But what was he doing in the Stab? Surely he, too, had not become addicted to the "demon drink" that was threatening to sink them all?

Bishop then recollected that Franklin was in London for his "Greater London Crusade" and had probably been mortally wounded by the slashing sarcasm of some of the press notices his first few nights at the Earl's Court arena had drawn.

The Daily Mirror had described Franklin as presenting Londoners with a "Honky Tonk Gospel," while the Sun's man had asked, "Why doesn't Franklin concentrate on solving the horrifying crime problem in America instead of telling us how to run our show?"

Time quickly moved back into motion, as Franklin, despite being repelled by the acrid smell of thick tobacco smoke and spilled booze, inquired of a reporter, downing the contents of a pint of bitter, "Sir, could you please direct me to Mr. William Doberman."

"Sure," he said gesturing with his head, "he's the portly chap over in the corner wearing the bow tie and smug grin."

Doberman was an acid-tongued columnist for the Daily Mirror who had, in recent days, made it his business to go for Franklin's jugular in his daily "Outburst" column.

"Verily, verily, Reverend Franklin," he had written irreverently for that morning's edition, "I challenge you to meet me on my own ground at one o'clock today, to answer my questions about what on earth thou art doing in Londinieum."

The arrogant and self-opinionated Doberman had stipulated that "his own ground" was to be "The Stab in the Back," being convinced that the evangelist would never venture into such a place. Franklin had decided that if he was to win over the British public, he had to do it through the press, and so he could not allow this challenge to "pass by on the other side."

Doberman spotted Franklin, but made no effort to move toward him. Instead, he allowed the American to weave his way through the stupefied journalists.

When Franklin arrived at Doberman's corner of the bar, which had a backdrop of framed photographs of "Stabbers" with some of their better-known victims, he held out his huge paw and gave a presidential-style greeting.

"Mr. Doberman," he said effusively, "it's a great pleasure to finally meet you." His voice oozed southern charm. "I've heard so much about you."

The overweight columnist met his eyes with a malicious gaze and countered with, "Not as much as I've heard about you, Mr. Franklin. Can I buy you a drink?" Doberman smiled at the evangelist in a way that was almost predatory.

"Sure, I'll have an orange juice," said the Southern gentleman.

"A bottle of champers for me and an orange juice for the pulpiteer," Doberman yelled to George behind the bar. "Be a dear and make it quick!"

Then Doberman hissed out of the side of his mouth to an adoring junior colleague, "Go and get a photographer," and then invited the spellbinder to "draw up a pew."

"You obviously didn't think I would come, Mr. Doberman," said Franklin, as he fixed his deep-blue eyes that blazed like the North Carolina sky in summer, on the plump and rather pompous figure before him. Doberman smiled, showing a set of slightly stained white teeth.

By now the bubbly was being poured for the star columnist and Franklin had taken his first modest sip from his orange juice that, as is the British tradition, was served without ice.

Many of the hacks began gathering around the pair to try to witness what promised to be an interesting, if not barbed, conversation.

Arch Bishop lifted his glass of "g & t" by the stem and sidled over to the center of the attention. His six feet four inches height gave him an advantage over the British who, for some reason, were much smaller in stature. In fact, his height had become something of a standing joke in the Stab. These jests had stopped abruptly, however, when he finally got mad at a Sunday Mirror hack.

Looking up at Bishop, David Peterson, the reporter, like many before him, had asked, "What's the weather like up there, Bishop?"

The American glared down at him and then, without warning, spat on his head.

"It's raining," he chortled, as a disgusted Peterson desperately began wiping the top of his head with his handkerchief.

Now the debate was about to begin and Bishop's extra inches meant that he did not need to crane his neck to watch the proceedings.

"Fire away, Mr. Doberman," said Franklin. "I'm all ears." (So were the assembled throng, as they inclined theirs to catch every word of what promised to be quite a verbal scrap.)

Doberman slowly and deliberately got out a cigarette from a gold container, fixed it into a holder and lit it. After taking a deep draw, he blew the smoke out sideways, and then delivered his first shot, which he felt would immediately draw blood from the well-groomed preacher.

"Well, Mr. Franklin," said Doberman, an insidious smirk playing about his lips, "many of my readers would like to know why you came to this country from New York on the luxury liner, the QE2, while your leader, Jesus Christ, came riding into Jerusalem on a donkey. How can you justify this?" He delivered the question with simmering hostility.

Bishop chuckled to himself. That'll teach Franklin to put himself in this situation, he thought maliciously. He'll never be able to get out of that one!

"Good question, Mr. Doberman. "I'm glad you asked it. It has a simple answer," said Franklin, bowing his head slightly toward him. "If you can find a donkey that can swim the Atlantic, I'd be happy to come across on it...." His answer brought cackles of hysterical laughter from the listening reporters.

"Touché," chuckled Frank Bramble, a Sunday People reporter, loudly. "That's what I call a Doberman-pincher..." When he saw the crowd was with him, Bramble added, "If you do find an ass that can swim the Atlantic, Doberman, make sure it is as pompous as you." With that he threw back his head in uproarious laughter, amazed at his own wit so early in the day.

The American evangelist, with one clever answer, had won over many of the assembled throng, though that was mainly because most of them despised Doberman for his arrogant attitude toward the rest of them. The columnist had made it clear that he considered his plumb-in-the-mouth way of speaking, and his upper-class private school education, elevated him to a cut above the rest of the hacks of the gutter press.

For some thirty minutes, Doberman blustered along amid the haze of the eye-stinging smoke, trying to trip up Franklin, but each time he was outmaneuvered by the preacher's answers. Whenever the American won another victory with a clever retort, a reporter chalked up the score on the nearby darts' scoreboard. Bishop allowed himself the luxury of a faint smile. He marveled at the degree of sophistication Franklin had acquired since he had last seen him in Brooklyn some eight years earlier. Then Franklin had been dubbed, "The Preaching Windmill," for his flamboyant and breathless presentations. But now he was somehow different.

Bishop then had been a fast-rising reporter on the Brooklyn Banner, his home-area paper, owned by San Francisco-based magnate Elmer Jansen III. It had been his first job in journalism after receiving his master's degree in Mass Communications from the University of New York. It was on this paper that he had quickly discovered that what he had learned in the classes bore little resemblance to the real world he would encounter as a scribe for the masses. His professors had not warned him about crooked politicians, mobsters and ego-crazed, insecure rock and movie stars.

Bishop then had been dispatched by his assignment editor to the Brooklyn Paramount Theater where Franklin was conducting a two-week crusade to save the souls of at least some of Brooklyn's four million chunk of the "Big Apple." He had managed to obtain a short interview with Franklin and had been impressed with his transparent answers. Bishop had been accompanied by a young trainee reporter on the paper, Gloria Jansen, who had been sent to the East Coast by her rich daddy to learn "all about the business of news."

Arch Bishop recalled that throughout the interview, Gloria kept nudging him because he had lit up one cigarette after another. She somehow had felt that this was not appropriate in the presence of the awe-inspiring evangelist.

Bishop's fondest memory, of that day, however, was that he had managed to get this lovely heiress out on a date. He had phoned-in his story from a nearby cocktail lounge, then they both got brightly incandescent on "g & t's" in the darkened atmosphere. The rest was predictable history. Even now, her lovely image rose before him as Doberman and Franklin continued to lock horns in front of an appreciative audience.

Doberman's wrinkled brow was by now awash with sweat. He was obviously uneasy with the way the interview was going and what made it was worse was that he was being "cut to ribbons" in front of his fellow "stabbers." It was not much fun being made a fool of by a "hick American preacher," while a bunch of jeering hacks savored his humiliation. Doberman desperately needed to save face.

"Well, Mr. Franklin, I realize you must go on to save some more unfortunate souls in our wicked city," said Doberman, getting up from his stool rather unsteadily in a punch-drunk manner and gazing with ill-disguised contempt at the preacher.

"Before you go, can I ask you one final question?" he said.

Franklin nodded without expression.

"Why on earth did you come here today?"

The American stood up to his full height and gazed down at the obese, quivering mass before him.

"Well, Mr. Doberman, Jesus drank with publicans and sinners. So why shouldn't I?"

The ghost of a smile on Doberman's face quickly disappeared. So did the evangelist, to the sound of hearty applause.

5
The Night Court With Gloria

The Stab was as quiet as a morgue. It was now the Wimbledon fortnight and many of the hacks were busy pursuing the latest bunch of stars to see if they could uncover scandals that would sell more papers. Most of the British hacks hunted in packs. They would devise plans to upset the tennis stars that poured into this south London suburb each July to take part in what was billed as the greatest tennis tournament in the world. And the women players were not exempt from their attentions. It was essential to prove that at least some of the top players were lesbians, so hours were spent in trying to uncover their lovers.

The New York Tribune had sent over two sports scribes for the event and so, after Bishop had settled them into their hotel and wearily briefed them on life in London, he let them get on with it.

After a couple of "g & t's," Bishop decided to dismiss himself from the deathly quiet of the pub and head for his Barbican flat. He stopped off on his twenty-minute walk to pick up a bottle of Gilbey's gin from an off-license liquor store, where the British buy most of their booze for home consumption.

A clinging humidity that reminded him of New York caused his shirt to cling to his back. The apartment was like a furnace as he walked through the front door.

"Why, oh why don't the Brits install air-conditioning?" he

sighed wearily as he mopped his brow with the sleeve of his jacket. The simple answer was that they never expected such hot weather in their cold, damp island. Arch Bishop flicked off his tie, threw his jacket on the nearby sofa and cracked the seal of the Gilbey's.

Rather than wash a glass, Bishop took a swig from the neck of the gin bottle. Washing dishes and glasses was never high on Bishop's agenda. He just let them pile up in the sink. He depended on his aristocratic lens girl to do that on the nights she came around to go over her photographs for the latest story. Tonight, he knew she would be drinking with the other hacks after a grueling day at the Center Court.

Bishop switched on the television and, as he sank back in a chair, the rotund and balding figure of "Lou Grant," filled the screen in the umpteenth repeat on that channel. Grant was as brusque as ever as he issued orders to a cub reporter on his make-believe newspaper.

"Take Miss Chambers down to the courthouse and show her the ropes," he spat.

"She's just started with the paper today. And O'Reilly, behave yourself."

The cocky TV character smiled at his city editor. "I'm not a cradle snatcher," he smirked.

"Since when?" snorted Grant, squinting at the young hack with a skeptical eye.

As the reporter took the enthusiastic young graduate on her first assignment, Bishop lit up a cigarette and allowed a hundred memories to shuffle through his mind like a doubled pack of cards. He remembered the first day he had met Gloria. Dave Farrow, the city editor of the Banner had taken her around the noisy newsroom, and on her brief tour, stopped at Bishop's untidy desk.

"Take your stupid feet off the desk," Farrow bellowed. His tone echoed a lifetime of insulting reporters. Then, with one lightning movement, he knocked Bishop's feet off the table.

"Why did you do that?" the reporter yelled back. "I'm trying to think through this story before the copy deadline."

Farrow leaned over the typewriter and began checking the copy:

The body of an attractive girl in her early twenties was found outside a Russian nightclub on First Street late last night. Police say Jane Clements, a cocktail waitress at a nearby bar, had been strangled.

This is the third time in two months that a young woman has been killed and had her body dumped in an alley behind The Babushka Club.

"Why don't you continue with your tour so I can complete my story," Bishop said, raising his eyes and staring with cool contempt at Farrow. The city editor ignored the gaze.

"Bishop, I'd like you to try and be nice to this young lady. She's just arrived from the West Coast and wants to learn all about the glamorous life we lead on The Banner."

Bishop held his gaze on Farrow, concentrating with disgust on the cigarette dangling on his boss's lower lip. He saw from Farrow's look of hostility that he was not pleased at his up-and-coming reporter's gauche manners.

Arch Bishop screwed up his eyes to look at the young lady standing open-mouthed before him. He had to agree she was lovely. She was elegantly dressed in a two-piece tweed suit and held him with beguiling deep hazel eyes. However, it was the sensuous face, and dark auburn hair, that attracted him.

Slowly, he eased himself out of his chair and stood before her. Taking her soft left hand in his, he leaned over and kissed it with mock reverence. He noted that she was not wearing a ring.

"Gloria, I'm so glad to meet you," he said softly as his expression changed to one of utmost charm. His face became smooth and impenetrable as a marble egg. The young lady felt her legs turn to jelly. This handsome young man was gazing deeply into her eyes and she had to avert hers in embarrassment. He was so different from the California "air-heads" she was used to. He appeared to have a depth to his personality, something she had not found in men on the West Coast.

Bishop pulled up a chair from an empty reporter's desk and motioned for her to sit down. He leaned over and took her hands in his and gave her another intense look that she found hard to handle.

"My dear, Miss Gloria," he said, a provocative smile playing about his lips and revealing his highly polished white teeth, "do you believe in love at first sight?"

She nodded weakly. "Why do you ask?"

"Well, I think I'm falling in love with you. You are without doubt the most beautiful creature I have ever met."

Farrow stood by watching this silver-tongued Italian Romeo with the non-Italian name, reciting a script he knew he had used many times before.

"Cut this out, Bishop," Farrow shouted as he cocked his head to the side to keep the smoke from the cigarette, attached to the corner of his mouth, from stinging his eyes. "Don't you know that this is Elmer Jansen III's only daughter? You'll get us all shut down if you carry on like this."

"Or," countered Bishop, "I'll get us all a raise!"

Bishop knew, only too well, whom he was talking to. He had heard that Daddy wanted Gloria to inherit his billion-dollar business that included twenty-six American newspapers from the West to the East Coast, three television and seven radio stations.

But first he had stipulated to his beautiful daughter that she had to learn all about the newspaper business. If she did well, then radio and TV would follow. Jansen had chosen for her to begin at the Brooklyn Banner because it was one of the most successful newspapers in his chain.

"Mr. Jansen doesn't want us to show his daughter any favors," Farrow continued, his cigarette still hanging from his lips, the ash by now getting perilously long.

"He wants her to start at the bottom, and you can't get much lower than you!"

The feisty city editor knew that Bishop could certainly give her a good insight to life as a reporter on the Banner. Ever since he had burst onto the paper three years previously, Bishop had shown an arrogance, yet a cunning brilliance in his performance. He had a motto: "It is better to smile someone in the back than to stab them in the back." Farrow rated Bishop highly because of the way he used his undoubted charm to pry information out of even the most hostile people.

"Take Miss Jansen to the Night Court tonight. That should be a good introduction for her to the scum of Brooklyn."

Bishop was not so sure. The Night Court might prove to be too much of a shock for this little girl from the sheltered opulence of Cinderella's Malibu home. As they arrived at the court located at 100 Center Street, a derelict weaved past them blearily isolated from the comings and goings of the building. All that mattered to him was the paper bag he tightly clutched with a bottle inside of it. In the reception area Gloria's eyes became as large as saucers as she caught sight of a drunken street person arguing with his Legal Aid attorney.

"Look," he shouted at the top of his voice, "I ain't gonna plead guilty for you or nobody." With that he took a wild swing with his fist at him. The attorney ducked just in time and the man fell to the floor.

As he slowly got to his feet, the man saw Gloria gaping at him. "Whatsamattawidyu?" he yelled. "Ain't you ever seen a street person before?"

Bishop grabbed the arm of heiress and propelled her away from the lobby with its strange assortment of characters - from prostitutes, to pimps and drug pushers.

"Just ignore him," he said as he grasped her moist hand reassuringly. "He's a regular here. He specializes in panhandling and then when the person goes to give him some money, he pulls a knife on them and takes their billfold."

As Gloria followed her escort into the shambling atmosphere of the court, Bishop nodded to the pallid bespectacled judge and sat down on the hard bench reserved for the press. Bishop deliberately kept his face expressionless. He got out his notebook and began taking copious notes on the case that was unfolding.

A Vietnam vet called Tony Argonzoni had been caught selling heroin to an undercover cop. The accused sat forlornly by his legal representatives, wearing an old army flak jacket and faded Levis. A Purple Heart was pinned to his jacket; the pusher was a real, live hero.

"Your honor, my client..." droned the attorney whose mind seemed to have retreated into the impenetrable indifference of a Public Defender's low fees, "was kinda injured in Vietnam outside of Danang. He caught a bullet in the leg and it changed his whole personality." With that he yawned and then turned to the former soldier and asked him to roll up his left trouser leg.

"Look, your honor, you can see the terrible wound he sustained fighting for his country. They gave him a Purple Heart for his bravery, but when he got back home nobody could care less."

Bishop leaned over and whispered in Gloria's ear, "The lawyer couldn't care less, either. He just wants his fee to plea-bargain the case for a quick end to it."

The journalist stopped speaking when he noticed that the veteran had sunk to his knee, closed his eyes and was praying out loud.

"Why is he doing that?" the judge asked the tired attorney.

"He is praying to God that you will show him mercy," said the legal eagle, amid a few snickers from the street-wise cops scattered around the court.

"It's not my job to show mercy," retorted the judge, "it's my job to enforce the law. I'll take a short recess and give my judgment." The assembled, which included others about to be tried who were sitting on a long, side bench, were asked to rise as his honor left for his chambers to consider the case.

The veteran looked agitated as he waited for the verdict. He appeared to have a nervous affliction in his head and kept shaking it, as if trying to get rid of a fly perched there. The head shaking got more violent as the judge returned to his bench. He peered over his half-glasses at the accused and cleared his throat.

"Right, I have considered this case and I do feel a certain sympathy for you," he said looking at the miserable man before him.

"But you can't just go around selling heroin. Don't you realize the damage you are doing?"

The vet was quickly on his feet. His face was flushed with anger. "It was Uncle Sam who introduced me to drugs in 'Nam,'" he yelled. "I'm not to blame - THE GOVERNMENT IS!"

Before he could go any further with his tirade, the judge interrupted him. "I cannot comment on that," he said. "All I know is you've broken the law and I am sentencing you to a year in jail. Next...." With that he banged his gavel firmly on the bench and signaled the court officials to take away the pathetic prisoner.

Gloria's wide hazel eyes became moist as the man was roughly marched to the holding cells below to await transport to Ryker's Island: two Puerto Rican youths moved from the side bench to take their place before the weary judge.

Bishop took her hand and whispered, "Don't take it so personally. This is life in this part of the world. It's a jungle out there and only the fittest survive. It's Darwin's theory come true. In this job," he added as an afterthought, "you've got to annihilate your emotions."

For three hours, the pair observed the ritual of criminals of all shapes, sizes and colors being defended by lawyers appointed by the court and mostly found guilty by the judge. The whole thing began to meld in a surrealist painting for Gloria as each drama unfolded before her.

As the court ultimately began to empty, Bishop signaled to Gloria that it was also time for them to leave. With that, he snapped his notebook shut and inserted his ballpoint pen into his top pocket.

"Let's go and get some food at Alfredo's all-night deli," he said to his exhausted companion. "They have sandwiches built like the Great Wall of China - as hard as a brick and 1000-years old! You need a snake's hinged jaw to eat one." He chuckled to himself.

Gloria was not sure if Bishop, himself, planned to strike.

6
Caught in the Trap

Thick slices of sausage and cheese hung like pennants in the window of the Italian grocery shop owned by Joseph Battiglia on Atlantic Avenue, Brooklyn. As Gloria Jansen tried to peer in through the plate glass window, she nearly tripped over the sacks of beans, grain and dried chestnuts that slumped among huge jars of cinnamon sticks, immense olives in wine, pignolia nuts and peppercorns set out in front of the store.

Some of the jars held neat little bundles of dried oregano and rosemary, while sticks of dried bacalao rose like strange, exotic plants.

Gloria turned as Arch Bishop paid off the cab driver who had brought them over from the *Brooklyn Banner* for her first meeting with his parents.

True to fashion, the cabby was disgruntled with the tip. "Take the bus next time; it's cheaper," he hissed through tobacco-stained teeth and huffily adjusted his checkered cap.

Bishop ignored the barb and joined Gloria in front of the shop. Her face was swept with a huge question mark as she looked at the sign over the door - "BATTIGLIA ITALIAN GROCERIES."

"But Archibald, I thought your name was Bishop?"

"It is.... now. I changed it."

Before he could explain further, a squat balding man with a

fringe of gray hair circling his head, waddled through the doorway and threw his arms around Bishop. He had a walrus mustache, huge jowls of fat on the side of his face and wet blue eyes.

"Joseph, my son, how are you? You hardly ever come to see your Mama and me since you became a big-time reporter," he said reprovingly, in a heavy Italian accent.

"Well, Papa, I've been very busy." Bishop reached out and put his hand on his father's shoulder. Then, turning to Gloria, who was wearing a polka dot dress, he said, "Papa, I want you to meet Miss Gloria Jansen. She's my new girlfriend."

Wiping his sweaty hands on the apron stretched over his beer belly, Papa took her right hand in his two hands and shook it warmly.

"My dear, I am so pleased to meet you. Joseph has told me about you on the phone."

He signaled them into the shop. As Gloria walked through the door, the smell suddenly hit her. It came from the edifices built high of Italian cheese and salamis, fortresses topping displays of proscuitto, mortadella and wrinkled sausages. And the dried fish? Ugh! She bit down on her lips, afraid that if she opened her mouth she might throw up.

"It smells like rotting garbage, doesn't it?" said Bishop brightly as her face turned paper white. "Don't worry honey, they tell me the only thing worse is when you have morning sickness!"

Mr. Battiglia served the last lingering customer of the evening and then shut up shop. The "SORRY, WE'RE CLOSED" sign was in the doorway window. The pair then followed him upstairs. He wheezed as he led the way to the cluttered apartment. As Gloria obediently followed Arch's father, she felt a sick thump in her head and her stomach began suddenly to churn.

In the kitchen Gloria was confronted by the disconcerting figure of Mama, an overbearing ocean liner of a woman with wide streaks of gray in her curly raven hair.

"Joseph," she shrieked, rushing clumsily toward her only son. "Let me look at you." His formidable Mama made him stand mutely in front of her as she inspected him from head to toe. He tried to smile, but it was a huge effort.

"Are you eating properly, Joseph?" Her large face was clouded with motherly concern. "You look terribly thin. You need some of Mama's cooking to put some meat back on your bones." Her mouth, suspended between two puckered cheeks, seemed to Gloria to be the only part of her face that moved.

Gloria could see Arch was deeply embarrassed with his stout and voluble mother, but he could not do anything about it. He had told her she was quite a matriarch who dominated him totally as a boy. Mama had drilled into him that he was different from the other boys in the neighborhood. He had to study harder than them to "make something of your life." His father had paid for his college education and then to take a degree in mass communications at the University of New York. Gloria could see that the black-clad Italian mother had ruled her boy with a rod of iron. It must have been quite a struggle for him to free himself from her total dominance of every area of his life.

"Mama," said Papa Battiglia, seeing that the tongue-tied Gloria was being left out of the conversation, "I want you to say hello to Miss Jansen. She's Joseph's latest young lady."

Gloria felt herself shiver involuntarily as "Mama" turned her dark, piercing eyes on her and appeared to be looking into her very soul. Those eyes then focused on her blonde hair with ill-disguised disapproval. Gloria found her hands beginning to shake uncontrollably.

"You're not Italian?" she observed, in a sharp, accusing tone.

Gloria shook her head lamely, feeling that she, by not being Italian, had some terrible social disease that meant she should carry a bell like the lepers of Bible times, ringing it as she called out, "Unclean, unclean."

"Are you pure?" Mama then asked abruptly.

Gloria searched for an adequate answer. There was a cold knot in the pit of her stomach. "Well, err...." she stammered with a sickly croak, as a deathly silence descended over the room. Gloria wanted to hit back but said nothing. Bishop felt it was time to intervene on behalf of Gloria, whose face was by now tombstone gray in color.

"Mama, does it matter?" he asked, holding up a placating palm. He felt his hackles rising at her rudeness. But he knew, too, she was only acting like any Italian mother who just wanted her son to marry a "good Italian girl," and produce a litter of children for her to fuss over.

Mama then looked disapprovingly at Gloria's skimpy dress and asked, "Aren't you afraid you'll catch your death of cold in that thing?"

Gloria was speechless. She could understand now why Bishop had decided finally to move into an apartment and live his own life in Brooklyn - free from the constraints and traditions of their small village just outside of Naples, where his parents came from.

Soon it was time to eat and they gathered around the table. However, the red, homemade wine and heavy pasta was too much for Gloria. With her hand held tightly over her mouth, she knew if she didn't make a dash for the bathroom, everything was going to come up at express speed all over the table.

"Are you all right, honey?" Bishop called after Gloria as she rushed toward the bathroom. He followed her.

Everything did come up and, as Gloria expelled her dinner,

Mama was not impressed. Standing outside the bathroom doors, she called to her son and said coldly. "How do you expect her to bear children if she can't even hold down her food?"

Bishop came out of the bathroom and shot Mama a look fit to kill. He went inside again and found Gloria weakly holding onto a shower rail to keep from falling. He kissed her affectionately on the forehead and told her "not to worry."

"Mama's a monster," he retorted angrily. "I'll never forgive her for this."

After a few more minutes, Arch gently guided Gloria back to the lounge and eased her onto the sofa, putting a cushion under her head as she stretched out. Papa realized that a little light relief was called for and, with the courage brought on by the red wine, he told how Mama and he had just returned from a bizarre trip back to the "old country." They had also visited England, France, Holland and Belgium.

"Your Mama made me very embarrassed," Papa said as the free-flowing wine continued to free up his usually reluctant tongue.

Arch smiled inwardly as his mother's face turned as black as thunder.

"Don't you dare repeat that story," she warned, fixing her husband with a withering stare.

But he did dare! "Son, she took a whole pile of paper clips with her. Mama had heard that there was a shortage of paper clips in Europe and decided to give them to everyone who performed a service for us, like taxi drivers and waiters.

"I can't tell you how embarrassed I was when she handed half a dozen paper clips as a tip to the taxi driver, who drove us from Heathrow Airport in London, in a black cab to our hotel He was speechless!"

"That was because he appreciated what I did," interjected Mama vehemently.

Tears began to roll down Bishop's face as he pictured the scene, and even the prostrate Gloria was able to crease her face into a faint smile.

"Mama, how could you?" With that he slapped his knee as the laughter around the table threatened to get completely out of control.

"It's a wonder he didn't give you a 'clip' around the ear."

Mama still could not see what was so funny. To her, she was performing a kindness to the "poor, unfortunate people still stuck in Europe" who she had read somewhere were "finding it impossible to lay their hands on paper clips."

The evening finally broke up with Battiglia and his son smoking convivial cigars in the lounge under the disapproving eye of Mama and her collection of religious figures painted in sentimental pale pinks and blues and displayed on the mantelpiece.

Arch and Gloria decided to walk home as hand-in-hand they began their trek through the lovely violet of dusk. Strength began to trickle back into her body as she felt she was coming out of a nightmare. They chuckled at Mama's paper clip episode. Gloria was enchanted with the sights, sounds and smells of this part of Brooklyn. Their footsteps echoed hollowly on the sidewalk as they strode for block after block in this fascinating microcosm of the world transplanted in this part of the USA.

They hurried past a chattering, laughing cavalcade of Slavic women returning home from their office cleaning jobs, with their wide, pale faces, greenish eyes and thin, light hair, covered with wool 'kerchiefs of floral peasant design.

There were also Hasidic young men in black-rimmed, satiny hats, silk coats, knee breaches and black socks striding purposefully toward the synagogue.

A few old black-clad Italian women, with dark thick, wavy hair that suited their significant faces, hastened nervously through the gathering dusk.

Tanned Puerto Rican children turned the fire hydrants on each other as they squealed with delight and jumped up and down with excitement, their clothes sopping wet.

"Arch," she suddenly said as she clasped his arm, "I am confused. How is it that your father and you have different names?"

"Oh, you noticed," he chortled, as the spray from a hydrant was turned on them and they received its cooling balm.

"Well, as you witnessed tonight, I have a mother who would have done well as an SS guard in one of Germany's concentration camps. She felt her mission in life was to pump me full of her guilty hang-ups."

"Oh, Arch, that's a bit cruel, isn't it?"

"Not really, honey."

Even now at the age of 28, the memory of his mother's smothering personality filled him with bitterness. He recalled for Gloria how, for the first few years of his life he had to report to Mama before leaving for school so she could inspect every visible part of him.

"She would check to see if I had clean fingernails and if I had washed behind my ears," said Arch as his face contorted in disgust.

"Then, when I got home from school, she would make me sit on her lap and tell her everything that happened that day.

"Mama had an all-consuming fear that I would get involved with a girl. Even though I was so young, she would warn me, 'Joseph, don't ever kiss a girl. That's how they get pregnant. And you can go blind, too.'"

Bishop laughed aloud. "You know, honey, I never kissed a girl until I was eighteen, because I was scared of making her pregnant. And I didn't want to lose my sight. Can you believe that?"

Gloria held tightly onto his arm, but said nothing.

"I guess the worse thing she ever did to me was when I was in the Cub Scouts. She heard that we were to have a Halloween costume party and so spent weeks making my costume!"

"What sort of costume?"

"Honey, she dressed me as Little Bo Peep and made me walk through the streets of Brooklyn in that awful outfit carrying a crook. Everyone laughed at me, but Mama didn't care. She even followed me to make sure I didn't try to sneak off.

"When I arrived at the Parish hall where we met, I discovered to my horror, that there was no costume party and I was the only one dressed up. All the boys laughed hilariously. I ran outside, crying my eyes out.

"I guess Mama always wanted a daughter and that's why she dressed me up that way."

Gloria looked stunned.

"Even as a young boy, I vowed to change my name and start again from scratch, with a new identity. Mama has never forgiven me for what I did, but Papa understands. He would like to get out from under her thumb, but it's too late for him. So he throws himself into his business...."

"And you throw yourself into your work?" Gloria interrupted.

"You've got it, babe!"

Gloria could see some of the hardness of Bishop's exterior shell beginning to crack. He was suddenly very fragile and vulnerable. A dullness veiled his eyes; there was a distance, a privacy that she could not yet penetrate.

"Where did you get your strange name from, Arch? What gave you the idea for it?" Her voice was by now as soft as silk.

Arch Bishop again laughed out aloud. "Babe, you're not going to believe this, but I got the idea from the British Archbishop of Canterbury when he paid a visit to New York."

Arch could see the question mark hanging on Gloria's face, so he continued.

"When he arrived here, I attended his press conference. I asked him, with a smile on my face, if he planned to attend any nightclubs while he was in New York.

"Looking rather ridiculous in his outfit which included gaiters, he asked innocently, 'Are there any night clubs in New York?'

"So I headlined my tongue-in-cheek story, '**ARCHBISHOP HITS 'BIG APPLE,' AND ASKS, 'WHERE ARE THE NIGHT CLUBS?'**'"

"My colleagues at the Banner thought that was so funny that they christened me, 'The Archbishop.' So I decided that I would change my name to Arch Bishop!"

Gloria was open-mouthed at his explanation. "You were making fun of a man of the cloth, Arch. Don't you think that's a bit cruel?" she asked.

"Come on, honey. Where's your sense of humor?"

* * * * *

Joey "The Weasel" Valenti looked decidedly nervous as Arch Bishop entered the dank, cool, silent world of the Shamrock Bar in Brooklyn Heights. His concern was because the reporter was not alone, but had an elegant leggy girl attached to his arm. Valenti cautiouslywaved to Bishop and, as he arrived beside him, "The Weasel" whispered out of the side of his mouth, "Hey, man, is this a set-up? I told you to come alone." His voice shook as he spoke at machine-gun speed.

The "squealer" did not like anyone else knowing about his risky business. He was aware that it was dangerous to allow confidences about "The Mob" go too far. Valenti knew that if it were discovered he was about to blow the whistle on a Mafia scandal, he would soon be lying dead in an alley, his body full of lead, or clad in cement at the bottom of Long Island Sound.

"Joey," said Bishop to the small, slightly bent-up man sitting in the darkened corner of the Irish bar, his face blue-stubbled and vulnerable with exhaustion, "you worry too much.

"Let me introduce you to Miss Gloria Jansen, who is helping me on the 'crime beat.' She's been working with me for six months now and is as discreet as a priest in the confessional."

"Well, I don't know, Mr. Bishop," said "The Weasel" as his beady eyes burned through the cigarette haze of the bar. In a nervous and hushed voice, he added. "You've never brought anyone along before when we've met." He was neurotically suspicious, but who could blame him? The stakes were high.

Gloria stood at the side of the table watching the scene, still holding tightly onto Bishop's arm.

"Look you two, if you would rather I leave, I'll...." Her voice was husky with hurt.

"Stay where you are, honey," said Bishop testily. "If Joey doesn't know by now that he can trust my word, I'll stop doing business with him."

The reporter took a $100 bill out of his wallet and flashed it in front of The Weasel's eyes.

"If you don't want anymore of my pay-offs, Joey, I'll just have to take my money elsewhere."

The greenback had the desired effect, and the "snitch" greedily snatched it from Bishop's hand and stuck it in a trouser pocket.

Six months on the crime beat with Bishop had caused Gloria to grow up quickly. For the first time in her life, cynicism had entered her emotions. She took an instant dislike to the sneaky little creature Bishop had come to do business with. To her, he was a Judas betraying his colleagues for a little more than thirty pieces of silver.

She hadn't liked too many of his informants. To her, they were grimy double-crossers who took money from their employers in "The Mob," and then from reporters like Arch Bishop at the other end of the spectrum. Her only feeling toward him was sick disgust. She realized that in the dark and secret world of a crime reporter, weasels were needed to provide leads for stories to bump up circulation figures. The readers apparently wanted a freak show of sex and violence in each edition. "Good news," as Daddy had told her on many occasions, "doesn't sell papers."

After ordering a "Bud" for the weasel, a "g & t" for himself and a glass of white wine for Gloria, Bishop sat down as Gloria joined him and got down to the business at hand.

"Okay, Joey, what have you got for me this time? It better be good. Your last tip didn't pan out, you know."

"This one will. It's a biggie, Mr. Bishop. I swear to it on my mother's grave." He paused to gaze into his beer then seized it firmly and gulped down the whole glass. Then he signaled to the cocktail waitress - an aging, frumpy lady in a short dress which stressed her tree-trunk legs - that he wanted a refill.

As the booze-bearer wearily trudged to the bar in her white, sensible shoes, Valenti leaned over to the pair seated across the small wooden table from him and began to speak in a conspiratorial tone.

"The story I've got for you, Mr. Bishop, is that Senator Mario de Rocca is about to take a big pay-off from 'The Mob' for doing them a favor."

"What kind of favor?" asked Bishop brusquely.

"They want him to 'lean' on the police chief to stop investigating 'The Mob's' protection rackets. I thought you would be interested because your Papa has been forced into paying 'protection' money to them. They have threatened to torch his shop if he doesn't continue to cooperate."

For a long moment Arch Bishop froze, then he exploded with anger. He had noticed Papa had been subdued on a recent visit to him, but he hadn't guessed it was because of this. If only for Papa, he had to put a stop to this racket that had plagued the area for so long. His mind suddenly shifted into top gear.

"What if we fitted you up with a tiny transmitter, Valenti?" he suggested. "You could then be in on a 'meet' with your guys and the senator? I could be in a car nearby taping the proceedings." Bishop ran an excited hand through his disheveled hair.

"The Weasel" wasn't sure. "What if they discover what I'm up to?" he asked nervously.

"They won't!" retorted Bishop confidently. "And I am sure I can persuade my paper to give you a big pay-off - bigger than anything you've ever received before."

After a few more hastily consumed beers, "The Weasel" finally agreed to the plan. They resolved to meet again soon, this time in a nearby alleyway, to finalize the plan. Then he gave "The Weasel" $2,500 "on account" with a promise of the same amount "once we get the evidence" and the story had "hit the streets."

Arch Bishop's hunter instincts were by now aroused. As on previous occasions, he was not looking upon the senator as a person with feelings, but an object to advance his career. Like a dog on a leash, he was again being let out after his quarry.

Still, Gloria felt apprehensive. For the first time in her life she was beginning to experience the bitter taste of fear. An inner sense of utter panic began to grip her.

* * * * *

Arch Bishop parked his pea-green Pinto just around the corner from the senator's headquarters on Third Street. He plugged a special radio receiver into his cassette tape recorder and nervously waited with Gloria for the transmission to begin. There was a strange sound as it came to life.

The micro transmitter had been taped under "The Weasel's" left armpit and they heard him visit the bathroom in the senator's office. Bishop chuckled as he heard the toilet flush and "The Weasel" clearing his voice.

The rest was left to Arch and Gloria's imagination as "The Weasel" entered the senator's reception office. He joined Al Licavoli and Guiseppi Angersola, the local Mafia boss and the person who was to offer the bribe to the politician.

A husky female voice announced to the trio, "The senator will see you now," and ceremoniously ushered them into de Rocca's office.

After some pro forma small talk about each other's families, they got down to serious business.

"Mr. Senator, before we hand you to you the $20,000, I want to know how we can be sure that you can stop O'Higgins from continuing his unfortunate probe of our activities," said Licavoli as droplets of sweat began breaking out on Arch Bishop's forehead. "After all he isn't Italian. He may not understand 'our way' of doing business."

There was a brief pause in the proceedings as the senator pondered the question. "Don't worry boys. O'Higgins owes me a favor for something I did for one of his guys some months back.

One of his officers got excited and shot two 'Spics' for turning a water hose on him. I spoke to the judge and the guy got off with a warning.

"So if I tell him to lay off your case, I know he'll listen. In my game it's a case of 'you scratch my back and I'll scratch yours.' No, gentlemen, you've got nothing to worry about."

Bishop and his companion heard some muffled whispering among the trio and then Angersola finally ordered "The Weasel" to count out the money in $100 bills. Arch Bishop's heart began to pound against the walls of his chest.

"Yes, it's all there, sir," said Valenti. "Count it for yourself." The senator did, and confirmed out loud that the $20,000 was "all there."

Bishop's large frame shivered with anticipatory excitement.

"You can keep on 'protecting' the neighborhood, boys," the senator chortled in a voice filled with satisfaction. "And I'll keep on 'protecting' you."

That was exactly what Arch Bishop wanted to hear. He enjoyed eavesdropping on the private lives of others and he punched the air in triumph and then threw his arms around Gloria who had sat stupefied at what she had been listening to. She already knew something of the "low-life" in Brooklyn, but this was more than she could comprehend. Arch had been a good teacher, but an elected official behaving in this way just threw her sideways. She was exhausted by the tension.

As Bishop planted a large kiss on her ripe, soft mouth, he began yelling as if the Yankees had just scored a home run, but she became deadly serious.

"Arch, don't you realize that if you go ahead and print this story, your life will be in danger?" she said nervously. "What you are planning to do is absurdly risky." Gloria felt her stomach churning with fear, and her face drained as pale as milk.

Bishop took a deep breath. He knew what she had said was true, but he didn't care. This was a big story and he was going to "publish and be damned" regardless of the consequences. He had a feeling he was invincible.

After a dramatic conference with the top brass at the Banner, Bishop went with a photographer to confront the senator with the taped evidence. Naturally, de Rocca vehemently denied everything - until Bishop produced the cassette and began playing it to him. As the damning evidence came from the tiny speaker, the politician clasped his hands on his ornate mahogany desk and stared at them silently, blinking, but not totally comprehending the seriousness of the situation.

Then it hit him and, without warning, he began to sob uncontrollably. As he thrust his head into his hands, the Banner's cameraman clicked away for a series of candid shots of the senator's misery.

Bishop measured the pain he had caused, but then left the senator to his despair and the comforting arms of his secretary who was desperately trying to console him by holding his head close to her and whispering, "There, there..."

The next morning, Arch Bishop's bylined story carried the startling headline: "**SENATOR MARIO DE ROCCA CAUGHT RED-HANDED TAKING BRIBE FROM THE MOB**." The story, illustrated by photographs, pictured the senator at first showing disbelief on his face and then holding his head in his hands. Bishop called for de Rocca's "immediate resignation and prosecution by the District Attorney."

The repercussions of Arch Bishop's story were startling to say the least. TV crews descended on Bishop to interview him, as did reporters from both Time and Newsweek. He even received a congratulatory letter from Elmer Jansen III - and the constant adoration of his only daughter.

Six months later, Arch Bishop was awarded the Pulitzer Prize for his "outstanding" reporting. When the award was announced, Gloria's eyes filled with a foolish, cow-like worship, and she presented him with a pair of diamond-studded cuff links.

This was the man she knew that she would marry.

7
A Shot in the Light

The shrill of his office phone interrupted Arch Bishop's thoughts as he put the final touches on his daily *Confidential* column for the *Brooklyn Banner*.

"Yep," he rasped impatiently into the instrument. "Who's this?"

A gruff voice that was desperately trying to be polite countered, "Is this Arch Bishop?"

"Yep, but who's this?"

"Mr. Bishop, my name is Al Farr from the *New York Tribune*." The rough-edged voice continued in an unnaturally friendly vein.

Before Farr could finish, Bishop snapped, "I've already got a subscription, Mr. Farr, so there's no need for you to give me your spiel."

Farr's control wavered momentarily and then an irritated edge came into his voice. "Mr. Bishop," he said, clearing his throat, "I'm not a salesman. I'm the news editor!"

Bishop's slapped his head at his stupidity.

"I'd like to meet with you as soon as possible to discuss a proposition that could be of mutual benefit to us," said Farr, undeterred.

Arch Bishop sat up straight in his leather chair. "What sort of proposition?" he asked, trying to sound matter-of-fact, but really feeling quite excited.

"Let's get together and I'll tell you about it. What about 'Elmers on Second Avenue on the East Side?"

Bishop was acquainted with the bar. He had once gone there to interview former Middleweight Champion of the World, Rocky Graziano, who "hung out" there with other old boxers, including Jake "Raging Bull" La Motta.

The pair agreed to meet up that night at eight o'clock and Farr explained that he would be standing by the bar with a copy of the *New York Tribune* laid out in front of him.

* * * * *

The quivering crew cut and the bull neck could only belong to Al Farr. There was only one Al Farr, a tough ex-marine who had entered journalism after serving with the "few and the proud" in Korea. He had become something of a legend in New York for his crusty manner, his omnipresent cigar, but also for his brilliant news sense.

Bishop walked firmly through the darkened bar toward the tree-trunk figure and lightly touched Farr on the shoulder just as Farr was about to take a drink of an ice-cold Bud.

Paraphrasing the words of Henry Stanley when he finally tracked down David Livingstone in Africa, Bishop said brightly, "Mr. Farr, I presume."

The man spun around and, at the same moment, inserted his huge cigar in his mouth. For a long moment he chewed on it and surveyed the sight before him.

"You presumed right, buddy," he said gruffly. "I guess you must be Arch Bishop. What's your poison?"

Bishop ordered a "g & t" while Farr had another Bud with a chaser of whisky-on-the-rocks. Arch Bishop was to discover that

Al Farr was a man who hated small talk. He believed in getting straight to the point.

"Well, Mr. Bishop," he barked as if giving an impersonation of George C. Scott playing Patton, "I've been following your career with great interest. Nice work you did in that 'de Rocca case.' I always guessed that rat was up to no good. I had a tail on him, but you beat us to the punch."

Bishop gently sipped on his "g. & t." and wondered what was coming next. He did not have to wait long.

"Well, Mr. Bishop, I'll come straight to the point. I like your work, especially your columns for the Banner. You seem just the sort of guy we need on the *Tribune*. How would you like to join my team?"

Bishop smiled inwardly and almost clicked his heels and rasped, "Yes, sir." But he managed to check himself. He didn't think that Farr would appreciate that response. Of course he would like to join "Farr's Platoon," as his team was called in the "Big Apple."

"What 'rank' would I have?"

"You'd be a senior reporter specializing in crime. After all, you seem to know what you're doing in that area."

Bishop felt his heart would burst with excitement. It had been his dream ever since that first day he had joined the *Banner*, five years previously, to hook up with a paper as prestigious as the *New York Tribune*. He knew his Pulitzer Prize had probably influenced Farr who prided himself on having what he considered the sharpest news crew in the United States. But still, Bishop thought he would play hard to get.

"What's the pay and perks, then?" he asked abrasively.

"What do you want?" countered Farr craftily.

The two verbally "fenced" with each other for another round of drinks and finally shook hands on a deal.

"Okay, Mr. Bishop, I'll look forward to having you in my 'platoon' one month from today." With that he firmly clasped Bishop's hand, almost crushing it in his vice-like grip.

The announcement of his appointment was certainly clear. "PULITZER PRIZEWINNER JOINS THE TRIBUNE'S CRIME BEAT," was how the *New York Tribune* headlined it. Of course the staff at the *Banner* was sorry to see him go, but they had been expecting this move since he had gained such national recognition.

Gloria also had mixed feelings about the appointment. She was obviously pleased that he was climbing the ladder of success; but she also feared that all this attention could turn his head. Already he was showing signs of becoming arrogant, even with her.

Still, she accompanied him to his first morning on the *Tribune* and kept her feelings to herself. A yellow cab dropped them off at the bustling intersection of 42nd Street and Times Square that gave them a short walk to the offices on West 43rd Street. It was 9:30 A.M. and the area was just filling up with the despicable life that inhabits much of the area.

"Like some grass, man?" whispered a black sidewalk "salesman," out of the side of his mouth, as the couple passed by.

"Get lost, slime," responded Bishop angrily. He hated drug pushers almost as much as his Mama.

"Scum," he hissed to Gloria as she clung on to his arm.

When they reached West 43rd Street, Gloria stopped her man momentarily and pulled him squarely in front of her. "Let me look at you," she said proudly as she fixed his tie and flicked some hair from his collar. Arch Bishop was immaculate in a dark, pinstriped suit and black patent leather shoes. "You look like the manager of the Chase Manhattan Bank," she chuckled. "But, you'll do. It's time to go and take New York by storm, you crazy guy."

Gloria told Arch she would not go any further. "You just go on in there and knock them dead!" she said, knowing that was just what he planned to do. With his ambition to succeed and his contacts, he could not really fail.

Arch tenderly leaned toward her and firmly kissed her pouting mouth. She was so fresh and innocent, like a fragile flower just coming into full bloom. Then he turned on his heels and strode purposefully toward the front entrance of the paper. As he came close to the doorway, a peculiar foreboding swept over him, but he was not able to pinpoint the cause of his anxiety.

"Pull yourself together, Archie boy," he muttered to himself, trying to alleviate the strange nervousness he felt deep in the pit of his stomach. "It's just first-day nerves," he continued, trying to reassure himself.

Gloria stood quietly amid the noise and bustle of Times Square watching her man approach the doorway of his new career. Her eyes were pinned so tightly on him that she had not noticed a sleek black Cadillac stretch-limo crawling along the street a few yards behind him. Sitting in the back seat, his arm resting on the divider, was a hit man called Mario Angelus, safely invisible behind the dark-brown bulletproof sunglass. His Gucci-clad feet twitched with eager anticipation.

Gloria blew him a kiss as Bishop finally reached his destination and he turned back and responded in like fashion. Just then he became aware of a large shadow gliding up behind him. Then a voice distracted him and he whirled around toward the limo as an electrically operated window slid down. "Hey Bishop, I've got a message for you from a friend." The hoarsely whispered shout hung heavily in the humidity of the morning.

As Bishop stood transfixed, the man wearing dark glasses raised, as if in slow motion, a 9-mm Parabellum pistol and squeezed the trigger.

Pssst... was all the sound that Bishop heard as the silencer effectively did its job. The hollow point lead bullet slammed into his left shoulder with such force it spun him half around and knocked him against the swing door. Then another bullet grazed his head, just behind the ear, causing his body to convulse spastically with its impact and his head to bang violently against the wall. Screaming with pain, Bishop slumped to the ground. Reality began to zoom down a dark black hole for him. He could feel pain, faint and far away, in his shoulder and head. It was spreading all over him...oblivion...void.

As blood spurted from his head and flowed like lava from a dying volcano, the squeal of tires heralded the fast escape of the hit man who watched the scene with satisfaction through the darkened rear window of the car. Angelus dialed a number on his cellular car-phone that connected him to his client.

"The job's done, Mr. de Rocca," he said in a businesslike manner. With that he pressed the "end" button and replaced the receiver.

Gloria had watched the shooting take place in shocked disbelief. It was if the scene was in a freeze frame in a motion picture. Surely this could not be real? But it was real; horribly real. Feeling an avalanche of horror envelop her whole body, she ran screaming hysterically toward the slumped figure of Arch Bishop who lay like a crumpled rag doll by the still moving swing doors of the newspaper, his left leg trapped under his body.

She rushed to cradle his head as security men began to clear a way through the crowd of gawkers that had appeared from nowhere.

"Call an ambulance," screamed Gloria as the transfixed crowd stood and stared. Her body was wracked with sobs as she gazed down at Arch's contorted face. For a brief moment, he managed to open his eyes, and then they began to roll helplessly in their sockets like a fear-maddened horse. Bishop tried to mouth, "I love you." With that his head fell back and he slid into a deep unconsciousness.

Gloria hardly noticed that her smart gray, two-piece suit was now covered in blood. She kept shouting, "Arch, you've got to live. For God's sake live."

God had not figured much in her life up until now. But as death hovered close by, she cried out desperately to Him.

"God, I don't really know who you are, but please save his life. Please.... I'll do anything if you'll just let him live."

A frantic siren, punctuated by a bleating Klaxon demanding a clear path through city traffic, suddenly broke into her desperate conversation with the Almighty as an ambulance, followed by another, appeared on the scene and two paramedics jumped out and knelt beside Arch and tried to stanch the flow of blood gushing from his gun-shot wounds.

Gloria watched transfixed as one of them began speaking into a mobile unit portable transceiver.

"Rampart, this is mobile unit one, do you copy?"

"We copy, go ahead please."

"Doctor," the paramedic said urgently, "the guy's losing an awful lot of blood. He's taken two bullets - one in the shoulder; the other grazed the side of his head. I think his clavicle is shattered and the bullet has possibly torn a large vein. Judging by his head wound, he also may have a fractured skull."

Gloria inclined her head to try to catch what the doctor was saying in reply. She caught the words, "Cut that out, Morris, I'll do the diagnosing...stabilize his condition before you move him" and "get the IV going. Just concentrate on stopping the bleeding and increasing the venous velum with plasma expander." Then another wailing police siren drowned out the rest of the instructions to the sidewalk paramedic.

A drip was set up and colorless liquid began slowly moving into Arch Bishop's un-responding body, via his left arm. A stretcher quickly appeared and Arch was gently lifted onto it and guided toward the ambulance, with one of the paramedics holding the drip. As they carefully walked toward the waiting ambulance, photographers from the *New York Tribune* recorded the scene for the next edition.

Gloria followed the stretcher to the back of the ambulance and looked imploringly at the medics.

"Please, let me come with him."

"Okay, lady hop in the back, but be quick."

* * * * *

Gloria paced the corridor outside the Emergency Trauma Unit where Arch was being worked on. The whole scene seemed to have a cold reality. Here was his life hanging by a thread and yet a constant drone of routine messages for hospital staff and relatives were continually relayed on the PA system. "Would Mrs. Ojarovsky please come to... would Nurse Simmons please...." She wanted to do something, anything, to help, but what could she do? Finally, she approached a starched nurse with a starched face at her station and implored, "Please tell me what is going on."

The nurse allowed her professional face to show a tiny tinge of compassion.

"Well, honey, they are doing all they can for him."

"Why not let me give my blood for him. Maybe we're compatible." Gloria's desperate expression touched a sympathetic chord with the nurse. "At least test me to see if we are the same blood group type."

The nurse, however, still was not sure. But just then Dr. Jon Johannsen, a Swede who had escaped from "Socialized medicine" to make his pile in New York, emerged from the unit. Gloria rushed toward him.

"Doctor, please test me to see if my blood is suitable for Arch. Oh, please...."

He scratched his head and looked at her face that was etched with despair.

"I understand. You feel helpless. You want to do something to help. Okay, follow me and we'll see what blood type you are." He knew that one unit of blood was not going to make a difference, but understood the gesture she was making.

A quick test in the lab at the downstairs clinic, revealed that Gloria was "A-Positive," that was exactly what was needed.

A nurse asked Gloria to lie on the bed so they could begin drawing her blood. She closed her eyes as a rubber tourniquet was tightened around her right arm and the unit nurse began gently slapping her veins until one began to pop up, blue and large. A dab of alcohol was applied and she gritted her teeth as the large needle was swiftly inserted into the vein. She dared not look at the plastic bag that was beginning to fill up with her blood that she knew would soon be surging into Arch's body. Gloria felt good that she was, at last, doing something positive to try to help an apparently hopeless situation.

* * * * *

Gloria leaned forward to dab the perspiration dotted about Arch's forehead as he continued to gaze unseeingly at the white hospital ceiling. The auditory signal of the cardiac monitor was turned down low. Doctor Johannsen had granted her VIP admission, contrary to the usual policy, and she had watched for hours the visual signal trace a repetitive fluorescent blip across the tiny screen. She tried to ignore the tube that had been inserted through his mouth to help him breathe with the assistance of a respirator. But she could not blot out the sound from the machine that sounded like a defective steam kettle with a sinus infection and looked, to her, like the dashboard of an expensive car.

"He's doing much better than we thought he would," said the white-starched nurse, Deborah Hall, another escapee from "Socialized medicine," this time from the National Health Service in England.

"To be honest dear, I'm more worried about you than Mr. Bishop," she added in a perfect English accent. "This is the second night you've sat here without any sleep."

Gloria turned her dark, sunken eyes on the duty nurse.

"I've got to be here when he wakes up. Otherwise he'll be frightened."

Nurse Hall looked at her with deep compassion in her eyes.

"My dear, you know the doctor says he may never come out of the coma. Even though you gave your blood, he has still got a long way to go.

"Now why don't you go and get some rest. I've made up a bed for you in a room down the hall. I promise to call you as soon as he shows any signs of regaining consciousness."

Gloria looked heavily through the dimmed lights of the ward at the man she loved so much. She could hardly bear to see him lying strapped as he was in a silver metal cot, with two intravenous lines, one running into his left arm, the other into his right, taking in saline with potassium directly into his heart. His wrists were held tightly by bandage restraints resting on wood splints because he had on several occasions begun flailing his arms wildly and had tried to rip the IVs from his arms, even with his heavily bandaged hand. He looked like a drugged tiger in a cage.

Bishop's large face - framed through his head dressing - looked pale and gaunt. There were black lines in a half-moon shape, drawn as if by an eye pencil, under both his eyes. Gloria saw them as semi-circles of pain. Was he going to die? She could literally taste death in the air in this Emergency Unit of the hospital.

It took all her self-control not to un-strap his hands and take out the needles and hold him.

"Okay, nurse, you win," she said as time had slowed to an inchworm crawl. "I'll try and lie down for a little while. But you must call me the moment he stirs."

"I promise," said the nurse as she went over and gently helped Gloria to her feet. She put her arm around her waist to steady her and Gloria walked through the door. Gloria almost tripped over the dozing cop, posted at the entrance to protect Arch Bishop from further attacks. Needing some light relief from the situation, she leaned over and, as the horrified nurse watched, Gloria shouted, "Stick 'em up, buster." With that she pointed her fingers, gun-like, at his temple and watched him snap back into panic-stricken consciousness.

"Oh, my God, lady, don't shoot," he yelled, raising his hands upward. "I've got a wife and kids to support."

She looked deadly serious. "If anything happens to Mr. Bishop, I will hold you directly responsible," she snapped as the officer was now sitting bolt upright.

* * * * *

Mama's face kept leering into Arch Bishop's subconscious mind.

Her multi-layered chin was shaking like jelly as her lips suspended between huge puckered cheeks kept moving and maniacally, bellowing, "Joseph, you're a bad boy. Mama's going to spank you again...and again...and again...."

Surrealist images of his short, stumpy legs flailing wildly as Mama pounded her pudgy hands with great force on his bare bottom veered in on him. No Singaporean flogging could compare with the beating Mama was giving him.

As he cried out for mercy, blubbering with dread, Mama yelled, "I'm just beating all the sin out of you. You're an evil, disgusting boy."

The beating seemed to go on for hours and the more he tried to free himself from her unbridled violence, the more he realized he could not move his hands - in fact he could not escape from Mama's cruelty.

"Stop!" he gurgled. The word suddenly moved from Bishop's subconscious to his mouth. The unearthly sound jolted the nurse who was studying his charts at the end of the bed. She stopped suddenly and adjusted her nylon uniform. Then she pressed a buzzer at the side of the bed summoning another nurse to watch the stirring patient. As soon as she arrived, she dashed out of the ward, past the startled cop, and into the guestroom where Gloria lay fully clothed, on top of the bed.

She took Gloria's arm violently. "Wake up, wake up, Miss Jansen."

Gloria started violently back from her fitful sleep, and sat up in a groggy consciousness.

"What? What?"

"Just follow me. Quickly, quickly. Mr. Bishop's just made a sound."

Gloria dashed into his private room followed by the nurses'

squeaking white crepe-soled shoes. There they found Arch mouthing over and over again, "Mama, don't hit me again. I'm cured. I'm cured."

She took his restrained left hand gently and rubbed it reassuringly. Then she traced her finger lightly around his fever-hot forehead.

"Arch, honey, can you hear me?" A weak smile trembled at the corners of his mouth as he continued with his incomprehensible croaks.

Squeezing his hand, she whispered in his ear, "Arch, it's me, Gloria."

Slowly, he opened his eyes and squinted as he tried to focus on the figure leaning over him. The outline of the face was certainly not that of his roly-poly Mama.

"Who are you?" he seemed to ask as a confused look spread across his face.

A tiny tear appeared in Gloria's reddened eyes. She looked desperately at the nurse at the other side of the bed. The nurse judged rightly that it was time for her to try to take charge of the situation.

"Mr. Bishop, you are in the hospital and this young lady is Gloria, your girlfriend. Someone shot you and you've been unconscious for thirty-six hours."

"Did Mama shoot me?" he mouthed.

"Of course not, Arch," said Gloria. "She loves you very much, and so do I." The voice floated down to him as if from a great distance.

As he gazed up, through screwed up eyes at the blurred image of his elegant young lady staring down at him, he summoned up a labored smile.

Gloria leaned over and kissed him affectionately on the

forehead. His eyelids felt as if they were weighted with lead.

"Why don't you sleep now?"

8
"For Better ... For Worse ..."

Arch Bishop's knuckles turned white as the countdown in the "America in the Morning" studio in New York began.

"Okay, Charlie, ten, nine...two, one," indicated the floor producer with his fingers to the genial breakfast TV host, Charlie Dibson, as the third segment of the daily show began.

Just then a candid shot of the nervous bandaged face of Arch Bishop moved slowly down to his shaking right hand then was pulled back to a long-shot of him trying to grip the sides of his wheelchair. This was flashed across the country.

"Ladies and gentlemen," said Dibson, "we have an extraordinary man in the studio with us this morning. He's a man who two months ago was shot by a hit man on his first morning with the *New York Tribune*.

"For several days, his life hung by a thread, but the love and concern of his fiancée, Gloria Jansen, has helped pull him through."

Dibson turned to Arch Bishop, whose throat was as dry as cotton, then smiled at Gloria who was sitting next to Arch in an upright chair.

"Welcome to you both."

Bishop nodded weakly, while Gloria smiled and then tightly clasped Arch's hand. She loved being known as his fiancée.

Dibson turned and asked to see the diamond ring that now adorned Gloria's third finger of her left hand. Camera three zoomed in on it and America was about to share in Gloria's pride.

"When's the big day?" asked Dibson with unaccustomed genuine interest.

Arch Bishop, trying to shield his eyes from the harsh lights, squinted at the host, and muttered in embarrassment, "When I can...." His speech suddenly stopped and a vacant stare came over his face. His arms then began to contract, as Dibson looked bewildered at Gloria. She smiled weakly as Arch again picked up the thread of what he was saying and added, "...when I can walk properly again."

Gloria butted in, realizing what had occurred. "That won't be long. The bullet that grazed his head has caused a paralysis in his legs, but every day he managed to go a little further. With his determination and my love, he'll do it."

The camera then turned to Al Farr, who sat impassively across from Charlie Dibson, an unlit cigar gripped firmly in his hand.

"Mr. Farr, you are the news editor of the *New York Tribune*. When will Mr. Bishop be able to start work?"

Farr smiled briefly. "We're in no rush. We want him to regain his strength and get better first. He's a courageous man and we will set him to work after he gets married to this lovely young lady. I predict that could be very soon indeed."

Even as he spoke, Bishop began to sob. Dibson, who asked for an update on the weather from a colleague who was standing by for such an eventuality, cut the interview short.

After the show, Farr asked Arch and Gloria if they would like to have a drink with him at the nearby O'Halloran's bar.

Farr ordered a Bud, while Bishop had his usual "g & t," and Gloria had a mineral water. After Farr finally left, Bishop wanted to continue his drinking "for a little longer." So he ordered several more drinks. Gloria noticed the more he consumed, the more vicious his tongue became.

When she tried to get him to stop, Bishop looked angrily at her and said, "Who do you think you are, woman? My mother? You don't own me. I'll drink as much as I want."

It was a further hour before - and with his head whirling - he finally agreed to let Gloria push him and the wheelchair out onto the street. She hailed a cab and the driver helped Arch into the taxi, then folded up his chair and put it into its trunk.

When they arrived at his apartment, the cabby helped put the wheelchair together and manhandled the very drunk Arch Bishop into it. Then he pushed them to the building and into the waiting elevator.

"Thank you," said a grateful Gloria as she paid him off. "I do appreciate your patience."

"Think nothing of it, sweetheart," said the cabby tipping his checkered cap. "I reckon he deserves a drink after what he's been through. I saw him on TV this morning."

Arch Bishop did not hear what was said - he had already sunk into a drunken stupor and was snoring loudly. In the apartment, Gloria managed to tip him from the wheelchair onto his bed and then turned him so he faced upward. As the raucous sound of his snoring continued unabated, she began looking around his rather untidy apartment. She was horrified to discover, as she checked the drawers, countless empty bottles of gin. Gloria knew that Arch liked to drink, and when they had said good-bye at night, she knew he had a "nightcap," but not whole bottles before going to sleep. Something was terribly wrong.

When he was sober, his personality was like the old, chirpy, Arch, but once the gin began to flow into his system, it was like a demon had gotten hold of him. Along with the alcohol problem, Gloria had noticed the blank stares and lapses in conversation had been increasing.

Dr. Johannsen had warned her about what to expect just before his release from the hospital.

"What has happened, Miss Jansen, is that the bullet has caused great pressure on the hypothalamus, which is just above the midbrain and contains an important group of nerves," he said, trying not to be too technical.

"Beneath it, the optic nerves from the eyes meet, and part of their fibers cross to the opposite sides.

"The thalamus which is found next to this group of nerve endings, contains another group of nuclei which integrate sensations of many sorts. Also, it is the site of a crude form of consciousness and plays a role in the production of emotion. When this part of the brain is injured, you can get crude emotional responses such as spontaneous laughter or crying. You will probably see a big change in his personality."

The Swedish doctor was not sure if she had understood what he was saying, but still he pressed on with the bad news. "I believe Mr. Bishop's head injury may cause epilepsy. However, in his case, it could come out in petit mal attacks, which is the mildest form of epilepsy. It will show itself in the loss of consciousness in fleeting ways, from one to 40 or 50 times a day. Quite often it may be so short that it goes unnoticed."

Feeling she now needed some encouragement, the doctor added, "This is usually controlled by drugs such as Dilantin and Phenobarbital. But he shouldn't drink any alcohol!"

Gloria needed to know more.

"Well, for instance his head may nod momentarily, the flow of his speech may halt a second or two and then may be normally resumed; or perhaps only a vacant stare marks the attack. Sometimes there are one or two contractions of the arms or the flickering of the eyelids.

"All I am saying to you, Miss Jansen, is be patient with him and don't let him get into stressful situations."

He paused and then continued. "Bit by bit, the wondrous entity of the human personality is being decoded. We have found discrete locations in the brain of an intricate system that serves, among other things, as the human moral compass. Largely in the prefrontal cortex, it is where reason is applied to complex social situations, where our personal scales of justice do their weighing. But this highest faculty can be as be as vulnerable as say a knee joint. It could be that the bullet injury could completely change Mr. Bishop's personality."

She waited patiently for Arch to wake from his alcohol-induced slumber to confront him with the bottles. But he was unrepentant.

"It's none of your business," he snarled as he held his thumping head. "My mother wanted to own me, now you do. Well, I've got news for you both; no one owns me - except me!"

"And the bottles?" said Gloria pointedly as she held up an empty Gilbey's. "What's happened to you, Arch? You never used to drink like this."

He stared defiantly at her. "I'll tell you what happened, honey. I got shot! That's what happened. This stuff kills the pain for me."

"Well, at least that's your excuse," she countered angrily.

For a few weeks, things began to improve after this confrontation. Bishop paid attention to learning to walk again. Each time he fell over at the hospital gym, she picked him up with the help of a male therapist and encouraged him not to give up. He didn't drink any more in front of Gloria and began to show some of his old affection for her.

The turning point came when he managed to walk some twenty yards unaided. With each step, perspiration poured from his pain-fevered brow. On his last step he fell into Gloria's waiting arms.

"That's it honey. I've done it," he said breathlessly. "If you'll still have me, let's make it legal as soon as possible."

Those lingering doubts were, at least, partially dispelled as she held him close. Obviously, his erratic behavior had only been a temporary lapse...she hoped against hope.

* * * * *

There was an expectant hush in St. John's Episcopal Church, Brooklyn, as Arch Bishop, wearing a white Tuxedo, began his unaided walk to the center aisle from a side entrance. He took his place at the front of the ornate church. Mama was distraught that they wouldn't be married in a Catholic church, and Gloria's Protestant family, who were footing the bill, did not want that. St. John's was a compromise that was both "Catholic" and "Protestant".

"Go to it, Arch," whispered his proud father as he turned his head to watch his son painfully put one leg after the other as he headed to the center aisle, where he was to receive his bride.

When he finally made it, his best man, Al Farr, looking surprisingly dapper, as he clasped Arch's arm and said, "Well done, kid. That's the spirit."

Farr felt gingerly inside the pocket of his rented penguin outfit to make sure he had the gold band safely stored there.

The church was filled with "Oohs" and "Aahs" as Gloria made her grand entrance, a white veil covering her flushed and excited face. A dress of Princess Di proportions, trailed behind her. The organist played, "Here Comes the Bride," and she was soon at her groom's side as her father stood proudly by Jayne, the third wife of Elmer Jansen III who suspiciously eyed his two ex-wives who were just a few feet across the aisle. Jansen had married each before the glamorous Jayne, then a young Hollywood starlet, and now Gloria's stepmother.

Both Arch and Gloria faced each other as they pledged their troth to each other "for richer for poorer, for better for worse, in sickness and in health...."

After all the formalities were completed, the priest intoned, "I now pronounce you man and wife. You may kiss the bride." He did!

On the outside steps, Mama edged close to her unfaithful and ungrateful son and kept her iron-grill smile going as the flashes of many cameras recorded the scene. Mama waited for her moment and then, while Gloria was being congratulated by her relatives, she hissed in his ear, "Joseph, how come you didn't have a Catholic priest and why couldn't you have married a good Italian girl, instead of a Protestant?"

Gritting his teeth, he turned to Mama and spat out, "Because nice Italian girls aren't filthy rich. Now quit bugging me, Mama."

After a lavish reception paid for by Elmer Jansen III, during which countless toasts were offered, to the "happy couple," Arch greedily gulped down the champagne as if it was going out of style.

He suddenly rose to his feet and said he would like to propose a toast to his mother. All conversation ceased as he lifted his glass and said, "I want you to raise your glasses and drink a toast to my big fat Mama. May she rot in hell!"

A shiver of shock ran through the assembled guests and Mama began to sob loudly. Then she stood up from her seat and screamed at Arch, "You ungrateful... I ought to skin you alive right now."

After this confrontation, the guests began drifting away, and Gloria finally persuaded Arch that it was time for them to leave in the white Cadillac stretch-limo for their honeymoon suite at the Waldorf Astoria.

* * * * *

"Come on, Arch," said Gloria in a strong, and nearly hysterical voice. "Let me undress you. Let's get to bed." She stood and watched him tottering in his addled state clutching a half-empty bottle of champagne.

"Don't order me around, woman," he slurred. "I'm going to have another drink and you won't stop me." He was already too drunk to see the apprehensive flicker in her eyes.

Bishop uncorked the bottle and slumped his bottom heavily down on the king-size bed. He started guzzling from the neck of the bottle until he had drained it dry, and then just fell back unconscious on the bed, still wearing his crumpled wedding suit. His top hat lay sadly on the floor at the foot of the bed.

Gloria joined him fully dressed on the bed and lay at his side, quietly weeping. Terror and loneliness began to surge up within her. Maybe, she thought for a desperate moment, it would have been better if he had died. At least he would be at peace.

* * * * *

Arch Bishop felt an uncontrollable anger rise up inside him when Al Farr threw him a simple re-write job.

"Look, Mr. Bigshot," he yelled petulantly across the news room, "I know I've only been back at work for a few weeks now, but why do you keep giving me all these stupid re-writes to do? I'm a

Pulitzer Prize winner, you know, not a cub reporter just starting in this game."

Farr chewed on his cigar and tried to keep control of his exasperation. Every day with Arch Bishop in the office was, for him, like trying to ride an unbroken colt.

"Stop feeling sorry for yourself," Farr snapped back at him. "When you're fit enough to do another 'biggie,' I'll send you on one. Now stop behaving like a spoiled brat."

Farr knew that he may never be able to send Bishop on any more of the "biggies" not only because he was still a bit shaky, but also because he had a habit of getting "tanked up" before an interview and then insulting the interviewee without mercy. He still had not started his "crime beat" because of the danger to him - and because of his erratic behavior.

Farr remembered with horror the call that had come from the secretary in the Mayor's office, asking that someone come and pick up, "Your drunken hero. He's just taken a swing at the Mayor."

Both Gloria and Arch began to settle into their sadness. Bishop drank himself into a stupor each night with the television set for company, while Gloria took a mass communications course at the University of New York. Gloria had decided that the newspaper business was not for her, but possibly television was, maybe as a news announcer at one of Daddy's TV stations in New York. Because she could not bear to see him destroying himself, she would sit quietly in the university library, her nose in the textbooks.

Al Farr eventually forced their hand by asking Bishop if he would like to "try his luck" at being the London correspondent for the paper. He hoped that a change of scene would be the boost that Bishop needed to shake this terrible drinking habit that was daily shortening his life. Farr had first of all called Gloria and told her he wanted to offer her husband the London post.

"Let him go and then join him a little later," said Farr reassuringly. "I think this move could turn him around."

That final night, in their thirty-third floor Manhattan apartment provided by Gloria's Daddy overlooking Central Park, was a disaster. Gloria wanted to comfort him in his despair, but he had just kept on drinking until he was incapable of uttering anything.

As he lay face down in a sodden slumber on the bed that had once been briefly a place of ecstatic joy for both of them, she hastily dressed, wiping the tears that slipped down her flushed cheeks with the sleeve of her blouse. His wife, who had once loved him so desperately, left him in his hopeless stupor. The last sounds she heard were heavy, alcohol-induced snores. Her tears welled up anew. She felt cold, weak and used up.

"Good-bye, you stupid fool," she whispered hoarsely, shaking her head despairingly. "I hope you find what you are looking for. I know I can't give it to you."

She lingered for a moment longer, gazing at him, and then slowly closed the door behind her. A sickening sense of futility swept over her. She had become Arch Bishop's *poor little rich girl*. Gloria never again was able to rid herself of that terrible sense of numbness.

Next morning, despite a paralyzing hangover, Arch Bishop packed up his life into boxes and prepared to move it 3,000 miles across the "Big Pond" to start over in the "Old World." He would faithfully report on life in the "scepter'd isle" and try to get his life into some sort of order.

9
"The Purpose of Terror is to Terrify"

Klaus Wagner had over 50,000 miles of excellent roads to choose from in the Irish Republic but, as always, he instructed Peter O'Reilly, his surly, black-clad driver, to cruise in his silver Mercedes the same twenty-five-mile-route from O'Connell House, his stately home in the rolling, deep green countryside of County Wicklow, to his machine-tool factory on the west side of the ancient capital of Dublin.

On that morning, Munich-born Wagner had a grim decision to make this day. A three-week strike for more pay for his three thousand Irish workers was beginning to bite deep into his profits. He had to decide whether to give in to union demands for a fifteen per cent pay hike, and one extra week a year vacation, or risk the plant being shut down.

Until now, Ireland's benevolent tax laws and incentives for foreign investors had provided him with a virtual license to print money. But now, this dispute was costing him dearly.

The obese, balding and elderly industrialist knew only too well how he would have dealt with trouble at the infamous Auschwitz Birkenau II vernictungslager in Poland, where he'd been commander of the "Canada Unit."

"Gassing would be too kind for these ungrateful 'Paddy's," Wagner hissed gutturally to Peter-of-the-grim-face, who winced at the insult to his compatriots but said nothing. The sleek Mercedes pulled up at the factory gates and Wagner was greeted with a wall of hatred, mainly inscribed on banners, but also yelled at him. What he saw and heard caused his face to turn purple with rage. His eyes began to draw down to ugly slits behind his huge thick-lens glasses that dwarfed his face and magnified his eyes.

One banner reading "Wagner is an exploiter" was waved at him by one of this volatile horde of what he considered to be "Irish barbarians." The German angrily pulled down his homburg that covered his shining pate, and adjusted his velvet-collared overcoat, when a placard declaring that "Wagner is a Nazi swinehund," suddenly crashed on the roof of his sleek driving machine.

That was enough for the Garda, (police) who had turned out in force each morning for this daily ritual of violence, to begin wading into the mob, lashing out with their nightsticks at ribs, armpits and leg jabs. As the battle erupted, a security man slid open the large iron gates to the spanking new factory, and Wagner's driver put his foot to the floor, causing the car to surge forward into the mass of rushing humanity, knocking both strikers and police to the ground.

Because of the mayhem, Wagner had not noticed the chopper whirring ominously above the factory, but a BBC Television crew covering the strike had not missed it. Suave reporter John Johnson-Jones brushed back his liberally sprayed hair and yelled to his camera operator to move the camera lens away from the fighting and zoom in on the helicopter, which now was landing on the soccer field behind Wagner Machine Tools.

The three-story building obscured the helicopter's landing, so the TV crew ran around to the back of the factory. Johnson-Jones quickly realized something rather dramatic was going on. As the television men reached a good vantage point at a break in the wooden fence surrounding the complex, they noticed three hooded gunmen begin firing at the car with Belgian FN-FAL automatic assault rifles. Suddenly Wagner's driver slumped sideways out of the car, on to the pavement, blood pouring out of a head wound, as he had desperately tried to escape the hail of fire. Then the terrorists moved toward the passenger door and grabbed Wagner roughly and propelled his short fat legs toward the waiting whirlybird.

"He's being kidnapped," yelled Johnson-Jones into his microphone during the live broadcast. "Ladies and gentlemen, you are witnessing the kidnapping of German industrialist Klaus Wagner." The usually composed, mannequin figure was no longer composed.

As Johnson-Jones breathlessly continued to report on the drama, a cluster of heavy thighed police officers were spilling wildly across the soccer field like shire horses in blue hats, their pistols drawn. One uniformed police officer was cut down like an axed tree after being hit in a barrage of fire from the hooded men.

The Garda officers fired futilely at the helicopter as it zoomed skyward. The humiliating response they received from the sky-borne kidnappers, were one-fisted salutes as they soared quickly out of range.

Wagner, his bullet-like head awash with cold sweat, had lost his beloved black hat in the struggle and was roughly slapped across the face by Randy Burke, the 30-year-old leader of the gang, as the green patchwork quilt of Ireland provided a strangely beautiful panorama below. But the view was lost on Burke as he tied his victim's hands behind his back with thick hemp.

As Wagner vainly struggled to free himself, Burke whipped off the German's thick-lens glasses that dominated his rubbery visage, dropped them to the floor of the chopper crushed them with a heavy boot, then tossed them out of the side door.

"Vy are you doing this to me?" Wagner gasped almost inaudibly, as a torrent of terror enveloped his corpulent frame. "Vot haf I done to deserve this?" A nervous tic became more and more frequent on Wagner's face and he began to cry great tearing sobs that seemed to be ripping him apart.

"Because you're filthy rich and we need some of that money," spat out Burke in a thick, Belfast accent. He leaned forward and pressed the cold muzzle of his weapon against Wagner's right temple.

"Wagner, you fat slob, if you want to come out of this alive, you had better cooperate fully with us, or you will get the same as your driver - a bullet through the brain. That's if he had a brain!"

A helpless victim, Wagner's mouth twisted down with the bitter taste of fear. He found his mind running wild with terrifying thoughts. The German knew that these men were not fooling. After all, hadn't he experienced that intoxicating surge of excitement of total power over others when he had sat watching, through his special vantage point, thousands of Jews die, choking from poisonous gas? The perverse thrill this had provided him was indescribable. Now he was, like them, a helpless victim.

Wagner knew only too well that these individuals had "tasted blood" and he could be the next to die, so he would have to go along with their every whim if he was to have even a chance of surviving much longer. He screwed up his eyes to focus in on the bizarre scene around him. He could just make out three hooded men caressing their guns and semi-automatics and a pilot wearing a baseball cap and chomping on a half-smoked cigar.

After about twenty minutes, the American pilot coolly put down the machine on a field. They were watched disinterestedly by some cud-chewing cows. Wagner was dragged out of the helicopter and his obese bulk shoved into an ancient farmhouse. Even before he was thrown onto the stone floor of the old, beamed building, the rotor blades were carrying the pilot upward and onward. Soon he would be out over the Irish Sea and landing at a quiet airfield near Lille in northern France.

Burke switched on an old black and white TV set standing on rickety legs by the fireplace in the lounge, and settled back to see how the story would be covered by Irish television. A hurling game was being transmitted live from Dublin's Croke Park. Burke chuckled at this uniquely Gaelic game, ruminating on the dangers of putting ashen clubs in the hands of opposing Irishmen. His smile grew even larger as the broadcast was interrupted with a news flash.

An excited Shaun O'Higgins, Ireland's best-known newsreader, came on the screen and said, "Three masked gunmen have kidnapped German industrialist Klaus Wagner a few minutes ago. Three hooded men in a helicopter dragged him away from his factory on the outskirts of Dublin. Wagner's driver, Peter O'Reilly, was shot and killed during the incident, as was a member of the Garda.

"Commander Patrick Moore, head of the Anti-Terrorist Squad, has just released the following statement from his headquarters in Dublin:

"'We believe this cowardly kidnapping to be the work of the Provisional Wing of the Irish Republican Army. We will stop at nothing to get Wagner back safely and punish the perpetrators of this crime. This kind of terrorism has got to be stopped. It brings nothing but shame to Ireland!'"

The three men laughed heartily. "It's you, Moore, who is the disgrace to Ireland," roared Jim O'Hara, a 17-year-old disciple of Burke, and one of the deadly troika.

"Did you hear that, Wagner?" said Burke, as he roughly cradled the German's chin in the palm of his hand and pulled his petrified face to his. "They say they will 'stop at nothing' to get you back."

"I heard," said Wagner, vainly trying to hold back the terror in his voice.

"It seems to me they face a real problem," said Burke. "And that is that we have you! We also have 'ways' of not insuring your safety." The others roared with laughter at his wit as Burke grinned with savage satisfaction.

"If you do exactly as you're told, fat man, you 'might' have a chance of living. If not, well, you will be blasted into eternity." Burke's eyes, as they peered through the slits in his mask, were dead and cold as icebergs.

Dave Hagan, a 19-year-old bricklayer from the decaying Falls Road area of Belfast, a Catholic ghetto, and the third Provo in the kidnap team, decided it was time to brew up some tea, so he began boiling water in an ancient kettle on the wheezing gas stove in the kitchen.

Burke began writing out, in black felt-tip letters, a message on a large piece of card. Then he untied Wagner's hands and instructed him to hold it up while he photographed the strange scene with a Polaroid camera. Wagner's face looked redder than usual as he stared into the lens of the camera. The message came out clearly on the instant picture. It read:

"Don't try to find me. Just pay these men what they want. Long live the Provo cause!"

The picture was "made available" by a Provo Public Relations Officer to various wire services in Dublin and, within hours, was carried on the front page of many major publications around the world. But, at least for the time being, no attempt was made by the Provos to contact Wagner's headquarters in Munich for the $5

111

million-dollar ransom they were to ask in return for the ex-Nazi.

Burke was determined to squeeze every bit of publicity value out of the situation. He recalled a statement of the Algerian FLM asking as early as 1955, "Is it better for our cause to kill ten of our enemies in a remote village where this will not cause comment, or to kill one man in Algiers where the American press will get hold of the story for next day?" Obviously the latter was the correct strategy.

Now that satellite communications could bring terrorist acts into the world's living rooms, Burke knew only too well how important it was to "cash in" on the new technology. There had been a lull in Provo activity of recent times due to the fact that so many of its leaders had been caught by British and Ulster intelligence and were behind bars. A desperate search had been on within the Provo ranks to root out the suspected "mole" that was turning in so many colleagues to the authorities. So far, no one had been "fingered" for this unforgivable action.

Burke had certainly come a long way since those heady days at Queen's University in Belfast where, as a milk-faced student in his early twenties, he had studied Political Science. A group sprang up there at Queen's called "People's Democracy," with one of its leaders being the diminutive Ulster fireball, Mary O'Shaughnessy. Although a Protestant himself, Burke had become pumped up with outrage at the way the Protestants had "misused" power in the Six Counties since the British split up Ireland in 1922 into the Irish Free State and Northern Ireland, meaning that the north stayed with Britain.

Randy Burke particularly despised Northern Ireland's "invisible government," the Orange Order, a fraternal organization founded in 1795, and pledged to defend "Protestantism" in Ulster against what they called the "Harlot of Rome," and to protect the

Protestant succession to the British throne. Burke's father belonged to this Order, so the young student was well acquainted with its inner workings - which were similar in some ways to the Masons, with its secret oaths, handshakes and prayers. Burke knew, from his father, a Belfast shoe shop owner, that for decades, all the Unionist representatives at the Northern Ireland parliament at Stormont Castle were "Orangemen." All of them upheld the founding principle that was allegiance to the Crown and upholding the Protestant Ascendancy. Randy Burke, however, considered that the Orange Order had "infected" and "poisoned" the very bloodstream of Ulster.

As a young idealist, he was appalled when he heard on the radio an Ulster Prime Minister urging employees to continue work discrimination against Catholics by saying they should be hiring "good Protestant lads and lassies."

The situation in Londonderry - "Derry" to the Catholics - was something that he considered to be "disgraceful." Although the city was almost two-thirds Catholic, the Protestants had resorted to "dubious" electoral practices to maintain control. While adults could vote for representatives to Westminster and Stormont, the Northern Ireland parliament, the rules were changed for local elections. The Protestant "masters" had decreed that only heads of households and their wives could vote. Youths of voting age living at home, and servants, could not. Business owners and their wives also received "extra votes," the rationale being they had a "greater stake" in the community. This naturally favored the "wealthy" over the "poor," and most of the Catholics belonged to the latter.

So, when Mary O'Shaughnessy began her barnstorming with the Northern Ireland Civil Rights Association (CRA) in 1967, he found a new "cause" to enthusiastically follow.

The group had decided that passing out leaflets and penning

letters to representatives at Stormont had not been very effective. So in August 1968, the CRA decided to hold its first demonstration, an historic march from Coalisland to the nearby village of Dungannon. Burke joined the thousands of people that milled around the hawkers selling civil rights-rosettes, and generally having a great time. After the march, a good-natured rally was held, songs were sung, and the rally broke up peacefully.

But soon the marches became violent and vicious. Burke remembered taking part in the "Long March" that began on New Year's Day, 1969. For three days they all had marched in good spirits, but as they neared Burntollet Bridge on the outskirts of Londonderry, a Paisleyite (followers of Protestant leader Ian Paisley) mob attacked them and began raining down boulders, bricks and bottles on them. Then wild hordes of screaming Protestants, wielding planks of wood, iron bars, crowbars, cudgels with nails, and bottles, attacked the group with fury.

The girls on the march were beaten as badly as the men. The police stood by and gleefully watched the violence. Soon, more of the unbridled beatings were directed at the Civil Rights marches and that caused Burke to "seethe" with anger.

Burke was, therefore, most interested when news came to his attention at the university that Seamus O'Shea and a number of others had walked out of the official IRA annual meeting in Dublin in late 1969. The "rebels" were appalled that the "officials" had given up their armed struggle back in 1962 and had, instead, opted for a "political solution," so they had established a "Provisional's' Army Council." Burke made discreet inquiries among other "Republican students" to find out how he could make contact with them. He realized that quick change would not come in Ireland through the ballot box, because that was being rigged. "It can only come through the barrel of a gun," he told O'Shea, who had taken an immediate liking to his new intellectual recruit.

"The IRA are a bunch of cowards who won't fight anymore," said the chain-smoking O'Shea. "That's why we broke away."

Then he looked at Burke and grinned maliciously, "Do you know what IRA now stands for?"

Burke shook his head.

"I RAN AWAY," he responded. With that they both roared with laughter at the man's sarcastic humor.

O'Shea decided to give Burke a "baptism of fire" and assigned the enthusiastic student to take part in a daring raid on a Belfast gun shop in which they were to steal a horde of weapons, as well as a large quantity of ammunition.

It was Burke who later called up the British Press Association reporter in Belfast, anonymously announcing that "ammunition and weapons" had been seized "in the name of the Provos."

The publicity had its desired effect, and soon several units of the official IRA began to switch their allegiance to the Provos and sent their weapons to Belfast. Burke watched O'Shea's eyes light up as he gleefully counted the thirty Thompson sub-machine guns, twenty-seven rifles and assorted pistols all captured in the raid.

O'Shea knew that if the Provos were to begin their campaign of terror in earnest, they needed cash, and quickly. So Burke was dispatched to New York, Boston and Chicago to address Irish-American groups on "the cruel way the Protestants, backed by the British, was repressing the Catholic minority in Northern Ireland."

Burke had been an articulate spokesman for the cause, and was able to raise over $200,000 during one month. He naturally promised that "every cent will go to the victims of British imperialism in Northern Ireland." In fact, all of it went toward buying more weapons.

It was while in New York that Burke had been approached by a reporter from the New York Tribune, Arch Bishop, for an interview about the "Irish troubles." It was several years before the 9/11 attack on New York and Bishop had received an anonymous tip from a man with a Belfast accent that Burke was, in fact, a terrorist, albeit a charming one. He decided to go to meet the Irishman without telling Farr. Sitting in the darkened bar of the Hotel Tudor, close to the United Nations building, Burke had used all his skills as an articulate spokesman for the cause of Irish unification.

"What really is your aim in Ireland?" Bishop had asked him pointedly as he sipped his third "g and t" and thoughtfully puffed a Camel.

Burke wore a brown stylish jacket, presenting an image more akin to that of a high school basketball coach than a "triggerman" for the Provos. He brooded briefly on the question, then replied, his fresh face breaking into a one-sided smile, "That's quite simple, my friend. We want a united Irish Socialist Republic."

"And are your friends using terrorist tactics to achieve that goal?" Bishop asked looking unblinkingly into Burke's green eyes.

"The purpose of terror is to terrify," said Burke, recalling Lenin's phrase. With that he gave a rather disturbing chuckle. It was a short, mirthless laugh.

That same chuckle had surfaced for Burke on another occasion when the pilot of the plane about to land at Belfast Airport said cheerily over the loudspeaker, "We are about to land in Ulster. Prepare to set your watches back three hundred years!"

* * * * *

The telephone shrilled in the London bureau of the New York Tribune. Finally a flustered Arch Bishop picked up the receiver, irritated that Beth, the operator, had not answered a call yet again. Why, he wondered, did she have to spend so much time powdering her nose in the bathroom, instead of making his life a little easier in the office?

"Yes," he grunted down the phone, as he drummed his fingertips on his desk.

"Is this Arch Bishop?" asked the refined Belfast voice at the other end.

"Who is this?"

After a moment of hesitation, the voice said, "Don't you recognize my voice? I'll give you a clue.... 'g & t's' in the Hotel Tudor."

Bishop searched his memory. Then he remembered the encounter earlier with the well-spoken Irishman.

"Burke, is that you? How's the revolution going?"

Totally ignoring the journalist's sarcasm, he continued, "Look, Mr. Bishop, you once did me a favor by treating me fairly in print," he said smoothly stroking Bishop's ego, "now I have something for you to repay your kindness."

"What's that?"

"How would you like a world exclusive? I can fix it for you to interview that German industrialist who was kidnapped two weeks ago in Dublin."

Bishop whistled aloud and dragged deeply on a cigarette,

"Interested, my friend?" asked Burke.

"Of course. But how?" He'd tried to sound normal but his voice was now pitched too high.

"Just listen. I want you to fly over to Dublin immediately, and meet me at 4:30 P.M. at the Guinness Museum in Watlin Street. It's close to the Heuston Railway Station. Just wander around there and pretend you're interested in the history of brewing in our fair land and I'll make contact with you.

"And later we'll have a few 'g & t's' to celebrate your scoop."

Then Burke's friendly tone changed. "Mr. Bishop, if you tell anyone about this, except maybe your photographer, who can come along, I'll make sure you'll get a different kind of poison in your drink," he warned.

With that, the phone line went dead, and Bishop slowly put down the receiver. He jumped up from his creaky chair and burst into Fida's darkroom where she was developing film of Queen Elizabeth greeting evangelist William Franklin at Buckingham Palace. The pair had been enjoying afternoon tea together.

"Come on, Fida, old sport; forget about your royal relative. We've got more important business to take care of over the Irish Sea."

Once again, Arch Bishop began to experience the surge of excitement most reporters feel when onto a big story. It was like a dog on a leash about to set out after a quarry.

10
No Innocents in War

Arch Bishop screwed up his eyes and blinked in disbelief as the blindfold that had tightly covered his eyes for the past 90 minutes, during the drive with Burke and Fida from Dublin, was removed by the Provo chieftain. Suddenly the macabre scene in front of him came into sharp focus. Lying on his side in a metal cage, six feet long by two feet wide and secured by a stout padlock, was the obese, frightened figure of the ancient Klaus Wagner. His right eye was closed, as if he had just gone fifteen rounds in a world title fight. His badly bruised face was etched with sharp terror.

Standing over his prostrate body were the menacing figures of two men clutching their semi-automatic weapons. Their faces were sinisterly obscured by ski masks but Bishop noted through the slits, a determined gleam in their eyes.

It was Fida's turn to have her blindfold taken off. As it came away, she let out a shrill scream when she saw what at first appeared to be a tortured grizzly bear. Her body began to shake as she let out another piercing shriek, then another. Her eyes were wide circles of fear, her voice high and strangled.

Burke stepped in front of her and promptly slapped her across the face. "Pull yourself together, woman. You're here as a professional to do a job; not to behave like a stupid school kid." The charm had left his voice and it was now edged with steel. The sharp pain of his blow only caused her to scream more, as her hands and feet turned as cold as gravestones.

"Give her a drink, Burke," shouted Bishop, angry at this savage display of violence by the man whom he had considered an educated and in control person. "You are not going to achieve anything by alienating someone who can help your cause."

Burke knew he was right. The American had touched a raw nerve. He knew the mass media could be the terrorist's best friend, and that this act of kidnapping was nothing without the accompanying publicity.

"Get her some 'gargle' to ease the pain," yelled Burke to one of his masked men. With that he put his arm around Fida's heaving shoulders and guided her to a shabby sofa that was located close to the cozy peat-burning fire.

"I'm sorry for doing that," he said quietly. "But I had to stop you from screaming."

Hagan, who was the cook for the kidnappers, put down his weapon and went over to a cupboard and found a half bottle of whisky.

"Will Johnnie Walker do?" he asked Burke.

"Yeah, hurry up!"

Hagan poured the whisky into a chipped china cup, and Burke helped her shaking hands guide the fiery, but soothing liquid, down her quivering throat. Fida winced as the powerful spirits flowed over her taste buds. It took a full ten minutes and several more gulps for her to stop shaking. Slowly, her slim frame began to compose.

Fida had enjoyed her job until now, and she could not help but recall that just the previous day she had been in the stronghold of British imperialism - Buckingham Palace - photographing Queen

Elizabeth, the very symbol of British rule in Northern Ireland. Her royal relative was actually most pleasant. What a contrast that was to this situation. Of course, Fida had read many stories about terrorists, but they had never seemed real to her before. The horror of seeing a fellow human being humiliated in this way chilled her to the bone.

A wave of compassion swept over Bishop as he watched his faithful photographer suffer. He realized how nasty he had been to her during their eighteen months of working together. But really, he figured, she had been partly to blame for this because of her tough exterior. Now, as she sat, fragile and vulnerable like an injured butterfly, he knew she did have deep feelings and her previous act had been just a cover-up for her true personality.

"Okay, Mr. Bishop, now that little drama is over, can we get down to the real reason you are here," said Burke, resuming his businesslike manner as he stood up and pointed to the shivering, Wagner whose teeth chattered uncontrollably.

"Oh, the German," stammered Bishop. It seemed the prisoner had been forgotten in all of the commotion.

The journalist went over to the cage and squatted down beside the prisoner. Wagner looked up at him, his eyes bulging with anguish. Bishop switched on his tiny Sony micro-cassette recorder and introduced himself.

"Herr Wagner, I'm Arch Bishop, a reporter for the *New York Tribune*. Can you tell me how you are feeling?"

Wagner looked at him incredulously. "Vot sort of stupid question is dat?" His mood had changed suddenly. "How vould you feel being caged up like an animal vit a bunch of baboons for company?"

Hagan was not going to take that from anyone. He viciously poked his captive in the ribs several times with the barrel of his weapon. "Don't ever say that again, you Kraut."

Burke moved into the situation and tried to calm his outraged colleague. "Not in front of the press," he hissed to the young guard. With that, Burke turned to Bishop and flashed a charming smile. "Right, Mr. Bishop, the floor's yours. Fire away!"

Bishop half smiled, feeling he would have phrased it differently. After checking that the miniature tape was still rolling, he then asked the German how he was being treated.

"Vell, you can see for yourself. These monsters keep me locked up in this contraption twenty-three hours a day and only let me out to use the bathroom and valk around the room. Then they handcuff me so I can't attack them."

Looking at this overweight, aging figure, Bishop did not think he would have much chance in any fight with these Provos, but still he understood that Wagner needed to have some self-respect that he was still a man.

"The food they give me is terrible," he continued. "The Irish may brew good beer, but their food is the vorst I've had any place in the vorld."

Burke looked anxiously at Hagan and with a nod warned him not to react. The young Irish "cook" clenched his fist to try to stop himself from hurting the corpulent German.

"Did you know the Provos have asked for a $5 million-dollar ransom for your safe return?" asked Bishop.

"I did."

"Do you think your colleagues in Munich should pay it?"

"Of course day should," the quivering captive exploded. "After all it is my money and if I vos not to be around, dere vould be no Wagner Machine Tools."

As Bishop continued the strange interview, he marveled at the apparent lack of understanding the industrialist had of his precarious predicament.

"Don't you realize that if they don't pay up soon, you could be executed by these men? Looking at them I think they are eminently capable of rubbing you out like a chalk mark."

On hearing this, Wagner's attitude suddenly changed. He began to sob deep, heavy sobs, as he gazed up at the reporter. "I know dat, Mr. Bishop, and I don't vant to die. I am scared of dying. Dis whole ting has become a terrible nightmare. I don't tink these men realize vot day are doing to me."

Burke cut in. "Herr Wagner. Did you ever consider what you and your Nazi thugs were doing to the innocent Jews during the war? I have done some checking on you and discovered that you showed no mercy to your victims. Why should we show you any mercy?""Because...because...."

This was the first Bishop had heard about Wagner's Nazi connections.

"Is it true what Mr. Burke says?" he asked the German.

"I vas just a soldier, that's all."

"That's a bare-faced lie, Wagner," yelled Burke with genuine indignation, his voice rising.

As the drama unfolded, Fida knelt beside the cage clicking away in black-and-white and color as she captured Wagner's tortured expressions on film. Her cameras were working overtime as she focused in on his bloated, unshaven face, his reddened, damaged, eyes, underlined by pouches of weariness his ordeal had accentuated. The lens appeared to be licking their lips as they sucked in the images of terror.

"You're lying," Burke shouted to Wagner. Then he turned to Bishop and said, "This beast lying in this cage was none other than 'The keeper of the ovens' at the Auschwitz Concentration Camp. He knows all about cooking, but he always 'overdid' the meat.

"Even a slow, painful death is too good for this monster," he added with venom.

"You haf no proof of dat," retorted Wagner at the top of his voice. He was pumped up with outrage at this slur on his character. "I have been an outstanding citizen of my country and no charges ver ever brought against me."

"Yes, and I know why," said Burke triumphantly. "I have some Israeli friends who have been chasing you for years. They tell me that at the end of the war you disappeared to Uruguay where you changed your name and had plastic surgery to change your appearance."

"Boy, what a mess they made of it," interrupted Hagan.

"Shut up!" ordered Burke. "Can't you see I'm talking?"

Hagan grimaced and left the room while Burke turned his attention back to the German.

"Don't go whining about our treatment of you. At least you are still breathing. Those you dealt with in Auschwitz don't have that privilege."

Bishop could see that if this was true, he had an even bigger story on his hands than he had bargained for. The adrenaline was beginning to surge through his veins and excite his imagination as he now viewed Wagner as a story, and no longer as a human being. This had happened to him many times; the tale had become all important, and the victims were of little importance although the good journalist will cleverly make the interviewed feel he really does care. Bishop gazed down at this victim totally trapped in and surrounded by steel and yet unable to feel an ounce of sympathy for him. Even Wagner's wracking sobs that shook his entire jelly-like body, did not seem to mean anything. This man had lived by the sword and now, one way or the other, he could die by it.

"How much longer are you going to keep Herr Wagner here?"

Bishop asked Burke, who was crouched down beside him, gloating over his prey.

"We have set a deadline of one more week. If the ransom is not paid in full, we will take him out over his factory and drop him out of the sky without having to shoot him. I somehow don't think he would survive that kind of drop."

"Good riddance to bad rubbish," muttered Hagan, who was at the old stove in the kitchen, cooking up some stew for the evening meal.

"Do you mean that you would actually kill him?" asked Bishop, a sharp edge coming into his voice.

"We wouldn't actually kill him; the fall would do that," said Burke. "But we hope it won't come to that. Once the world reads your story and realizes that he wants his colleagues in Munich to pay the 'fee' we are asking, he will be released. Then the Israelis can do what they like with him. The money is more important to our cause at this point in time than having another carcass on our hands.

"You know, Wagner," Burke said turning towards the quivering German and chuckling out loud in a manic way, "if I were a betting man, and most Irishmen are, I wouldn't lay odds against you lasting much longer.

"I would think a few fires are being stoked up down there right now!"

Burke then signaled to Bishop and Fida, whose faces were flushed with the drama of the occasion, that the interview was now over.

"I'm afraid we'll have to put the blindfolds back on you two." His voice was soft again. "I hope you understand. We can't run the risk of you discovering where this place is."

Bishop did not care any more. He had gotten one of the biggest stories of his life. It was a world exclusive for the *New York Tribune*. He knew that Gloria still read the paper every day, and maybe when she saw it she would be proud of him. Maybe he would call her in New York after the paper had hit the streets and casually ask her what she thought of what he had written.

Bishop stuck his hand through the cage to Wagner and said, "Well, sir, thank you for the interview. It's been most enlightening."

Fida blew a kiss to the cage. "Good luck, Herr Wagner. Thank you for the pictures. I'll let you have a set."

"Don't bother," responded the scowling prisoner. "Tanks for nothing."

* * * * *

The phone rang in Arch Bishop's hotel room in Dublin. Bishop picked up the receiver and snapped, "Yeah."

It was Al Farr calling from New York. "Bishop, what are you doing there? I've been trying to contact you since yesterday. I've got a story for you in that dull city of Birmingham. Jimmy Carter is speaking at the university there and...."

"Why," thought Bishop, "is Al Farr always so stupid?" "Look, you lunatic, if you'll just shut your big mouth for a moment, I'll tell you about the biggest story you've had from me since I've been in Europe!"

"Oh, yeah. You've got an exclusive interview with Adolf Hitler after discovering that he didn't die in the Berlin bunker?"

Trying to suppress his distaste for this man who he considered to be a "beer-swilling moron" who enjoyed nothing better than baiting his reporters, Bishop snapped, "Look Mr. Big Mouth, I've just had 'words' with that German whom the Provos kidnapped. It turns out that he's a Nazi war criminal. He's being kept in a cage by the Provos in a farmhouse some place outside of Dublin."

"Have you got pictures?" By now Farr appeared to be mildly impressed.

"We've got scores of them. Fida went through I don't know how many rolls of film."

"How quickly can you file and get the pictures to us?"

"We'll wire the photos from here and I'll email you the words in about 30 minutes. I've already got it mapped out in my head."

With that Bishop slammed down the receiver and looked at Fida, who was sitting on the edge of the bed in the room of their hotel close to O'Connell Street.

"Don't think that I'm going to do anything," Bishop told her. "This is just a business relationship. You should know that by now." Then, as an afterthought, he added, "I guess we could, at least, be friends, especially if we have to spend so much time together."

Fida was not sure if she could just be a friend with Bishop. She had, for some time, desperately tried to keep a grip on her feelings toward him. However, she also knew that he could not free himself from the vision of Gloria. One night Bishop had sat down with her in "The Stab" and told her part of the story. As the "g & t's" had taken hold of his befuddled brain, he had become more and more maudlin about his former wife.

"I don't think I will ever get over her," he said as he gazed sadly into his glass. "Now that the divorce is final, I've decided to be married to my work and this - booze. At least this stuff doesn't nag back at you."

Bishop gave Fida instructions where to get her films processed and wire the prints to New York, via a local news agency, then settled down at the writing table to compose his story.

He lit up a cigarette and soon his fingers began to race over the keys of his lap-top.

"I can exclusively reveal today that Klaus Wagner, the German industrialist kidnapped from his Dublin factory two weeks ago by the Provisional IRA, is a suspected war criminal being sought by Nazi hunters from Israel...," he began the story. (see above)

After 20 minutes of frantic composing, the insistent ring of his phone stopped his free flow of words.

"Yeah," he spat down the receiver.

"It's Burke. I'm back in town. How's it going?"

"Well, New York's excited and I think I can confidently tell you that the story will be the front page lead in tomorrow's paper. That's if you'll let me finish it."

"Okay, okay. I get the message. I just wanted to invite you and your delightful Fida for a few drinks when you are finished. I'll be downstairs in the bar when you're ready. See you then."

Bishop could not think of a more pleasant way to end an excellent day of story hunting. A few "g & t's" with Fida and a chat with this extraordinary Irishman would be interesting, he thought. He typed at the bottom of his copy, "If you need me any more, I'll be in the hotel bar." With that he hooked up his modem and sent it to New York.

* * * * *

Bishop looked vainly around the shadowy bar for Burke, but could not see him anywhere. Then he spotted a finger beckoning him. It belonged to a long-haired man with a droopy Mexican mustache.

"Mr. Bishop, over here," said a voice that sounded familiar. "Do you like the disguise?"

The American laughed out loud when he realized that Burke had transformed his appearance for the meeting.

"I can't take any chances here in Dublin," he said. "I'm too well-known to Special Branch. I think they already suspect that I had something to do with Wagner's kidnapping."

Burke smiled and then asked the American journalist, "Do you take a drink?"

"Sure do."

"Well, don't take mine." With that Burke laughed out loud. "Do you like that one, Mr. Bishop? I heard it on the radio driving here."

Bishop didn't like it. But to make up for his "bit of fun," Burke ordered three doubles of Bishop's medicine of "g. & t's" which he lined up in front of him, while he began sipping the thick, creamy froth off the top of a Guinness.

"I have to help the Irish economy," he explained, a twinkle in his eye. "This country runs on this stuff, you know."

It was not long before Fida joined them, her face flushed with the success of the project.

"Daahlings, the pictures were absolutely marvelous...oh yes; I'll have a sherry, Mr. Burke."

Bishop began to study Burke. His thoughts whirled as he wondered how a sophisticated, educated man, could have become so involved with a bunch of thugs, which was how he viewed all terrorists.

"An Irish penny for your thoughts, daahling?" asked Fida, as she settled down on the hard wooden seat in the darkened corner of the bar.

"Well, to be honest, they concern Mr. Burke."

The Irishman looked puzzled.

"Yes, I would like to understand why a person like you is involved with the Provos. Surely, with your education, you could be out earning an honest living."

Burke gave him a fake pained expression.

"You mean like you?"

"Ouch!" laughed Bishop.

"No, but seriously, when I hear of the atrocities that you people commit, I find it hard to understand the logic behind it all."

"For instance?"

"Well, the murder of Earl Mountbatten in 1979 on that fishing boat that you apparently blew up at sea."

"Well, I didn't actually do it."

"No, but you know what I mean. Mountbatten was 79 years old. What possible threat was he to Ireland? In fact, I understand he enjoyed nothing more than coming here."

"Look, Mr. Bishop, Mountbatten went up in smoke because he represented British Imperialism. We needed a victim and he was the best we could get."

"But," said Bishop, a consuming anger welling up inside of him, "you also killed his 14-year-old grandson and a 15-year-old passenger. Surely they were innocent victims of your terrorism."

Burke's face was deadly serious. "Well, Mr. Bishop, you're learning an important lesson tonight. There are no innocents in war."

"Are you saying that your whole campaign is conducted with the media in mind? Mountbatten's murder was a publicity stunt?"

"You've got it! That's why we try to focus as much of our activities as possible on the British and in Britain itself. You may recall that the bombing at Harrods in London as well as the one in the Manchester city center brought a few headlines for us.

"We realize that one bomb in Harrods or in Manchester is worth ten in Belfast or Derry."

Bishop was feeling uncomfortable, knowing he was now being used by the Provos, although, he too, was using them to further his career. A story like this could possibly win him another award back in the States.

"Violence," continued Burke, "is the only language that the British and other Western countries can understand. Power really does come down the barrel of the gun."

"But power for whom?"

"In this case, power for the Irish people."

Bishop saw a big flaw in that argument. For after all, what about the Protestant majority in Ulster, or the many in the south that abhorred what the Provos were doing?

"Okay, I'll ask you one more question before I turn in for the night."

"Fire away."

Bishop winced, wishing Burke would not use that expression. "Aren't you really fighting a war for communism? Isn't it true that your real aim is to set up a Marxist, Cuba-like state in Ireland?"

"Well," said Burke, a wry smile moving across his impish face, "if that is true, and I'm not admitting to any of it, you and your capitalistic newspapers are helping them greatly.

"I have read the Communist Manifesto by Karl Marx and Friedrich Engels. In it they say, to paraphrase, that modern capitalists are making money from their enemies and in so doing are in fact becoming their own gravediggers.

"How does it feel to be a gravedigger, Mr. Bishop?"

With that Bishop angrily rose to his feet, drained the remainder of his third "g & t" and turned to Fida. "Are you coming up?" he snapped.

"No, Arch. I'll have another drink with Mr. Burke...then I'll be up."

"Okay, but be careful he doesn't blow you up!"

With that, Arch wearily made his way, via the elevator, to his third floor room and a relatively early night. It had been quite a day and he was confused now about what he had done. Had he been a pawn in this instance, or were Burke and the Provos his pawns? Ah, well, who cares? It was a good story, he assured himself. That justified everything.

* * * * *

The radio back in Arch Bishop's London apartment brought the news some days later that the ransom had been paid for Herr Wagner and he had been released close to the gates of his factory. But not before one of the Provos had "kneecapped" him.

"Shortly after his release, the German industrialist was kidnapped again, this time by Israeli agents who have announced that he is now on his way to Israel to stand trial for his war crimes," said the announcer.

Bishop scratched his head, and then said aloud, "There are truly no innocents in war."

11
The Day God Cried For Ireland

God blinked his eyes and began to pour out his tears, through leaden clouds. The rain soaked the sad, black-clad group gathered around a large open grave in Shankhill Cemetery.

"The Lord gives, and the Lord taketh away. Blessed be the Name of the Lord," intoned the Rev. Robert Patterson, the Presbyterian minister, as the steel-gray curtain of rain parted his Brylcreamed hair in a way even he couldn't have predestined.

Unsteadily supporting himself on his crutches, David Burke stared, without blinking, at the two coffins with rain bouncing off the light brown varnish, waiting to be dropped into the sodden hole. Around him stood Uncle Joe and Uncle Allen looking slightly silly in their Orange Order black bowlers and sashes slung across their pin-striped suits, their wives obediently at their sides, buried beneath warm coats. Even in death, the men felt they had to uphold the purity of their Ulster secret society.

Standing in a muddy puddle, just in earshot, was a gravedigger who looked vaguely familiar to the despairing mourners. He leaned against his shovel, cap in hand, as the Reverend Patterson completed the formalities. The man's face and hair dripped of "God's tears." His eyes looked tired and his face was in need of a shave.

Then there was a blur of movement and, as if from nowhere,

four masked figures appeared on the scene, raised the cold steel of their rifles to the darkened sky. The assembled group heard a metallic click as safety catches were released and they shouted, "For God and Ulster." Then there was the crack of rifle shots echoing eerily through the graveyard, as a round of volleys was fired in respect to the pair who were about to be laid in their final rest.

The shadowy gunmen shook hands with David and the others around the grave and then raced off into a blue Ford mini-van parked nearby, ripping off their gray woolen masks as the vehicle pulled away.

The gravedigger was still motionless as two colleagues eased the caskets slowly on green straps to their final resting places, side by side below. David and the assembled group then dropped pieces of mud onto each side of them.

As David Burke maneuvered his walking aids to hobble toward the funeral limo, he nodded knowingly at the gravedigger who touched his wrinkled brow in response.

The black Daimler containing the party, headed at a snail's pace toward Uncle Joe's East Belfast terraced home where they would have sandwiches and hot tea. Back at the cemetery, the gravedigger picked up his shovel and shuffled toward the rain-filled grave. Conscience-stricken, he gazed down at the two oak caskets containing the mangled bodies of his parents.

"Good-bye Mom and Dad," he whispered, wiping the salty tears that mingled with God's on his care-worn face. "I know I wasn't much of a son while you were alive, but I'm going to make it up to you." A sense of guilt wrapped itself around the gravedigger, and nothing seemed to ease its stranglehold on him. Finally, in an anguished cry, he uttered, "One day, one day, you're going to be proud of me. I'm going to show you."

He stood for a long moment caught up in his own anguished thoughts, and had not noticed the police officer slip by his side.

"Did you know them?" asked the Royal Ulster Constabulary officer, puffing heavily on a damp cigarette as the heavens continued to rain "cats and dogs."

"A little," he replied hesitantly.

"Good folks," continued the officer as he looked into the unshaven face of the gravedigger. "Salt of the earth, in fact.

"Pity about their son, Randy, though. He joined the Provos, you know." The lines on his forehead knitted together as if to emphasize the point.

"Is that right?"

"Yes, a right black sheep he was. But we'll get him - dead or alive! You mark my words." His voice was resonant and determined.

"Well, good hunting, sir," said the gravedigger, extending a damp hand. "I've heard about him. He deserves all that's coming to him."

With that, he frenetically shoveled the muddy earth into the hole, as if the surrounding tombstones were urging him on. With deep anger and grief, he continued moving the deep brown, clinging mud until the hole was no more.

Not realizing the officer was still observing him; the grave digger wiped his brow and began to walk across the rain-swept cemetery. When he saw the officer gazing at him he bit his lower lip in a bid to control the urge to succumb to minor panic.

"Like a spot of tea in my car?" the policeman asked in a still friendly tone. "I always carry a thermos of the wonderful stuff with me."

The gravedigger was not sure why the policeman was acting so kind, but he had to admit that he was in need of something hot and wet. The biting wind and rain had caused his legs to become numb with cold, and his teeth were clenched to keep from chattering.

The policeman pointed to his sky-blue "Panda" car parked just down the hill from the lonely graves and began his slither down the incline, indicating to the gravedigger to follow him.

The car radio crackled with a message from the local station. It was not for him. The officer smiled at the man by his side and began unscrewing the cup of the flask and poured the steaming liquid into it. Before handing him the tea, he opened up his black tunic and pulled from an inside pocket of his black tunic a flask of whisky.

"Here, son, you have some of this. It'll warm the cockles of your heart. I often have a nip when on duty. It dulls the pain of this job."

As the cold rain outside blew against the windshield and condensation was forced inside the glass, the gravedigger gratefully swallowed the mix of tea and Scotch, while the officer lit up another cheap cigarette and filled his mouth with the powerful taste of it.

"Would you like a ciggie?" he asked, offering his companion a Player's from his pocket.

The gravedigger leaned over and took one and soon the two of them were cozily blowing smoke into the confines of the car and watching it slowly snake out through a small opening in the window on the driver's side that was wound down just a little.

"How long have you been digging graves then, son?" asked the policeman, taking off his peaked cap and tossing it onto the rear passenger seat. Before he could answer, he added, "Bit of a dead end job, eh?" With that he burst into laughter, amazed at his own wit, slapped his knee, and laughed again.

The gravedigger smiled weakly as a little warmth eased back into his bones and a mustache of sweat appeared on his upper lip.

"Were you at the whole funeral?" asked the gravedigger.

"Yes, son. I sat here in the car just in case there was trouble."

"Well, who were those men who fired the shots in the air?"

The officer looked into the gravedigger's red-rimmed eyes with a quizzical stare.

"Come on, lad. Where have you been all these years?" he asked incredulously. "They were the lads of the U.D.A. Two of them were from my station. They moonlight for them. Mainly teaching them how to use weapons and passing on tips to them on where they can ambush the Provos...."

The police officer looked at the gravedigger.

"Are you new around here? I thought everyone on the Shankhill knew what was going on."

"Oh...I have been away for a while," he said purposefully keeping his voice natural, emotionless. "I had a sort of a breakdown and went to England. When I left, things were very different around here."

Then the gravedigger pointed down to his mud-caked shoes. "I got them some years ago from the man they just buried. He used to sell great shoes. I put them on today as a special tribute to him."

The officer's eyes lit up. "See them boots, son," he said, inclining his eyes downwards, "I also got them from old Mr. Burke. He used to give us lads in the R.U.C. a special deal. The chaps at our station would buy all our boots from him, because he'd throw in a spare pair for nothing."

Taking another quick drag, he added, "I've kicked a good few 'Fenians' (Republicans) with these, you know."

The gravedigger's expression suddenly changed.

"Do you think you'll finally win the war with the Provos?" he asked a look of innocence sweeping his face.

"No doubt about it," the policeman answered confidently.

"Do you know, son, more and more people are defecting from their ranks and giving the British intelligence people good info. Still, it's small cheese at the moment. They're after someone who is close to the inner workings and not just connected with one of the cells."

He took the empty cup from the gravedigger's hands, poured more tea into it and then emptied the final contents of the whisky into it. The heady aroma made the gravedigger feel a little dizzy.

"But isn't it dangerous for someone from the Provos to squeal?"

"Sure it is. But there are those who are finally waking up to the fact that the Provos want more than just a united Ireland. Yes, they are beginning to see that this really is a revolution that doesn't just want a united Ireland, but wants a Red Ireland.

"Get my drift, son. The Irish won't run Ireland if they win."

"Is that a fact? So how do these squealers make contact with the intelligence people?" asked the inquisitive gravedigger.

The officer paused for a moment, frowning, and then looked quizzically at him. "For a man who digs holes you ask a lot of questions."

"Doesn't mean because I do this job that I'm completely stupid," he responded, a note of anger rising in his voice. "I read the papers, you know."

The officer raised his hand in defense as if parrying an attack. Then his eyes drew down into slits. "Anyway, why do you want to know?" he asked curtly.

"Well, I have a friend who might have some information that could help them."

"I see. Well, he could call the terrorist hotline."

"No, he doesn't want to do that. It's too impersonal...he told me so. He wants to talk face-to-face with someone."The officer scratched his head. "Well, that could be tricky. The British normally only talk with the biggies. What sort of information does this friend of yours have to give them?"

"Well, I can't speak for him, but I think it is something that could maybe turn the tide here."

Burke could almost see the computer clicking way in the police officer's head behind his heavy eyes. He pulled out a crumpled flyer from his pocket and handed it to Burke. It read, "If you know anything about terrorist activities - threats, murders or explosions - please speak now to the confidential telephone - Belfast 652155.

"Get your friend to phone this number and ask for 'Mr. Howells.' He can arrange for your friend to meet with someone important.

"Well, son, I must be about my business. There's a lot of nasty people around this town that need a kick in the rear from Mr. Burke's boots."

With that, the pair shook hands and the gravedigger headed out into the rain still pouring down like sheet metal from the darkened sky. He folded the flyer and slipped it into his back pocket.

* * * * *

David Burke munched a cucumber-and cheese sandwich as the assembled group at the funeral "wake" was beginning to run out of nice things to say about his mother and father.

"Pity your brother turned out the way he did," said Uncle Joe belligerently, as he slipped his arm around David's shoulder. "It just goes to show that all that book learning isn't always good for you."

"Seems to me," interjected Uncle Allen still wearing the Orange Order sash around his suit, "we shouldn't even be mentioning his name at a time like this. He's a dead man as far as I'm concerned.

What do you say, David?"

The younger son stared at him without answering, his mouth tight and grim. Then, in a calm voice, he asked, "Don't you believe that God can forgive Randy? You go to church every Sunday, yet you preach hate during the week. That's not what Jesus did."

Uncle Allen felt his face flush with anger. "Don't talk to me like that you young punk." A truculent expression now covered his rubbery face and his veins began to stand out on the side of his forehead like strands of spaghetti.

"You talk about God, yet you go around with your U.D.A. pals shooting Catholics." David Burke's voice had now turned raspingly sarcastic. "You lot in the U.D.A. aren't much better than the Provos." With some difficulty, Uncle Allen suppressed the urge to slap his nephew.

The wives, who sat straight-backed in a corner, became concerned with this little shouting match and tried to stop the row between David and his Uncle.

"Now, now, lads. Let's have no more of this talk," said Aunt Martha, Allen's frumpy wife, as she fixed the protagonists with a reproachful eye.

Uncle Joe tried to lighten the proceedings with a story he had heard last week at the Lodge: "Sam Paisley was telling me about a chap he knew who didn't believe in heaven or hell. When he died, the family was viewing the body in the coffin. He looked so smart in his best suit and tie. One of the group said, 'Look at him. All dressed up and nowhere to go....'" They all broke into peals of laughter. But David did not smile.

Just then the phone rang shrilly in the hallway, jangling David Burke's taut nerves. Seconds later, one of the women shouted into the room, "It's for you, David. Sounds like an American."

Giving his uncle a look fit to kill, David stormed from the room.

His aunt handed him the phone gingerly as if it were something unsavory.

"Yes," he hissed curtly into the receiver.

"Is that Mr. David Burke?" said the mid-Atlantic voice at the other end of the line.

"Yes, who is this?" he rasped impatiently into the instrument.

"It's me, Randy." A slightly nasal voice came on the line. "Do you like my accent? I picked it up from those Downtown Radio disc jockeys."

"Randy," said David lowering his voice to almost a whisper, "I told you never to call here. This bunch would lynch you if they could."

"They'd have to find me, first. None of them recognized me at the funeral, did they?"

"You were just lucky."

"Look, David, could you meet me in thirty minutes at the gravediggers hut? I have something important I want to talk over with you."

With that the line went dead, leaving David gazing down at the receiver for a long, silent moment. He marched back into the room.

"Who was it, David?" asked his Aunt Martha.

"Oh, just a friend who had heard about the funeral. He wants to have a chat. So, if you'll excuse me, I'll be off."

David went around the room and kissed the women on the cheek and shook hands with the men. "Let's call a truce," he told Uncle Allen. Uncle Allen nodded his head in reluctant agreement.

* * * * *

The heavy clouds were scudding through the dark sky as a half-crescent moon tried to peek through onto "Bomb City." David could just make out the weak yellow light from a solitary bulb that threw a glow as thin as buttermilk through the window of the wooden hut as he approached it and knocked on the door.

"Come.... It's open," a voice whispered hoarsely from inside.

David slid open the door that creaked badly on its hinges and threw himself into Randy's arms. They held each other tight for about two minutes. There were no words, but the communication was total. David pushed his brother away, as he became aware of the smell of whisky on the gravedigger's breath.

"Have you been drinking, Randy?"

"Does that shock you? I went to the off-license and got myself a bottle of J & B. There's plenty left for the two of us to finish off."

Randy slowly released himself from David's grip and picked up the bottle. He began pouring the golden liquid into a plastic cup and handed it to his brother.

"I think you deserve this, David. I don't think I could have put up with those relatives for long."

"You're right, Randy. I need a drink. You know, when you phoned I was about to 'punch out' Uncle Allen. He's not exactly your greatest fan, you know."

"Nor am I," said the gravedigger pointedly.

David winced as he swallowed the fiery liquid, tears stinging his eyes.

"You're not used to it. It's the great pain killer. I know!"

David took another uncertain sip and found his cheeks begin to redden.

"You know our tee-total relatives call this stuff, 'The Devil's Spittle.'" With that he took a swallow of his drink and sank into the battered armchair opposite him. With a sweep of his hand, he motioned for David to sit on the ancient leather couch opposite him.

The "gravedigger" laughed as the layers of memory from his childhood were peeled away to when he was in the temperance group, the Band of Hope. For a brief instant, he was a boy again. It seemed like eons ago when he had signed the pledge never to allow "strong drink" to pass his lips. He told David how he had watched with fascination one evening at the Shankhill Road Mission Hall during a temperance rally, when the long-faced speaker had poured some whisky into a glass and then unceremoniously dropped a wriggling worm into the contents. Within seconds the writhing creature gave up the ghost.

"Now," said the speaker, a hint of triumph in his voice, "you have seen what strong drink did to this worm. Imagine what this vile stuff will do to your insides."

The leader of the class rose from her seat on the platform and encouraged the wide-eyed children packing the hall to break into rapturous applause.

As the hand-clapping subsided, the speaker asked all the children to get to their feet and repeat after him, "I promise...never to allow...strong drink...to pass my lips." Randy enthusiastically joined in with the "pledge" at that moment, caught up in the fervor of the event. Mimeographed pledges were passed around the room and the boys and girls were asked to sign them as their promise to never to drink alcohol. Of course, Randy, like all of the others, signed up.

He thought of that worm as he drained the contents of his cup and filled it up again. "Poor thing," he mused. Then he chuckled out loud as he added, "But what a way to go!"

David took another sip of whisky and then asked Randy why he so urgently wanted to see him.

"Well, brother, I've come to a decision. As I stood there today in the rain and watched our mother and father lowered into the ground, I knew I had to do something to make up to them all that I've done over the past few years."

David sat up, wondering what was going to come next.

"Yes, I know I'm a little drunk, but I am deadly serious when I say that I want to become a squealer. I know who killed them and they were supposed to be my colleagues. Some colleagues! I serve their group and they kill my folks. I can give the British intelligence people inside information that will blow their minds.

"David, I want you to phone this number," he said taking out the flyer from his back pocket and unfolding it. "Call a 'Mr. Howells' and tell him that you know someone who could help him with info on the inner workings of the Provos."

"Are you sure you know what you are getting into, Randy? This could cost you your life."

Randy took a deep breath, feeling a deep weariness heavy within him.

"I know what I'm doing and I am aware of the risks," he said in a voice barely under control.

David thought, "You are probably digging your own grave by doing this." But he kept that disturbing thought to himself.

He turned to look at his brother. Randy's eyes were distant, almost as if he were looking to a world beyond his ken. That look gave David a sharp feeling of apprehension and an awareness of impending disaster.

Then God again began crying for Ireland and those tears began pounding on the roof of the hut.

12
The Meeting

"The Meeting" was one that Reem Salameh would remember for ever. For, gathered with her around a table in a five-star hotel in Damascus were a powerful group of men, who had one purpose - to restructure the world and herald in Islamic dominance of the Western World and the take-over of Jerusalem.

Reem, like the others, had a lot of "stock" invested in "the plan" that had entered her brain as she joined thousands of joyous Palestinians in Gaza City on that Tuesday night in July of 1998 just hours after an attack on the 110 storey, neo-gothic "New York Building," that housed a "secret" group of US intelligence officers. The main entrance at Broadway resembled European Cathedral entrances and was decorated with many symbols, like salamanders and owls, but now the whole building lay in total destruction.

She had heard that a faction of disaffected Saudi's called "Wahabi Warriors" were planning to hijack a plane from the Middle East just after it took off from John F. Kennedy International Airport and then crash it into this famous old building to show the U.S. that it was capable to hitting at the heart of Manhattan's skyline – and also kill many of its intelligence community.

People around the world, including Reem, had watched the events unfold on television. Along with Ibrahim and his wife, she screamed with excitement as an airliner crashed into the building. A while later, an announcer came on the screen saying that the plane brought had brought the huge building toppling down.

Soon, it became clear that the world would never be the same again. Thousands of people had perished in the attack, including many intelligence officers and many innocent officer workers.

As the sound of gunfire and honking horns filled the streets outside their home, Reem grabbed her AK-47 and rushed outside to join the joyous celebration. Soon she was squeezing the trigger of her weapon and firing it into the air. The cacophony of the shouts of support for the highjackers, the never-ending blare of car horns and the screams of joy, were intoxicating to Reem.

Then she spotted a cameraman shooting footage of the scene. She rushed over to him and pointed her weapon at his head and shouted, "Stop filming or I'll kill you."

He paused for a moment, but could see from her blazing eyes that she was serious. He stopped what he was doing and ran into the crush of the crowd.

Reem then joined the crowd singing the praises of terrorist mastermind Osama bin Laden. "He is our hero,' she and the crowd kept chanting. "He has struck a death blow to the American fascists and Zion lovers."

As she danced and sang, a plan suddenly came into her tortured brain. What if she could put together an operation to go even further than bin Laden, and wipe out the leaders of the developed world as well as the Prime Minister of Israel?

"We could call it 'Operation Red Dagger,'" she whispered under her breath. "I know just the person who could help me put this together…"

* * * * *

Smoke filled the room as the team got down to business. There were just five people seated around the table, but they knew that if they got the plan right, they could change world history.

Ibrahim Rudeniah took his seat at the head of table as chairman of the meeting. Seated to the left of him was his wife and next to her was Mahmoud Mustapha, 35, who sported a shaggy black beard. Reem sat across the table and next to her was Hussam Muhsein, a cold-hearted killer who claimed to have murdered some 20 IDF soldiers over the past few years.

"Well my friends," Ibrahim began as he surveyed the group before him, "I think the time has come for us to finalize our plans."

With that, he handed out documents which had "Top Secret" stamped on them, and each began studying them.

"You will be glad to hear that now we have the funding to move ahead," he continued. "It has come from our friends in Tehran. They are sick of being told what to do with their nuclear program."

He then turned to the smiling Reem and explained that she had been busy in gathering together "an extraordinary" team of trained killers from the crème de la crème of Western terrorist groups.

"Reem," he said nodding his head towards her, "the floor is yours."

"Thank you," she said as she rose to her feet. She winced as Hussam Muhsein took out a Turkish cigarette from a gold container, flicked on his lighter, held it to the cigarette and lit up. He took a long, deep, draw from it and blew the blue smoke out of the side of his mouth. The others looked in disgust at the man, but no one protested.

"I would like to begin with a poem written by the great Russian writer, Alexander Pushkin," she announced.

With that she took a piece of paper from her file lying on the table and read:

What to do? We have lost our way.
From afar, the Demon cries out.
He is leading us astray.

"I think we all know who that 'Demon' is?" she continued. "It is the Zionists, and their blind supporters in the West."

There were smiles all around the table as Reem continued her tirade about all that was bad in the Western World.

"To add to all of this, our people are suffering as never before. There are no jobs while the Zionists continue to get fat with the support they get from America."

She then quoted more from Pushkin's poem:

Skyward soar the whirling demons,
Shrouded by the following snow,
And the plaintive, awful howling
Fills my heart with dread and woe.

"My friends," she added, "our mission is urgent!"

Reem then got down to the business at hand.

"I have found a friend in Northern Ireland who is on board with our plan," she said. "I met him some time ago at a training camp in Syria. A few weeks ago he called me in Gaza and invited me to visit him in Belfast. My dear father had provided me with an American passport, so I went to see him. He has terrific contacts with many of the groups that we need to carry out our plan. Since I saw him, he has been visiting them and has received their commitment to join with us. These freedom fighters want to get rid of their leaders and will provide their best person to assassinate their leader."

She was trawling the darker emotional currents of humiliation and impotence coursing through her veins.

After some thirty minutes of detailed explanation about who had been recruited and what their role would be in the assassination of the different "hated" political leaders, she sat down.

Ibrahim beamed with pride as she ended her speech. "You can only gain power in this world through the barrel of a gun. That's why we must proceed with this plan," he said taking a sip of warm sugary tea from a glass before him. "That was a most encouraging report. I propose that we give you the authority to finalize your arrangements. All those in favor say 'Aye.'"

The vote was unanimous. Then Ibrahim said it was important that they now concentrate on the "sleeper cells" in the various countries so they could immediately start a reign of terror in the capital cities. They would also be in place in Washington, London, Rome, Paris, Madrid, Athens and Bonn, to seize key military targets and ensure "total chaos" in their cities.

After some four hours of intensive discussion, the chairman closed the meeting, and the group retired to an adjacent room for refreshments and some soft drinks. It had been a good meeting and celebration of "the victory" would begin!

* * * * *

After the meeting, Reem moved quickly. She took a flight that brought her back to Belfast, via Dublin, where she was met by Randy Burke. The Irishman was his usual charming self as he drove her to a hotel he had secured for her close to the Grand Opera House.

As she unpacked, he suggested they go for a walk so they could not be overheard.

After a few minutes, they arrived at the three-story Ulster Museum located at the southwest corner of the Botanic Gardens.

Burke guided her through the first floor exhibit that colorfully traced the rise of Belfast's crafts, trade, and industry. But she was more interested in the display that told the story of the Nationalist movement and explained the separation of the north from the rest of the country.

"You can see why we are fighting for our freedom," Burke told his Palestinian friend. "The British partitioned our country and we want to be a united Ireland."

They finally arrived at the small café on level three of the museum and Burke ordered coffee for both of them.

"Well, Reem, tell me how your meeting went," he said after checking that no one was near enough to hear their discussion.

"It went very well," she began, taking a sip of the hot, milky brew. "We are ready to move ahead with the plan, but we need your help."

He leaned closer to not miss a word of what she was going say.

"Yes, my friends have asked if you would take it upon yourself to bring a group of your friends together in a place that you choose so we can brief them on the plan."

Reem took another sip of coffee and then continued. "There is a G7 summit coming up in Vienna soon and we feel that would be the time for the lethal strike. Do you think you could organize some key people to be at a planning meeting before then?"

Burke smiled and told her, "Well, I think that Prague would be a good place for us to have this gathering. It is close to Vienna and I have in mind some terrific people who could join us there."

Reem pondered for a moment and then said, "Prague…that's the capital city of the Czech Republic. Yes, I think that's a good choice. May we make a quick trip there so I can see where we might hold our meeting?"

"Not a problem," he said. "But if we go, I want to introduce you to vodka. I know you are a Muslim who is not supposed to drink, but I think you will enjoy the experience."

Reem smiled and replied, "I'm not really a Muslim. I have just embraced their cause."

* * * * *

Two days later, after a relatively short flight to Prague, the couple found themselves in a smoke-filled hotel restaurant in this historic city. Burke ordered up a bottle of Symphony Vodka.

"Reem, this is good stuff," he said. "It was first produced in the 18th Century and has a long and rich tradition. It conjures up images of the great performers who are connected with the Czech Republic, as well as those master composers who were creating their beautiful symphonies at the time."

He poured a generous amount into a large glass and handed it to her. She closed he eyes, gulped it down, shook her head violently, grimaced briefly at its expected near-lethal punch, then smiled triumphantly at surviving her first taste of vodka.

"Right, Mr. Burke, it's your turn."

With that she filled up Burke's glass in the restaurant where they were meeting, and sat back to see how the Irishman would cope with the "firewater." Randy Burke looked around the room, and realized that almost every eye was focused on him.

Burke picked up the glass, closed his eyes and threw the vodka down his gullet. Almost immediately he coughed violently. Reem indicated to the watching audience that they should clap to cover his embarrassment. They did, and as Burke's spluttering continued, the assembled throng dissolved into friendly laughter.

"Here, Mr. Burke, have a sniff of the crusty bread. It will help quench the fire now raging in your throat."

She joined in the chortles as Burke ripped off a piece of bread from the loaf offered him and champed on it. It had a moist, rich, sweet-sour taste, but still did little to solve his problem.

By now the vodka-induced tears continued to well up in Burke's eyes and were proving a great embarrassment to him. After all, was not he supposed to be the tough, ruthless urban terrorist who had become a Provo legend in his own land? He wondered if Reem was trying to humiliate him. Or was it just innocent fun she was expected to enjoy before they got down to the real business of her visit.

"Have a pickled cucumber, Mr. Burke. That should do the trick," she said, wiping the tears that rolled down her reddened face.

The Irishman did, but then began to cough again uncontrollably. As he turned blue, an onlooker jumped up from his seat and slapped him violently on the back. Finally Burke composed himself and smiled weakly at the Palestinian. He had thought she would have the problem with the vodka, but somehow he had become of the worse of the two.

"I'm afraid," he spluttered, "Guinness is more my kind of drink!"

"I quite understand, Mr. Burke. If I ever visit your beautiful country, I would join you in the drink I have heard so much about.

Throughout the evening, Burke had, much against his better judgment, endured the much more unpleasant vodka - on ten more occasions to be precise. That night, as the room began to spin crazily before him, he asked Reem if he might be excused.

"But," she protested. "The night is young! It is only midnight. I once read that that once a bottle is uncorked, it has to be finished.

There is one that still has some left!"

Burke put up his arms in mock self-defense.

"Are you trying to get me drunk?" he spluttered.

"Now, would I do something like that?" she laughed.

Burke knew the answer lay in the affirmative, but was not going to say so.

"Okay, Mr. Burke, I'll let you get to bed, but not before I propose a toast to you. The toast, my dear friend, is to you, coupled with the great success of your Irish revolution," she said raising her glass inches off the table.

Burke steeled himself for one more shot of vodka. He chinked his glass with mock festivity against that of the Palestinian, drained the contents and lurched out of the hotel restaurant and into the lobby.

As he lay on his bed in the hotel, he tried to gather his thoughts about this young woman and how they had first met in Syria. He had returned to Ireland from that trip with all kinds of goodies that could help the cause. The Provo leaders were delighted with a glossy catalogue he had brought back with him, illustrating the wares available from an arms factory in Prague. There were rocket launchers, hand grenades, bazookas, guns and ammunition.

"It's like Christmas," shouted a triumphant O'Shea as he excitedly flicked through the brochure. Then, turning to Burke, he asked: "Will they supply them to us?"

Burke smiled wryly. "They sure will, and at very favorable terms."

As he sat in on their Provo High Command planning session held in their farm headquarters, Burke looked around at his grim colleagues and wondered if they really knew what they were doing. What was he to do? He was in the Provos too deep now to withdraw. Even the suspicion of his double dealing would mean certain death from any of those cold killers in that room. He knew only too well that there would be many volunteers to put a bullet in his head, as he had become the target of much hateful jealousy because of his active debating in the meetings. Many of them in the high command resented the fact that O'Shea made no secret that he liked Burke and often singled him out for special attention. They would regularly go off into the peaceful, often misty, countryside around the farm retreat to walk and talk about future tactics on Ireland's soil, described by Ulster poet Seamus Heaney as "black butter/Melting and opening underfoot."

On a trip to Belfast, in his usual disguise of longhaired wig and droopy mustache, Burke decided on his next course of action. He had read an ad only that morning in the Belfast Telegraph, which urged people to "Call the terrorist hotline NOW!" The British Army, along with the RUC, had set up a special phone-line for people to call in with anonymous information on terrorist activity and give the names of Provisional IRA suspects or those killers from within the Protestant community.

On hearing the pips, he nervously slipped in a five-penny piece into the pay-phone slot.

"Hotline, how may I help you?" asked a friendly "Colleen" at the end of the line.

Burke had expected a brick-hard man to answer the phone and was surprised to hear her silky, soft voice. Clever ploy, he thought. That would immediately put a caller at ease. But he did not feel at ease, so he firmly slammed down the receiver.

"This is madness," he gasped out loud. "I can't go informing on my comrades." Randy Burke felt by now he was dancing on the edge of a pin.

* * * * *

The next morning, Burke gazed into the bathroom mirror at his bloodshot eyes, and he felt angry that he had allowed himself to get into such a state. He threw cold water over his face to try and bring a little sanity back into his befuddled brain.

13
Island of Hate

"BILLY, BILLY, BILLY," rhythmically chanted the hyped-up audience in the tiny studio of *London Television* as bizarre talk-show host Billy Windsor stood up, with his arms held high to acknowledge the adulation of his adoring audience. With an affectation, he brushed back his died-black hair with his left hand and then made sure the red rose in the left lapel of his dark pin-striped suit was in place. The adrenaline was again flowing in Windsor's brain. Another live show of conflict and invective and the ever-present threat of violence was again being beamed into five million British homes.

"Britain is number one; do you agree?" he shouted to the monkey-faced skinheads sitting in the front row as they waved their plastic Union Jacks and shouted their obscenities in unison.

Arch Bishop stood bemused at the side of the set. He had been sent there by Al Farr to report on this new free-swinging, vitriolic television phenomenon that was sweeping Britain into an anti-immigrant fervor. Billy Windsor, a now decrepit former newsreader for the BBC was now the darling of Britain's extreme right-wing, with his bizarre late Saturday-night show, "Electric Chair." With a sense of pure political theater, he took on guests he was opposed to and waded into them like a world champ with a bewildering barrage of insults, usually knocking then out cold and then ordering them off the show. They would be escorted from the studio by a bevy of burly brown-shirted security guards with prominent Union Jack flags sewn on the shoulders of their shirts.

This night's show promised to be as wild as ever with "the conservative inquisitor," whom Bishop considered to be somewhat to the right of Attila the Hun, taking Khalid Amin, the Pakistan-born leader of the British Muslim Party. The second guest was to be old Etonian, David Farquhar-Smith, who was leading the "Legalize Marijuana Campaign."

To add to this "strange brew" was a delegation from the Anti-Fascist League who carried banners with them like "Smash the Nazis," "Remember the Holocaust" and "Stop Racist Attacks." This, thought Bishop, was definitely going to be an evening when anything could happen.

After the credits had rolled, this right-wing zealot was again ready to do battle with the "forces of evil."

"Okay Peter, who is to be the first up tonight to be sizzled in my electric chair?" Windsor asked his much milder co-host, Peter Davis, a former Conservative M.P. who years earlier had been kicked out of the party for having had an affair with a young lady who had been his election manager.

"Well, Billy," said Davis, in rather effeminate tones, "I know you're going to be just wild about this gentleman."

"Don't call him a gentleman..." interrupted Windsor, "he's nothing but a dirty troublemaker."

The Neanderthal supporters of Windsor, many completely hairless, their heads egg like, erupted with wild applause at Billy's comments. He, again, stood up to acknowledge their support. He looked like a boxer who had just won a title fight. Revulsion was theatrically written all over Windsor's face as he curled up his lip and rolled his eyes upwards.

"Dirty Packie, dirty Packie," parts of the audience derisively chanted in unison as Amin made his way to the "Electric Chair," a prop that had previously only been used by the station's drama department.

"Don't let him intimidate you, Khalid," yelled one of the members of the Anti-Fascist League from the back of the studio.

Bishop noted down in his reporter's notebook that many of the skinheads had tattoos on their pale gray shaved domes bearing slogans like ANARCHY and HATE. They also wore tight dungarees that were too short, only reaching the tops of their vicious high-laced boots. To him, fascism was bred from the despair and political bankruptcy that Britain had seen in its more recent years. The British, he reasoned, were an island people who did not know how to handle the fact that Indians and Pakistanis had "invaded" their land and brought with them ideas and religions that were "not usual" to that land. It was one thing for the British to take around the world their ideas of civilization, but the talk-show host could not tolerate it especially when these "foreigners" challenged that and settled in the inner cities of the UK and built their mosques and temples.

The American was not impressed with Windsor. He thought the man was cynically manipulating his audience like monkeys on a string.

"Right Amin, strap yourself in, you vermin," he yelled at the nervous guest who was already regretting that he had come on the show instead of staying at his office in Brick Lane.

A long camera shot of Windsor revealed to viewers that behind him was a large color picture of the Queen, a giant British flag and the slogan, "Britain for the British." Behind Billy Windsor stood two enormous "Brown Shirts," one on either side of him. They were there not only to give an effect to the show, but also to protect

Billy. He had received several death threats during his stormy nine months on the air.

Davis, by now had given up on trying to introduce the Pakistani, so Billy again slicked back his died-black hair, and did the formalities himself.

"Tonight, my loyal friends, we have a man who represents all that is bad about Britain today. One of the worst guests I have ever had the dubious pleasure to have in the Electric Chair," he railed with high decibel fulminations. "He's a man who is a disgrace to Britain because he has brought an alien way of life here. What do you say to that, Amin?"

"Well, Mr. Windsor," he began hesitantly with a thick East Asian accent, "if you can stop those baboons out there yelling I'll answer that question." He swiveled around to size up the crowd. The skinheads, who came mainly from the docklands area of London, looked back without exception with hostile eyes. Several stood to their feet and shouted "Sieg Heil" as they gave the fascist salute with their right arms.

With that Windsor was again on his feet behind his stage desk and pandemonium broke out in the audience as the grunts and chants got louder and louder. It was pure "Rocky Horror Show." One group of well-dressed men began singing, "There'll always be an England."

Windsor raised his hands and shouted, "Look you idiot, don't you insult my audience like that." He had all the subtlety of a pile driver as his right hand began to jab the air. "They are some of the brightest people around. I hope your friends in Mecca are watching this show. Then they will see what Britain is really made of."

Bishop scanned the audience. Many of them looked to him like a supercharged bunch of thugs at a soccer game spoiling for trouble. Amin shivered as one punk raced from his seat and aimed a kick at him. He was removed from the studio screaming insults, as the camera zoomed in on a large button which bore the sickening face - to Bishop - of his megalomaniac hero, Billy Windsor.

"God help Merrie England if this is their cream," Bishop thought as he whistled through his teeth in disgust.

The American had observed, with concern, the recent growth of quasi-fascism in Britain and Windsor was, in a frightening manner, verbalizing the fears of many good British people who were concerned with the way the country had been invaded by different forces from the old Empire. Now the Empire had "struck back" and many did not like it. In a country once known for its tolerance, sense of justice, and love of fair play, this seemed to Bishop to be a circus of naked fascism that disturbed him deeply. He jotted a reminder in his notebook to nominate Windsor for the "Hall of Phonies."

After allowing the insults to be screamed at Amin for a full two minutes, Billy Windsor again signaled the crowd to "Cool it." They did and obediently sat down in their seats. Windsor looked, with all the hate he could muster in his face, at the Muslim leader. "If you insult my audience one more time I'm throwing you off the show," he hissed.

During the yelling and screaming, the nervous Pakistani lit up a cigarette to try to calm himself and hawk-eyed Billy noticed it.

"Put that cigarette out, you scum," he shouted, his voice rising several decibels. "There's no smoking allowed in this studio."

Surprisingly, Amin obediently dropped the cigarette to the floor and stamped on it. Then he looked across at Windsor's face, by now contorted into a theatrical look that showed how much he despised him.

Trying to compose himself, Amin pointed behind his adversary. "I see you have a picture of *our* Queen," he said calmly in his pronounced accent.

"She's not *your* Queen, you vile pig."

"What I was trying to say..."

"Spit it out."

"What I was trying to say was, I'm surprised you haven't got a picture of Adolf Hitler alongside it. He's your real hero isn't he, Windsor. Admit it!"

The talk-show host was really wild now and his face contorted into purple rage.

"Did you hear that?" he screeched to his audience. Windsor got up from behind the table that had on it a large black-and-white photograph of Winston Churchill, a cigar in his mouth and giving his famous "V" for victory sign. He stormed over to Amin and grabbed him by the collar and pulled his face close to his.

"I ought to smash in your despicable face right now," he yelled loudly enough for his radio-mike to relay the words to his adoring television audience across the country.

"I fought for this country against Hitler...."

"Then why do you have these 'British Front' fascists from docklands in your audience?" screamed Amin, spitting out the words as he tried to extricate himself from Windsor's vice-like grip around his neck. Amin then got to his feet and stormed over to a group of well-dressed men at the back of the studio.

The camera followed him as he pointed out Jeremiah Smith, leader of the British Front, an extreme right-wing group that encouraged its followers to "Make Britain Great Again," by beating up West Indians, Indians, Pakistanis and Jews."I happen to know, Windsor, that you are a card-carrying member of the British Front," said Amin. With that he dramatically pulled out a piece of paper from his inside pocket and held up a photocopy of Windsor's membership card. He then carefully showed it to the lens of the camera.

"Go on, show that across the country," Amin dared the camera-man. George Smith who was operating camera-one desperately struggled to get his close-up shot in focus.

Jeremiah Smith was not going to allow any more of this and so moved from his seat and dived at the Pakistani, landing a vicious blow full in his face. With this, the studio erupted into savage violence. As Amin lay groaning on the floor, hefty kicks were rained into his ribs by a host of heaving jackboots. At the same time frenzied fists with HATE inscribed across knuckles in blue ink repeatedly pummeled his writhing body.

"We'll go over to a commercial break, **NOW!**" yelled a flustered Billy Windsor, trying to bring back a semblance of order to the proceedings which had by now gotten totally out of control.

Windsor summoned up all his cynical "sincerity," and looked straight into a camera and smiled sickly. "Don't go away, my friends. We will be right back after these important messages," he intoned. Before he could finish his words, a banner, bearing the slogan, "Kill the Packies," crashed down on his head and he slumped to the floor. It had been aimed at Amin but, in the confusion, had hit Windsor instead.

As the commercials rolled, a group of Bobbies who had been enjoying the show on a monitor in the foyer of Capital Television, woke up to what was happening and rushed into the studio, their truncheons drawn. They began wading into the melee, whacking everyone in sight. Blood streamed from cracked skulls as the "men in blue" fought to clear a way to the unconscious Pakistani.

Others went to the aid of Windsor, who was lying on the floor of the studio, blood trickling from his purple lips. His face was an ashen gray, his lips faintly blue, and he was making strange gurgling sounds. Bishop also dashed over to him and loosened his tie.

"Get a doctor and an ambulance," he yelled urgently. "Get help, somebody. The guy's having a heart attack."

A Bobbie radioed for help. As he did, the red light came on again and viewers were shown Bishop leaning over the prostrate figure of Billy Windsor, whose body had now gone still and lifeless.

They saw Bishop giving him the mouth-to-mouth resuscitation and then desperately thumping down on Billy Windsor's chest. But he did not respond. He just lay there on his back, his deep blue-eyes staring glassily upwards.

"He's dead," announced Bishop after several minutes as the cameras zeroed in on his anguished face. "My God, he's dead."

A white-coated doctor rushed into the studio followed by medics bearing resuscitation equipment. As they feverishly tried to revive Billy Windsor, Davis, his face a whiter-shade-of-pale, picked up a microphone and looked directly into the camera.

"Ladies and gentlemen," he said, his voice pitched on the edge of hysteria, "this is terrible. Billy Windsor is dead! He's the only person who could lead this country back into greatness."

The doctor frantically continued to try to bring life back into Windsor, but without success. One of the skinheads, bearing on his head the inscription "KICK IT TO DEATH," stood over the body. He closed his eyes, embarrassed by the unwanted dampness in his eyes. He took out a handkerchief and wiped the coagulating blood from a nasty wound at the side of Windsor's right eye. He snatched the large red-white-and-blue Union Jack flag at the back of Windsor's set, pulled out the pole it was attached to, and draped it over his hero's corpse.

"Pull your shot back," David Lee-Jones, the show's producer shouted down his microphone to the man controlling camera three.

"Get a shot of them carrying Billy's body out on the stretcher with the flag on it."

Handkerchiefs across Britain wiped away tears as the incredible scene in the studio was beamed live into millions of living rooms. One person watching the drama unfold and wiping away tears from crimson eyes opened to their physical limits, was American news anchor, Gloria Jansen. However, the tears were not for Windsor, but for her distraught ex-husband.

She had arrived in London that afternoon on from New York to do a report on some of London's fashion moguls. Gloria had been debating whether or not to call up her ex-husband. She guessed at this late hour that he would be drinking alone in his flat. She hated to speak to him while he was in the maudlin state that his "g & t's" usually produced. What a tragedy his life had turned into, she thought. That cocky, confident, silver-tongued reporter, who had breezed into her life in Brooklyn, was now a gaunt, tragic shadow of his former self.

She wanted to remember only those times of fun that they had enjoyed together when she had trailed after with him as he interviewed rock stars, fighters, hoods and politicians for the *Brooklyn Banner*.

Gloria had instinctively turned on the TV set with the channel changer in her Savoy hotel suite, and cried out when she saw Arch leaning over the prostrate figure of the silver-haired talk-show host. She uttered a shriek when she heard him make the "he's dead" announcement. It brought back painful memories of his own near-fatal shooting.

A camera had followed the medical team as they carried Windsor's body, still draped with the large red-white-and-blue British flag, out to a waiting ambulance. Gloria watched her husband jump into the back of the ambulance and the vehicle roar off into the night, its sirens wailing at full pitch.

A smiling picture of Billy Windsor was flashed onto the screen and a solemn announcer said, "Ladies and gentlemen, Billy Windsor died at 11:10 P.M. tonight during his `Electric Chair' show. His body is at this very moment being taken to the morgue at St. Thomas's Hospital in Westminster."

With her heart pounding at over one hundred beats to the minute, she grabbed her overcoat and rushed down to the front of the hotel. She jumped into the nearest black cab.

"Where to, Miss?" asked the affable driver, jauntily adjusting his cap.

"St. Thomas's Hospital!"

The cabby dropped his flag and pulled sharply away from the front of the Savoy, turned the circle of the front area and turned left into The Strand. They sped down Whitehall, past Downing Street, and left onto Westminster Bridge, with the imposing Houses of Parliament rising up to the right.

A large crowd had gathered at the emergency entrance of the hospital where nursing legend, Florence Nightingale, the "Lady with the Lamp," had served as a young lady.

Gloria handed the driver a crumpled five-pound note for the two-pound fare, telling him to "keep the change" and then began to push her way through the thick crowd, many of whom had rushed from the studio in a convoy of cars and were still waving their Union Jack flags.

A burly policeman barred her way as she tried to force her way through to the main entrance of the casualty department.

"I'm sorry, Miss, but no one is allowed in."

"But my husband is in there...."

Just then she spotted Arch to her right. He was surrounded by cameras and lights and was being interviewed.

"Arch," she shrieked as her heart melted at the sight of him. With that she pushed through the knot of media people and then swept him up into her arms, showering kisses all over his face. As she did, his expression lit up like Florence Nightingale's lamp.

"Are you all right, honey?" she asked, as he was overcome by a turmoil of emotion.

"Do you mind, lady?" rasped an annoyed Capital TV reporter. "We are trying to conduct an interview...."

Arch had now abandoned the interview and held his wife close and began to weep.

"Gloria, what are you doing here, you crazy kid?"

"I saw you on television. I came straight over. I'm in London for a few days doing a segment on some of the beautiful fashion people here in London."

She noticed that Arch's hands were trembling. It was obvious that he was barely in control of himself.

"Look lady, do you mind leaving your reunion until we've finished this 'take.' Then you can go and celebrate." By now the BBC reporter was hopping mad.

"The interview's over," snapped Bishop. "I've got some more important business to take care of.

"Come on Mrs. Bishop, let's go and have a drink."

With that Gloria's face dropped.

"Please, not tonight, Arch. Please...." He held her tightly. Neither said a word, but the communication was total.

"Okay, honey. You win. No drinks tonight!"

14
Stabbed in the Back

Gloria could hear insistent knocking at the door of her suite at The Savoy.

"Who is it?" she shouted.

"Who do you think it is?" yelled back her ex-husband.

Gloria had told Arch that she wanted to stay on her own after they had had some coffee at the hotel the previous night and he had surprisingly agreed to it.

She opened the door for him. "Time to get ready and let me show you London," he said brightly. Gloria had already showered and dried her hair and was now putting on her face. She had been so proud of him. He had not had even one drink! Arch appeared to have reverted to the fun-loving ways of their early relationship, joking about her new curly hair-style and also the "excessive rouge" on her cheeks.

"You don't look at all like the girl I married. I hardly recognize you," he chuckled, playfully squeezing her reddened cheeks as they sat on an elegant couch together.

"Is that a compliment or not?" she responded.

"A compliment; of course!"

"Why don't you wait for me in the coffee shop while I finish getting ready," Gloria suggested. "Go and get the papers and see what they have written about you."

Fifteen record-breaking minutes later, Gloria joined Arch and began reading copies of the *Sunday Times* and the *Sunday People*.

"Hey, Arch," she said excitedly, "the *Sunday People* says you made a heroic attempt to save the life of Billy Windsor, while the *Sunday Times* declares that you provided the 'only moment of sanity in a terrible evening of hatred.' Both of them carry a front-page picture of you leaning over that guy, Windsor, giving him mouth-to-mouth resuscitation.

"Hey, I'm jealous!"

For a short moment, the years had rolled back. After an English-style breakfast of eggs, bacon, and baked beans, with toast and marmalade and a pot each of hot tea, Bishop suggested they start their tour of the British capital at Speakers' Corner in Hyde Park.

"That place is something else. Talk about loony tunes," he bubbled affably.

Gloria was fascinatedm at first, with this unique forum of free speech. As always the "corner" was packed with orators of all shapes and sizes; of every religious and political persuasion. There were Arabs attacking the State of Israel, Jews verbally insulting the PLO, blacks yelling at whites, and whites insulting blacks. Not even the Queen of England was spared from the barbs of one speaker from the "Anti-Monarchist League."

The couple strolled hand in hand in between the knots of listeners and professional hecklers. They roared with laughter as a man wearing a pin-striped business suit, bowler hat and carrying a rolled umbrella, stopped by the side of a drunk who was desperately trying to say something but the words would not come out, and mimicked his actions.

Then he boomed out and cut through the babble as he said, "Everyone who's intelligent, come over here." His voice was so loud that it reached right across the corner. People in the scores left their speakers and hurried over to the pin-striped crier. When some two-hundred gawkers had gathered around him as well as the poor drunk, who was still waving his arms like a windmill, he promptly left. This meant the drunk had possibly the largest audience of his life, yet he had nothing to say. As he struggled to form his words, the crowds cheered then jeered.

"Silly old fool," shouted a skinhead wearing black leathers and a swastika earring dangling from one earlobe. "Let's teach him a lesson, lads," he added, signaling to his two friends. He was after another ill-tempered rumble that would give his deranged brain a charge.

Bishop unclasped his hand from Gloria's and rushed in front of the swaying drunk.

"If you guys touch this old fellah, I'll deck you," he warned the ring-leader.

"You and who's army, Yank. I can't see any missiles in your pocket."

Just as the three bald-headed men advanced menacingly towards Bishop, someone in the crowd shouted, "Hey that's the man who tried to save the life of Billy Windsor."

The punks stopped in their tracks.

"Is that true?" their leader asked.

"I guess so."

With that, he walked forward and warmly pumped Bishop's hand. The others followed suit, wanting to seek out some further mischief.

"Billy was our hero," said the skinhead leader. "He would have known how to deal with scum like this wino here."

"Yeah, he'd put 'im in the gas chamber!" said one of his companions.

"Reckon we'll give you a break this time, Mister American."

With that the vicious trio, all looking like clones of each other with their black uniforms and Union Jacks sewn on their backs, walked away.

Bishop turned to the rest of the crowd and shouted, "Okay gang, you've had your bit of fun, now leave the old guy in peace."

The drunk looked up at him with tears in his eyes. He then put his hand in his pocket and pulled out a brown paper bag containing a bottle of Methylated spirits and handed it to Arch. He nodded his head as if to say, "Go on, 'ave a drink on me."

Bishop politely refused and opened his wallet and handed the man a ten-pound note.

"Here, old fellah, go and get yourself something to eat. I reckon you could do with a square meal."

Gloria tugged at Bishop's hand and squeezed it urgently. "Let's move on," she said. Watching the old drunk had sent chills down the back of her spine. For she was acutely aware that the way her estranged husband had been going, he could end up in the same state in a few years time. She felt Arch had helped him only because of the deep guilt he felt about his own drinking problem, but she kept her thoughts to herself.

For the remaining hour, the pair wandered aimlessly around "Speakers' Corner," and continued to be subjected to a barrage of conflicting and often hate-filled views that really disturbed Gloria.

They were momentarily fascinated with a dark-suited preacher clasping a large, black Bible, who, from his soapbox vantage point was describing the "last days."

"Ladies and gentlemen, I want to tell you that in the last days there will be wailing and gnashing of teeth."

A wag in the crowd shot up his hand and yelled out, "That's all right mate. I ain't got no teeth."

Quick as a flash, the preacher said firmly, not a flicker of a smile crossing his face, "Teeth will be provided...."

The crowd erupted into hilarious laughter and the wag slipped away, to try his "wit" on another speaker, hoping for better fortune next time.

The largest group of all surrounded a man standing on a wooden platform dominated by a large red flag with a hammer and sickle emblazoned on it.

Tie-less, and wearing a shabby Harris Tweed jacket and un-pressed brown trousers, the man was certainly a spellbinder in a rough, working-class sort of way.

"We, in the People's Revolutionary Party, want *you*, yes all of you, to have the power in Britain," he roared with a strong Cockney accent as his voice built up to a crescendo. "No longer will the privileged classes push us around and exploit us," he continued in his well-rehearsed monologue. A ripple of unconvinced applause broke out in the gathering.

"Power to the people!" shouted a scruffy man at the edge of the crowd who was selling literature with Karl Marx's picture on it. Bishop thought the man was an obvious plant to encourage the speakers as he continued to unleash his diatribe against capitalism.

"Thank you, comrade," acknowledged the speaker.

"Now, are there any questions?"

Bishop shot up his hand as Gloria's face went deep red with embarrassment.

"I'd like to know what you are doing here. Hasn't anyone told you that communism has gone - kaput!"

"Oh, I see we have with us today a political student and a Yankee Imperialist to boot."

"No, I'm not a Yankee imperialist as you say. I'm just someone who would like an honest answer to my question. When there was communism in Russia, they enforced their ideology through the

KGB, psychiatric hospitals and Siberian labor camps."

Another ripple of applause broke out, this time from Americans in the crowd.

"My friend," said the speaker, trying to wrest the initiative back from the journalist, "you are misinformed. And anyway, the 'People's Paradise' will soon be back in Russia. You mark my word."

"That's dead right, bruvver," shouted the magazine seller from the edge of the crowd.

Gloria was now feeling decidedly uncomfortable. She knew Arch was spoiling for a verbal fight and could see that his temper was burning on a short fuse.

"That's enough, Arch, let's go," she said. With that she pulled him away and he reluctantly followed.

"See that, ladies and gentlemen. The Yank gives up when he knows he's beaten," the triumphant speaker yelled after him and jeers rang in Arch's ears.

"The man's a lunatic," Arch muttered loudly as Gloria guided her seething ex away from the crowd. "These British baffle me. Don't they realize that if he and his comrades ever got power, they would never be allowed to even use Speakers' Corner?"

"Arch," Gloria scolded, "I don't want to spend this time with you watching you argue with people. I just want to be with you."

Arch smiled apologetically. "I know honey. But these guys make me so mad."

"I know. I know. Now where should we go?"

Bishop checked his watch; it was well past noon.

"I know where we can go. Let's go to my 'private club.' It's by Fleet Street, where I work."

"Sounds fun," said Gloria, eager to go any place that was far away from Speakers' Corner.

The black cab pulled up a few minutes later in New Fetter Lane, just inside the ancient city of London, and dropped the couple outside the Stab in the Back.

"Oh no, not a pub," said Gloria, pleasure fading from her face to be replaced with a look of harried despair.

"Yes, honey. A real English pub! It's quite a special place. We could get some 'pub grub' and you could meet some of the strange creatures that pass for journalists in this neck of the woods."

"Couldn't we go some place that doesn't serve booze?" she implored, feeling as if a knife had been plunged into her heart.

"Come on, honey," said Arch. "It's just for an hour or so!"

Not convinced that she wanted to go inside, Gloria reluctantly followed Bishop through the door and into the smoke-filled bar which was already full of scribes who had descended into the pub like a bunch of barbarians, all anxious to "wet their whistles" and catch up on the latest Sunday lunch-time scandal.

As Bishop approached the bar and asked for his "usual" and then ordered a club soda for his teetotal wife, George, the main barman, beamed with obvious pride at the sight of the pub's pet Yank.

"Mr. Bishop," he said extending his large sweaty paw over the counter, "I want to congratulate you on what you did last night." He dropped a sliced lemon in the fizzy "g & t" and said with a wink, "This one is on me, Mr. B."

Bishop introduced Gloria to the "blade" behind the bar. "Charmed, I'm sure," he said as he leaned over shook her hand and then kissed it.

"Welcome to the Stab."

Just then the flustered figure of Fida appeared through the door.

"Arch, where on earth have you been?" she said, her face flushed with the unusually warm weather London was experiencing. "Farr's been trying to find you everywhere. He has been calling me every hour on the hour all through the night.

"They want to know why you haven't filed a story on last night's incident with Billy Windsor. It's been on all the wire services."

"Oh, no," said Bishop thumping his forehead. "I clean forgot to write a story."

He went to the pay phone in the pub and placed a call to New York.

Fida moved to Gloria's side. "I don't think we've been introduced, have we daahling?" she cooed.

"No," said Gloria, a bit taken aback by this affected creature. "That was very remiss of my husband."

"Your ex-husband? Don't tell me that you are the famous Gloria from New York."

Mrs. Bishop nodded and smiled. "Live and in person!"

Fida's jaw dropped in unfeigned surprise. "But I thought you two had split up years ago," she said her voice rising stridently. "What are you doing back with him?"

Gloria wondered who this pushy lady was who was giving her the third degree. "Do you mind telling me just who you are?"

"She's Arch's favorite lady," lied William Doberman, the bow-tied man standing at the bar to Gloria's left. Then he held out his hand for her to shake and introduced himself.

"Doberman," snapped Fida, "why don't you go and play in the traffic." She was angry at her least favorite hack for interrupting their conversation.

"Now, now, sweetie, there's no need to get upset because you've got a bit of competition. Everyone knows you have a crush on him and he would not give you the time of day. I can now understand why. With this vision of loveliness for a wife, you never stood a chance."

Suddenly they stopped their bitchy exchange of barbs as they overheard Arch's voice shouting down the receiver, "I was back with Gloria. That's why I didn't file my story, you stupid man," he yelled as all conversation stopped and the hacks tuned their ears to what they were hearing.

Fida felt like going over to Bishop and slapping him. How could he do this to her? She was being publicly humiliated so, in order, to try and save face, Fida turned to Gloria and said, "How would you like to see London with me as your guide? Maybe we could have tea and crumpets with Mummy, as well."

Gloria was not sure what to say, so she mumbled, "I do appreciate your offer, but I need to see what Arch wants to do first." Fida stood by Gloria and ordered a dry white wine and tried to block her ears to Bishop's shouting across the Atlantic. He was yelling with such vehemence that even Gloria was startled.

Bishop finally slammed down the phone and returned to his wife and Doberman, who was trying to nibble at Gloria's ear.

"Fatman, you disgusting animal, go and disturb somebody else and leave my wife alone," shouted Bishop when he saw what was going on.

"No need to be so touchy, old man. I was only trying to show this lovely lady some good, old fashioned British hospitality." Seeing the anger in Bishop's face, he backed away, beer in hand, and joined another group of "Stabbers."

Gloria was near to tears, as was Fida. After such a beautiful reunion on the previous night, Gloria felt this was turning into a nightmare. And as for Fida, her uncouth colleague was publicly shaming her.

"Well, I'm orf," Fida said, finishing off her glass of wine. "I've got an important date to go to." Her voice was just loud enough for the "Stabbers" to overhear.

With that, she departed, leaving Arch alone with Gloria.

"Can't we go somewhere decent and talk? This place gives me the creeps," said Gloria.

"It's not that bad, honey. It sort of grows on you."

"You mean like a cancer!" said Gloria as she glared at him.

Arch shouted across the bar to George for a "double of the usual." Double followed double and within the period of an hour, he had consumed twelve "g. & t's".

Gloria was, by now, in total despair as she watched her ex-husband drink as if it was going out of fashion. As it continued unabated, Gloria noticed a long-haired handsome man whose eyes were bearing in on her husband through the cigarette haze from across the bar. She thought, somehow, that the style of his hair and his droopy mustache did not fit the shape of his youthful face.

"Arch, there's a guy over there who keeps staring at you."

Bishop angled his head and peered through the gloomy, smoky, atmosphere until his eyes fixed on none other than the dapper figure of Randy Burke wearing a conservative pin-striped suit that made him look as if he had just stepped out of the London stock exchange. Burke nodded and smiled in his direction and then threaded his way through the literary lushes.

"My dear friend, it's so good to see you again," he said extending an exuberant hand toward the American.

"I couldn't help noticing this charming young lady by your side. I hope you will introduce me to her. She is easily the most beautiful woman I have seen all lunchtime."

Bishop did the required introductions and then chuckled as he added, "Those of us who know Mr. Burke call him Mr. Kneecaps."

Gloria was puzzled, so her husband added, with a wink at Burke's direction, "It's a private joke."

Then Bishop stared at the Ulsterman through his reddened, drink-blurred eyes and asked him what he was doing in London."

"Oh, Mr. B., I've got some private business to take care of."

"I hope it doesn't involve Harrods," said Bishop, almost choking with laughter at his own sick humor.

"Not, this time, Mr. B. Not this time." With that he turned to Gloria and said, "I'm charmed to meet you my dear. I hope we'll meet again soon." He then wheeled around and left the "Stab" for some more of his "dirty business."

"Who on earth was that?" asked a bemused Gloria, her head reeling at meeting so many strange people.

"Oh, that's Mr. Burke - he's a terrorist. His specialty is 'Kneecapping' his victims.

"He's one of those people who doesn't just talk about his revolution, he kills people for it."

Meanwhile, George continued to fill up Bishop's empty glass as Gloria felt a total revulsion at what was going on. Arch's drinking had gotten even worse than during the bad times in New York. It was 2:30 in the afternoon and her ex-husband was "legless." She wanted to both hit him and mother him at the same time. A thousand conflicting emotions clouded her mind. What was going to happen to him?

Gloria looked around the bar at the snickering groups of people all apparently enjoying hearing about the misfortune of others. She recalled hearing as a child, from the Bible, something about "the blind leading the blind," and if this happened each of them would "fall in a ditch." These were the people who were blindly leading a nation toward what? From her short sojourn in the Stab, she could see that an awful lot of people were about to fall into an awful lot of abysses if these journalists were a sample of the leaders.

Gloria knew her only escape from this was to leave, so she asked to be excused to go to the ladies' room. As this was located adjacent to the front door of the "Stab," she headed toward it, but just kept going, and out into New Fetter Lane. She turned right, walked to the corner of Holborn, and then flagged down a cab.

"To The Savoy," she curtly instructed the cabby, as black despair pressed behind her eyes and a sick thumping in her head made her dizzy.

When the taxi pulled away from the curb, she noticed the tottering figure of her husband literally fall through the door of the pub and crash awkwardly onto the sidewalk.

The cabby noticed what had happened and asked, "Is he a friend of yours, Miss?"

Her eyes took on a sheen of tears as she replied, "He used to be...."

Jekyll and Hyde still lived in the form of Archibald Bishop.

15
A Bishop in Prague

Reem Rudeniah was wearing a stunning long Western-style red dress and carried with her a purse that contained money, a ball-point pen and notebook. She settled back in her plush seat in the front row of the Tyl Theater, the oldest opera house in Prague, to enjoy a performance of *Don Giovanni,* and plan … mayhem.

Then a slightly scruffy man crudely pushed his way past the other opera lovers and dropped heavily into the seat next to her. Fida, who took the seat to his right, joined him.

"Hi," he said loudly, "my name's Arch Bishop. What's yours?"

Reem froze in her seat. She did not like people talking to her without a formal introduction so she tried to ignore his question. But the American did not appear to notice her reticence to talk.

"I'm from the *New York Tribune* and I'm doing a travel piece on Prague with my lovely photographer here, Fida. She's related to the Queen of England, you know," the uncouth man continued, extending his hand.

She looked at him with disgust and reluctantly shook his proffered giant paw.

"Did you know that Prague was the only place where Mozart felt he and his music were fully appreciated? He wrote *Don Giovanni* for this very theater." Bishop added in a voice that carried throughout the hushed auditorium.

Reem's expressionless face turned toward Fida and observed her delicate face that was well made up. Then she gave a swift sideways glance at Bishop. Maybe, she thought, this "American fool" would shut up if she just ignored him.

"Where are you from?" asked Bishop, not easily deterred.

"Why do you ask?" Reem growled stiffly, burying her face in the program.

"Well, you look like you are from the Middle East, and if you are, I'm fascinated by your part of the world."

"If you must know, I'm from the Middle East," she finally responded in a voice that wavered just a little.

"What kind of business are you in?" the journalist probed just as the lights went down and the opera began. Reem smiled slightly to herself and whispered almost inaudibly, "DEATH."

Despite the swelling of the music, Bishop overheard the word and felt a shiver run down his spine. Was this woman joking? He had not spent much time with Middle Eastern women, so was not sure how to react to this one.

When the lights came up for the first of two intervals, Reem found her mind snapping back from "Operation Red Dagger." She had been trying to figure out how Burke could recruit more leaders from the mainly left-wing terrorist groups in the Western world, and then persuade them to be a part of her deadly plan.

"Hey, Ms. Death, do you wanna drink?" asked Bishop.

With her brain racing, she tried to find a way to keep quiet this American with such gauche manners.

"No, thank you," she snapped as civilly as she could under the circumstances. Reem wanted to remain in her seat, so she could scribble down in Arabic the names of some of the groups and leaders she thought the Irishman could contact.

"Why don't you take your young lady? I would think she'd need a drink, having to put up with your manners," she said coldly, looking over a pair of designer eyeglasses she had just put on.

"Suit yourself," said Bishop trying not to sound offended.

As Bishop and Fida left for the bar, Reem began writing down the names of Pierre Rowlands, leader of the French Black October group, Guiseppi Palumbo of the Italian Red Fist group, Carlos Rodrigues of the Basque Separatists and George Markos of the Greek Liberation Organization (GLO).

"Must get the name of an American group," she hastily wrote on her note pad in Arabic as people began returning for the next part of the performance. With that, she ripped off the page, neatly folded it and stuffed it into her program. Then she took off her glasses, closed them and put them into her purse.

The pair soon returned and pushed past her to their seats. "You missed a real treat," said Bishop. "The Czechs were giving free drinks to Middle Easterners as a 'thank you,' for all the peace you have brought to the world," he chortled sarcastically.

Reem pretended not to hear and stared firmly at the stage. When the time came for the next break, the irascible American again offered her a drink.

"In the cause of *détente* between America and whatever country you come from, I urge you to accept my offer," Bishop said. "Look, I'm only trying to be friendly. And," he added, a broad smile sweeping his face, "I'll charge it to the *New York Tribune.*"

Seeing the comical side of having chilled vodka at the expense of one of America's most famous newspapers, Reem finally relented and moved with them to the lounge. Bishop elbowed his way to the bar to order the drinks, while Reem and Fida stood awkwardly in a corner. The Palestinian turned to the photographer, who had two cameras dangling around her neck, and said, "I didn't get your full name."

Fida chuckled, and replied with a mischievous twinkle in her eyes, "I'll tell you mine, if you'll tell me yours."

"Okay. I'm Kareema Jabir," she lied. You may have heard of me."

"No, sorry, it doesn't ring a bell with me." Then she added, with a toothy grin, "I'm Lady Philda Tintagel, and I'm a second cousin to the Queen of England."

After weaving his way through the chattering crowd, bearing a tray with three short-glasses of vodka perched on top of it, Arch Bishop appeared at the corner of the room where they were standing.

"Take one of these demons, each of you," he suggested, offering the drinks to them. With that he set the tray on the table, clinked his glass with theirs, and with a jerk of the head greedily threw down his drink in one gulp. Fida followed suit, as did Reem, but in a more civilized manner, only taking a sip.

Bishop smiled at the Palestinian and said, "I don't trust someone until you I have gotten drunk with them," he chortled.

Reem remained silent.

"Well, Ms. Middle Easterner, I've been thinking about what you said. Death. Hmmm. You are either an undertaker or up to no good. Which is it?" he asked in a deceptively soft voice.

Again Reem said nothing and took another sip of her colorless firewater.

Bishop eyed Reem's dazzling red dress, and said, his voice turning raspingly sarcastic, "Well, I would say that you are not an undertaker."

"So you're an expert at these matters, Mr. Bishop?" responded Reem with a wry smile.

The American was enjoying dueling with this fascinating and disturbing woman. "Don't you know that a journalist is an expert at absolutely everything? That's what we get paid huge amounts of money for."

Bishop roared at his own black humor.

Reem was becoming bored with Bishop's silly prattle. Still, maybe she could use him to solve a problem. She had been wracking her brain for the name of a group in the United States that had been involved in terrorist activity.

"Mr. Bishop," she said, facing the American eyeball-to-eyeball. "You obviously *do* know everything." The barbed remark showed her contempt for the Western press, who were always prying and demanding answers.

Bishop, however, was not daunted at all. "You are a person after my own heart," he responded, draining the last contents of his glass and pretending to accept the remark as a compliment.

"A friend and I are in the midst of a disagreement," she said. "He says the USA has never had an internal terrorist group. I say you have. It's gotten to the point where we have put a month's coffee rations on the line. Which one of us is right?"

Bishop pondered the peculiar question for a moment, then replied, "Well, get ready to have a coffee drinking binge, Ms. Middle Easterner. You are right. In the sixties, we had a particularly repulsive group called the 'Weather Underground,' who wreaked havoc all over the country. They got the name because their leader, Brent Fox, was once a weatherman at a New England TV station. I interviewed him one time. He was quite mad. He even tried, among other gruesome things, to assassinate Richard Nixon when he was still president.

"Come to think of it, maybe he wasn't so mad after all." Bishop chuckled. He then added, "Fox is about to be paroled from Attica Prison in New York State. I can't imagine why they would ever let out such a psychopath. He's sure to kill again."

The lights flashed on and off in the bar for the intermission to end and the trio trooped back into the auditorium. Reem Rudeniah was pleased she now had the name of a key person who might just be the man she needed to take care of President Lincoln Patrick, who had been such a supporter of the Zionists.

As the spectacular performance ended, Reem stood erect, stiffly shook hands with her Western acquaintances and headed out of the theater. "Maybe we will meet again, some time," was her parting remark.

Bishop stood up to leave and, as he began to move to his right, tripped over Fida's camera bag.

"You stupid woman," he yelled as he crashed onto the floor in between the red velvet seats. As he struggled to get up, he noticed a neatly folded piece of paper lying under the seat where Reem Rudeniah had been sitting. He reached over to pick it up. Unfolding it, he tried to decipher its hieroglyphics. Fida looked at the piece of paper and smiled. She had once taken an Arabic course at Oxford University. With her rudimentary understanding of the language, she made out a French name and an Italian name, with asterisks next to each one. She also noticed the Arabic for "USA" in bold letters and underlined twice, followed by a question mark.

Bishop took the folded piece of paper and said to Fida, "Let's go back to the hotel and see if we can make more sense of this. I reckon that lady is a real weirdo - a dangerous one at that."

He decided that when he got back to London he would talk with Bill Ehrlich, an ex-CIA operative now running an import-export business from Pimlico, to see if he knew anything about this lady with death on her mind.

But even he could see that all the names written down by Reem were of terrorist groups in Western countries.

Arch Bishop had stumbled onto something big - really big. He needed to know more about this mysterious woman.

* * * * *

Reem Rudeniah picked up the program from the opera and shook it. Nothing fell out. Alarm bells began ringing in her mind. She wondered about the piece of paper she had torn out of her notebook in the Tyl Theater?

"That's strange," she muttered aloud as she again checked her pockets. "It must have dropped out along the way."

With so much on her mind, Reem decided it was no big deal.

"After all," she reasoned, "if anyone could decipher my Arabic handwriting, they would have to be a genius."

Still, Reem was annoyed with her carelessness and mentally kicked herself in the rear.

16
The Paddy Factor

Jeremy Brett-King could taste the Scottish fog as it rolled in off the sea as he checked his wristwatch for the fifth time in an hour. "Where is that infernal Irishman?" he spluttered impatiently. "I bet he's changed his mind."

The tall, distinguished looking Englishman, with a sharp, intelligent face, opened his gold-plated cigarette case and brought out a silver-tipped cigarette. He shielded the flame from his monogrammed lighter, lit up and then drew deeply.

Brett-King, a Cambridge graduate now in his early sixties, had peered through the mist as The *Iris* arrived from Larne and disgorged its passengers, many of whom were swaying not just from the stormy crossing, but also from the beer they had consumed. It was now half and hour since everyone had left and there was still was no sign of the man he had come to meet. He shivered as the biting wind groaned through the Stranraer ferry terminal making the tip of his nose turn red.

"Where's the Paddy got to?" he whispered into the microphone concealed in his rolled umbrella. "Hold on. Stand by, number-two."

A bearded man furtively appeared out of the gloom. "Do you have a light?" he asked in a soft, Belfast accent.

"Why do you ask?" Brett-King responded, wondering if this

might be the man.

"Because I want to set fire to the men with no ideas," said Burke, his eyes fervently locked onto those of the Englishman.

With that, Brett-King fumbled for his lighter. "Welcome to Scotland, Mr. Burke. Thank you for coming. I have a car, a safe house."

Burke said nothing, and instinctively looked around in case he was being followed. When he could not see anyone, he climbed into Brett-King's gray Jaguar.

The Englishman switched on the ignition and as the engine came to powerful life, he effortlessly pushed the stick shift through the gears until they were roaring along at seventy miles an hour around the slick roads of Loch Ryan.

"They must pay you well in MI6," observed Burke with a confrontational tone rising in his voice as the car squealed around corners on the narrow road that took them out of the hammerhead-shaped peninsula.

"It's an 'office car,' old boy," Brett-King said out of the side of his mouth. "Is it better than the kind you get in your little group?"

Burke was not sure if he liked this man, who represented all he despised about the English. But still, he was quite a contrast to the people he had been with earlier that day. He thought back to the funeral he had attended at Belfast's Catholic Milltown Cemetery. There had been the full panoply of IRA ritual-black berets, the tricolor and a volley over the grave. Little did his IRA colleagues know that he, Randy Burke, had personally assassinated the two men who had killed his parents. The idea of taking matters into his own hands had been an increasingly enjoyable task for him. He and his brother David had made it look like a revenge attack, by Protestants, on the men who were leaving a drinking club in the Ardoyne. He laughed callously, as the two terrorists, eyes bulging from the pain, crumpled to the ground, blood pouring from the part of their faces that still remained. It never ceased to amaze Randy Burke just how much damage a few blasts from his Ingram MAC-10/11 could inflict.

"You will never know what it did to me when you killed my Ma and Pa," he had said in a cold and murderous voice as he stood over the bodies. With the deed done, he turned and sprinted to his brother's blue Cortina and they sped away.

"We are truly brothers-in-arms now, David," said Randy, breathing heavily.

"We sure are," interjected David. "But our next job is to find out who was really behind the killing; to discover who pulled the strings and gave the order."

As the coffins of Billy Loughran and Harry Boland were lowered below the ground and the Provo volley rang out over the cemetery, Burke muttered under his breath with savage satisfaction, "Good riddance!"

Representing the inner circle of the Provos, Burke had shook hands with colleagues from the West Belfast cell and headed out of the cemetery to his car.

"I have an urgent meeting that will turn this war around," explained Burke to Brendan O'Reilly, the cell commander. "Please give my heartfelt condolences to the families."

As Randy Burke drove out of the Catholic ghetto with its broken windows and slogans like GOD SAVE THE POPE; past the British soldiers crouched in doorways, Armalite rifles poised; he realized the death of his parents had had a cathartic effect on him. But he never could have guessed where that jolt would take him. One thing he knew for sure, however, was that he had to do what he could to stop the men who, he knew, would stop at nothing to unite Ireland under the hammer-and-sickle.

He would never agree with the Protestant secret societies that he felt "plagued" Ulster society: with men dressing up, making rules, beating drums, swearing oaths and inventing passwords. These groups never achieved much, being more like cozy men's clubs than front-line fighters. But even that was preferable to what the Provos wanted for Ireland - the People's Republic of Ireland.

An armored car rolled past him, with wire skirts beneath the chassis so that firebombs could not be rolled under them, and he was soon out in the lush green Ulster countryside. For a short while, the sun tried to break through the heavy clouds, but then the rain poured down again, flattening the buttercups in the fields.

Burke had stopped along the way to change the plates on his car, then continued down the side of Larne Lough into Larne, where he could hear the boat's horn echo all over the dark brown waterfront. The ferry was just arriving from Scotland. The Ulsterman parked the car and made his way to the terminal watched over by the dockside cranes that appeared to him to be crucifixes.

Burke waited in line to go through the security check. "What is your purpose in going to Scotland?" asked the RUC officer, his mouth tight and grim, as he poked through Burke's carry-on bag.

"Some business and lots of pleasure," he replied.

"Well, don't enjoy yourself too much. Next!"

* * * * *

Brett-King was getting decidedly angry with Burke. He felt his jaw tighten as he said brusquely, "Look, we can't give you immunity. You know we can't make deals."

"Don't give me that rubbish," said Burke indignantly, his eyes red with fury, his voice shrill and strident. The Irishman dug in his heels. "You either play this my way, or you get no help from me.

Just say you won't and I'll go straight back across the Irish Sea."

Burke was getting rather fed up being treated as a species of foreign barbarian who must be taught how to behave in a civilized society.

He leaped to his feet like a boxer at the sound of the bell and pointed a quivering finger at Paul Howells, the enigmatic officer with whom he had first talked in Belfast, who had been waiting at the hideout for his arrival.

"Howells," he said, moving menacingly towards him, "you promised that if I worked with you, I would not be prosecuted. Now this pompous man says there can be no deal." Howells nervously followed Burke's gyrations with his eyes.

"Who's in charge here, anyway?" asked Burke, his face contorted with rage.

Howells was embarrassed and tried to calm Burke with an upraised hand. He *had* made this promise, because he viewed Burke as a great "catch" for British counter-intelligence, but now, due to the intransigence of his colleague, it looked as if everything would fall apart. There was an awkward silence, and then he looked daggers at Brett-King and said, "Let's step outside for a moment. We need to talk." Brett-King reluctantly agreed. Burke's dramatics were beginning to set his nerves on edge.

As the back door was wrenched open and slammed shut, the outside wind sent the clouds scudding across the half moon. Howells blew up. "Look, Brett-King, I know you have a higher rank than me, but I'm telling you, I know more about these people than you do. You have to deal with Burke or you will lose him. Don't mess this up by being so stuffy." Howells paused for a moment to give his statement greater importance.

"Keep your hat on, old boy," Brett-King countered by raising his hand in the air. "I want to make sure that the information he will give is accurate. He could be a plant by the Provo's."

Howells took his colleague by the arm. "He could be, but it's more likely that he is on the level. So why don't you just go along with him for now and just see how much he really knows."

The two men eventually returned to the room and smiled at the Irishman. "Mr. Burke, you are right," said Brett-King. "I understand you don't want to be locked up for your part in what you are about to tell us.

"You have my word that you will not be prosecuted."

"That's not enough," snapped Burke. "I need it in writing. I am also going to need a new identity and a one-way ticket to somewhere that is a long way from Ireland."

Brett-King was again becoming annoyed with this man, but could see Burke's temper was boiling again, so he agreed to his terms and hand-wrote the guarantee that Burke would not be prosecuted for any crimes he implicated himself in.

"You don't trust me, do you?" said Jeremy Brett-King, handing Burke the single sheet of paper.

"It's my business not to," Burke said shrewdly. "My life depends upon it."

The Englishman smiled, then went over to a corner of the room and produced three bottles of Guinness. He deftly flicked off the caps with a bottle opener.

"Let's have a drink, old boy, and then we can get started," he said. With that he toasted Burke and said, "Here's to a relationship that will do great damage to the bombers of Ireland - the men who killed your parents in cold blood!"

The three "clicked bottles" and got down to the business at hand. Brett-King leaned back in the easy chair and began. "Mr. Burke, I'm aware that there are people in Iran and Syria who have some input with the Provos, but what about Colonel Khaddafi of Libya?

What role does he play?"

Burke smiled. "That madman would like to play a bigger role. But he's done his bit in the war against you people. I was first aware of his involvement back in 1977. We had a chap who had just come out of prison, and he managed to get a clean Irish passport by taking the name of a dead Dublin man. He set up a business called the Tower Bridge Electro Company. The major purpose of the company was to ship two three-ton transformers to Nicosia, Cyprus, for repairs.

"Once they arrived there, we had a team gut the transformers and then fill them with arms, all supplied by Khaddafi."

"What sort of arms are we talking about?" asked Brett-King.

"A considerable shipment: seven rocket-launchers, twenty French-made MAT sub-machine-guns, two .303 Bren guns, twenty-nine 9-mm Machine-pistols, twenty-nine Kalashnikov AK-47 assault rifles, eighteen boxes of grenades, 11,000 rounds of SLR ammunition, 360 kg. of 9 mm ammunition, sixty rockets, 4 kegs of TNT and about 75 lbs. of plastic explosive in 1 and 5 lb. packs, along with enough ferang pins to blast open every door at Buckingham Palace. How does that grab you for starters?"

Brett-King was pleased, but wanted to know who had arranged the shipment.

"It was between us and members of Khaddafi's agents in Cyprus," said the Irishman. "Our guys there loaded the transformers on a boat called *London Bridge* which was bound for Antwerp, then eventually Dublin."

"I seem to recall that something went wrong," said Brett-King.

"Yes, the Israelis blew the whistle," said Burke. "They were swarming around Cyprus and passed this information on to several potentially interested intelligence services, including yours, and before we knew it the ship was intercepted by the Dutch and the cargo was confiscated."

Burke took a swig from the dark brown bottle, and continued. "It was never difficult for us to get arms, especially in the United States. I would go over there to raise funds and then buy. There is an underground, but widespread market in M-16 replacement parts for the legal semi-automatic AR-15 rifles. These parts are illegal because they turn an AR-15 into a full-automatic M-16.

"We also managed to get hold of a large supply of the AR-180, which folds up and fits inside a box of cornflakes. Besides being collapsible, it has several other ideal characteristics for our needs in Ulster. It is single-shot or semi-automatic eliminating blockages and wasted ammunition. It also has a high muzzle velocity and a flat trajectory, but most important, the .223 caliber A.P. bullet could puncture both British army body armor and the sides of armored personnel carriers."

Burke emptied the contents of his Guinness bottle and asked for another. "Mr. Englishmen, I'm going to tell you something very funny now. Did you know that our great Provo leader, Seamus O'Shea, is actually Alfred Wright, born in Leeds? He's not Irish at all.

"There's been a power struggle going on within the GHQ staff and O'Shea has been ousted by a psychopath called Michael O'Hanlon, who's gone round telling everyone that O'Shea is an impostor. O'Hanlon had somehow got hold of his actual birth certificate and found out that O'Shea was raised in an orphanage in Belfast, but was born of English parents. He had just assumed the Irish name because he wanted acceptance.

"Do you remember when O'Shea was on his so-called hunger strike to death in the Maze prison? Well, it was then that O'Hanlon discovered the English background of his rival. That, along with O'Shea's giving up his 'fast,' destroyed his influence in the

Provos. O'Shea has been smashed by what I call the 'Paddy Factor.'

"You have to be Irish to fight the British."

"Will he be killed?" asked Brett-King.

"I doubt it," said Burke. "Something worse will happen to him. He'll continue to be treated with derision. There is no worse sin in the Provos than to be discovered you are actually English."

* * * * *

Two days of intensive questioning had elapsed when Brett-King finally got around to the main point of the discussion. "Mr. Burke, we know you have been to Syria for training, and we have been following the travels around Eastern Europe for some time. We have become aware of a lady called Reem Rudeniah. Do you know her?"

Burke nodded. "She's a tough one. I took an instant dislike to her when I first met her. She's the Devil Incarnate. She's also a snake. You don't know from what direction she's coming at you."

The Irishman stopped for a moment, then asked, "But why are you so interested in her?"

"Well, I'll come straight to the point, Mr. Burke," he said looking sharply at the Irishman. "We have reason to believe she is masterminding a plan to take out the leadership of the Western world at the upcoming Vienna summit. Do you know anything about this plan?"

Randy Burke's eyes flickered. "Where would you like me to start?"

"At the beginning, Mr. Burke, I think that would be a good place."

Burke nodded his head and began his explanation. "This thing is so serious that you could have a massive conflagration on your hands." The Ulsterman then outlined "Operation Red Dagger," and how that, in a few weeks time, there would be a meeting of representatives of key terrorists groups in Prague to finalize the attack.

Brett-King and Howells listened with great interest, but then Brett-King voiced a fatal flaw he saw in the plan. "Mr. Burke, why would these people use foreign terrorists to do such a thing?"

"Good question," responded Burke. "I had to ask myself that when I first got involved. The simple answer is that this group is deadly serious in becoming even more notorious than Osama bin Laden. They see that his group has started what could be a Holy Jihad that could topple the West as we know it and herald in their world domination.

"That would then give them time to carry out whatever evil deeds they had in mind. In fact, I suspect that they have 'sleepers' ready for action who are trained to infiltrate foreign cultures and are prepared to assassinate key leaders and officials. They would move in with their mayhem as the West is reeling from what had happened."

Brett-King accepted the explanation, and realized that Burke still had to be part of this plan. "Of course, you *must* be there for the Provo's," he said. "We will provide you with information that can help to destabilize Rudeniah. I think you'll enjoy reading it."

Brett-King's eyes narrowed as he delivered his final question. "Mr. Burke, please give me your personal assessment of this woman."

Burke paused briefly, and then said, "All I can say is that if Machiavelli were alive today, he would be a student of this woman, not her teacher!"

17
The Package Deal

Reem Rudeniah was in a hurry that fateful morning. She had an appointment with a group of killers but, as she stepped through the front door of the Prague apartment she had rented for a few weeks, she stopped in her tracks when she spotted a brown, padded package lying on the floor in front of her. Picking it up, she read the words, "To Reem from a friend."

"Strange," she mused as she impatiently ripped it open. "Hardly anyone knows I'm staying here."

Randy Burke did, however, as did Jeremy Brett-King. A tail had been on her since Burke had told the Englishman what he knew about her. Brett-King had also been alerted by former CIA operative called Bill Ehrlich who showed him a copy of a note that an American journalist had given him.

Brett-King and Ehrlich had met in the hushed surroundings of the "smoking room" of the British Officers Club in Pall Mall, London. All around were "Major Bloodnocks," warrior dinosaurs that spent hours re-living long-forgotten battles fought on behalf of the British Empire in places as diverse as India, Malaya (now called Malaysia) and North Africa.

Today, this pair ignored the old "duffers," having more urgent up-to-date business to discuss. Ehrlich then handed Brett-King a scrap of paper.

"Arch Bishop, a reporter from the *New York Tribune* picked this up from the floor of a Prague opera house and told me it was written by a strange lady called Reem Rudeniah," said Ehrlich.

"Bishop told me he was sitting next to her and he suspects that she's up to no good. Do you know anything about her?"

Brett-King pondered the loaded question. "Are *your* people interested in her, then?" he countered warily.

"Well," said Ehrlich, sipping the thick liquid he had just poured from a new-fangled coffee maker in the club, "as you know I'm officially retired, but you never really leave 'The Firm.' I still keep my hand in from time to time. I would think *we* would definitely be interested in a person like this."

Brett-King, an Arabic-language expert, took out his eye-glasses from his top pocket and scrutinized the note. He managed to make out the names of Pierre Rowlands and Guiseppi Palumbo as well as a reference to the USA.

"Very interesting," he verbalized. "These are two particularly nasty people. They must be part of her plan for the Vienna summit and I wonder what the USA reference means?

"Maybe we should work together on this one. You can tell *your* people that we are onto something big!"

* * * * *

Randy Burke's disguise as a janitor *was* successful as he casually brushed-up some trash from the corridor where Reem Rudeniah was picking up the package. Burke was in Prague to attend the special planning session for *Operation Red Dagger*, in a suite of rooms rented at Hradcany Castle and Brett-King had kindly supplied him with this special "gift" for Reem.

Just minutes before he had dropped the large envelope by her furnished apartment.

His uncombed hair drooped, and he found he could not suppress a smile as he heard the door slam shut. He tried to imagine what was going on behind the door and he guessed Reem's heart must have frozen for a moment as she brought out a series of black-and-white photographs. There were pictures of her stepfather in compromising positions with a young woman. It was obvious that neither participant was aware of the shots being taken. She stumbled backwards into her bedroom and sank heavily onto the creaking bed.

A handwritten note accompanying the photographs, stated, "Ibrahim Rudeniah is a gigolo, a cheat and a traitor. He has been having an affair for two years with this woman, Mary Luther, an American-born secretary at the US Embassy in Tel Aviv."

Also enclosed were copies of papers detailing a numbered bank account in Zurich, Switzerland. "You will see that he has also been receiving payment from the West American government for several years," the writer continued. "He's been supplying them with vital information about Red Dagger activities in the Middle East."

Reem felt all the blood drain from her face. She stared at the materials, trying to take in the meaning of what she was seeing. How could this be true? She had modeled herself on her stepfather, taking his views about a love of the Palestinian cause from him. Now it seemed his words were just a charade. How could he have betrayed her and his beloved homeland in this way? *No, there must be a mistake*, she thought desperately. But then she gazed again at the pictures. The paunch certainly looked like that of her stepfather. The bank account was undoubtedly incriminating, though she could not say if it was her stepfather's because it was the kind of account that could be claimed by anyone who possessed the correct numbers and password.

With glutted exhaustion, Reem thought back on how she had sat in the back of her stepfather's black limousine in the "good old days" as the driver took them to an expensive restaurant in a Gaza hotel.

They had smiled together from the warmth of the luxury vehicle as her step-father pointed out the young children from the Gaza Beach Refugee Camp coming home from school, their back-packs filled with school work.

"Do you know, Reem, these are our future suicide bombers," he had told her smugly. "If you continue in the way you are going, you will never have to experience what these kids are going through, but you will be able to continue to enjoy this lifestyle for yourself."

Reem had become part of the stratum of Gaza society that went through the motions of fighting for what it coveted. Yet, while criticizing the bourgeois way of life of the West, its main passion was to possess it. This privileged class attacked "consumerism" as a "Western Philistine psychology," yet valued the consumer goods and comforts of the West above all else.

Still, the effect of the package on Reem was dramatic and sent her into a state of deep depression. She felt betrayed by the man who had raised her, the one she called father. Reem headed out into the street feeling in desperate need of a drink and a place to think.

She soon found a quiet bar and, taking a corner table to herself, ordered a shot of vodka from the surly bartender. Before long, she swallowed another, and another. Pictures from her past, both disturbing and haunting, came flooding into her mind.

"My God," she cried out, "I killed my parents."

Throwing down some money on the table, Reem stumbled out

into the street and kept walking. There was no plan; she knew she just had to keep on moving. Maybe she would eventually discover what she should do to sort out this mess.

After about thirty minutes, she spotted a Catholic Church and, after checking that she was not being followed, ducked inside. There were a few old people sitting in the quietude of the pews, while others were lighting candles. She bowed, knelt, and rose again in imitation of the other worshipers. She had never been in this kind of church before, having been raised briefly in an unregistered fellowship. She was taken aback with the beauty of the building, its chandeliers, the lighted candles, and magnificent stained-glass windows with scenes from the Bible.

The peace of that sanctuary contrasted with the turmoil in her own heart. For years, she thought bitterly, she had given herself totally over to the Soviet system, using her stepfather as her role model. She had learned her lessons from him on how to rise and survive in the higher echelons of Palestinian society. Ibrahim had told her that she should always remain loyal to the ideals of the struggle. Yet, it appeared he was not? It seemed that her stepfather had been playing a dangerous game to gain his high rank in Red Dagger that brought with it financial security, and the prospect of still further advancement.

In return for the rewards, Reem had allowed her mind to be kept under lock and key. "My God, it's all been a farce," she said to herself as she sat devastated in a pew. "What a mess. Both my parents are dead and now my stepfather is a traitor."

Finally, Reem had begun to awaken from a deep sleep. She unsteadily rose to her feet and headed outside and wandered into the church's graveyard.

She shivered as she came across the gravestone of a couple who had been buried side by side. As she stood shivering looking at the white headstone, she suddenly realized that her parents didn't even have anything to mark their graves. Having perished in their home on that fateful evening, they would be lying in cold, unmarked graves somewhere in the Gaza Strip.

As Reem stood there, fighting back the tears, a woman with a scythe came into view as she began cutting the grass around the graves. Her only comfort was the fact that her parents believed that death was not the end, but the beginning of a new life for them!

With that she left the graveyard and headed out onto the busy street.

Unsettling questions became her constant companion during the next few days. They were like a nagging headache that would not go away. She began to think that the struggle was a cause that had robbed her people materially while impoverishing their spirit with deceit and corruption. That night she could not sleep as she was tormented with self-doubt.

The next morning, Reem ate breakfast in the crowded coffee shop of the Prague Continental Hotel, when a young man came over to her.

"Excuse me, madam. Do you speak English?" he asked.

She nodded.

"Looks like you have the only table here with a spare chair," explained the man in an American accent. "Can I join you?"

Reem reluctantly agreed and the man introduced himself as Grady McKeown.

"I'm with the American evangelist William Franklin," said McKeown as he made himself comfortable opposite the troubled woman. "Mr. Franklin is hoping to have a crusade here. I'm part of his advance team."

She couldn't have cared less. She was wrapped up in her own problems.

"Mr. Franklin wants to bring the *Good News* to the people of this part of the world," continued the American who Ms. Rudeniah decided was in his early thirties. "I guess that's something we can all use. What do you say?"

McKeown stopped briefly and looked directly at Rudeniah, who wished this man would just go away.

"I suppose...so," Reem finally stammered.

"Let me give you a tract that explains how anyone can receive that Good News," he said, pulling out a four-page leaflet entitled, "How *you* can become a Christian."

Reem stuffed it in her purse and mumbled her thanks. She then signaled the waiter for her bill.

"It's been very interesting, Mr. McKeown, but I must be off now," she said abruptly as the bill arrived. With that she put enough money down to cover it, along with a tip, and left.

Reem returned to her apartment to pick up her documents for the urgent meeting at the castle. It was to be a vital gathering for *Operation Red Dagger*, and she was going to share with the terrorist leaders that once their people had taken out the various Western leaders, members of various Islamic sleeper cells loyal to Red Dagger would already be in place in London, Paris, Rome, Brussels, Bonn and Washington, D.C., to move in and cause mayhem.

This "army" would wage war on an invisible front by assassinating or kidnapping key military leaders and attacking vital units and installations, and providing timely, accurate intelligence.

Her step-father, who had briefed her on what was going to happen after the mass assassinations, had said, "*Operation Red Dagger* will be our biggest jewel ever. Can you imagine the impact that it will have on the balance of world power? In just a few hours, we will control the whole of the Western world."

One by one, the terrorist leaders arrived in Prague, and were greeted by Rudeniah, as she installed them in their comfortable quarters in the ancient castle. She had decided that she would let things take their natural flow and on the first evening, sat talking with the Provo's man, Randy Burke, in a quiet corner of the lounge, which like the rest of the quarters, was especially secure from prying ears. This sound-proof windowless lair was double-walled with an air space through which low music played constantly; loudspeaker transducers were affixed to the doors to prevent eavesdropping.

As the sounds of specially prepared music tapes floated through into the room, Burke took the bottle of vodka, thoughtfully provided by the hosts, and poured some into Ms. Rudeniah's empty glass. He then half-filled his own glass and leaned forward and clinked it with hers. Although she was a Muslim; she was finding solace in the alcohol and was becoming afraid that she was enjoying its effects a little too much.

"Here's to some really good meetings," said Burke, brightly. "And also, here's to you, Ms. Rudeniah."

"Thank you, Mr. Burke," she responded lamely. The Irishman noted her subdued mood.

Burke was feeling chirpy, knowing that Rudeniah's long face was probably due to the package he had "delivered" earlier. He decided to play the situation coolly, try to relax her, and then make his play.

"Reem, have you heard any good Irish jokes lately?" he sparkled.

The Russian shook her head.

"Well, I'll tell you a good one I heard recently. Murphy was picked up by the police in Dublin for drunken driving. He had been weaving all over the road when they stopped his car.

"The policeman said to him, 'Murphy, you're drunk!'

"Murphy replied, 'Oh, thank the Lord. I thought the steering had gone.'"

Burke broke into uncontrollable laughter, while Reem looked blankly at him, her eyes not focusing. She did not get the joke and, even if she had, she was not in the mood for laughter.

"Well, I think I'll turn in for the night, before I get arrested for 'drunk walking,'" said Burke, smoothing his hair and fixing his tie. With that he got up and left.

Reem Rudeniah knew it was going to be a long and restless night for her back at her apartment. After several hours of tossing and turning, she turned on the bedside lamp and went over to her suit jacket and pulled out the tract the American had given her. In simple terms, she read how Jesus Christ had come to earth to become the Savior of Humanity. She was familiar with the language and understood what the writer was saying. But what was she to do?

Generously sprinkled throughout the tract were verses from the Bible that she recognized from her childhood. She was particularly taken with John 6:37: "*He who comes to me I will in no wise cast out.*" (NIV.)

Reem Rudeniah could see the emptiness of her life and the impotence of her political philosophy. She knew she had to finally "meet" the Truth. To add to her torment, ghostly figures of those Christians she had killed drifted into her mind.

She got out of bed and sank to her knees and cried out, "God, You've got to help me." She began to tell God of all her "rotten" past and then she asked for forgiveness. After what might have been an hour, she could not recall, she stood up feeling a different person. She had once studied Marxist-Leninism at the Islamic University and she recalled reading what Lenin had once said:

"Every flirtation with God is unutterable vileness." But she did not care anymore.

Now what was she to do? She was masterminding a plan that had all the potential to provoke World War III, yet Jesus had told His disciples to "turn the other cheek."

As hot tears stung her cheeks, she called out, "Not mine, but Thy will be done."

Reem was not sure how this mess could be resolved; she just knew that she was now on a different track.

18
Russian Roulette With a Loaded Gun

A slowly receding sinus-like headache let Arch Bishop know that he should stop drinking so heavily. He took a deep draw from his butt and then laid it on the ashtray at his side.

The crotchety scribe switched on his lap-top computer in his London office after it had booted into "Windows" he inserted a floppy disk into drive A and loaded the file labeled, **Rudeniah, Reem**. Bishop scrolled through the words he had already pounded into it about this strange Middle Eastern female who had begun to consume all his waking thoughts. Bishop noted his initial message: *Find out more about this woman.*

Bishop took another drag from his cigarette, turned to some Xeroxed pages on his desk and began studying them. They had been passed to him the previous night by his drinking buddy, Bill Ehrlich, and revealed that the CIA had been building up their own dossier on the mysterious lady.

"Reem Rudeniah is the adopted daughter of Ibrahim Rudeniah, a high-living Palestinian official who has been having an affair with an American secretary in Tel Aviv," he read. "She does not appear to have any other hobbies, except torture. Gaza contacts say she has made a detailed study of the Spanish Inquisition and has electronically refined what she has learned to extract information from mainly religious prisoners.

"She seems to have a deep-seated hatred for Christians."

Bishop's eyes then alighted on: "Wherever Reem Rudeniah goes, there are unsolved murders. In Gaza City, the local police found three pastors, who had been tortured, dead on the beach. It is thought that their bodies were dropped off there. "No proof was ever found to link her to the crime, but we suspect this is because of her high connections in Gaza. We know she was pretty high up in the Red Dagger organization."

The file spoke about Rudeniah's "new project." She had been seen in the company of several terrorist leaders and concluded, "She appears to be especially targeting the Provisional IRA for this plan."

Just then Fida walked through the door. She had shot a couple of rolls of film at Heathrow Airport, where Madonna had arrived on the Concorde from New York with her latest boyfriend.

"This stuff is dynamite," Bishop shouted across to her, as she took off her overcoat.

"What stuff?" Fida asked, as she walked over and ran her hands through his unruly hair. Normally, he would have exploded with anger at her action, but this time he had something more important on his mind.

"This file," he said handing it to her. "Do you remember Reem Rudeniah, that strange lady we met at the opera in Prague? Well, I have been looking into her. She's up to no good. She's a killer on the loose."

Fida felt all the blood drain from her face.

Arch Bishop turned his heavy eyes on Fida. "Do you know where Randy Burke is these days? I know that rogue has a special place in your heart."

Fida ignored the insult, and reached into her purse for her little black book. She flicked the pages and found Burke's home number.

"Do you want me to call him?"

"Sure. Tell him I would like to see him next time he's in London."

Fida dialed the Dublin number and was surprised to hear Burke's soft accent come on the line. "Is that the infamous Randolph Casanova Burke?" she asked provocatively into the receiver. "This is a friend from your dark past."

"I don't have a dark past," Burke responded coolly.

"Come off it, Randy daahling, we all know all about your treatment of a certain German businessman."

"Is that you, Fida?" he asked, breaking into a chuckle, adding, "How did you get my number?"

"That's not important," she laughed. "Arch and I were wondering when you are going to be in London next. We'd love to see you again."

* * * * *

Fida and Bishop sat in the lobby in the Park Lane Hilton Hotel facing the main entrance, waiting for their Irish contact to arrive. It was three weeks later and Burke was to be in London for a "business appointment." He had called her to meet afterward at 8:00 P.M. for a meal.

It was 8:15 and Arch Bishop was getting edgy and thirsty for a drink. Just then a page came over the hotel PA system for him. He left his seat and picked up a house phone and was told by the operator that "a Mr. Burke had called and said he wanted to meet them in the lobby of The Ritz in an hour's time."

Bishop decided to grab a drink to prepare for his meeting with Burke and went to the bar and ordered a double gin and tonic for himself and a glass of sweet white wine for Fida. He briefly nursed the drink, then greedily gulped it down and asked for a refill.

"Arch, be careful," warned Fida, knowing that the night was young, and one drink would lead to another, and another. That, she realized, meant she would have to once more drag him home and dump him on his bed as he passed into sodden slumber.

"Shut up, and relax," Bishop snapped. "You'll be seeing your Randy friend again in a few minutes."

After four more doubles, Bishop grabbed Fida's arm and snapped, "Let's walk to The Ritz." They headed out onto darkened Park Lane, the black cabs pulling in with their "fares." Fida breathlessly tried to keep up with Arch. They turned left at Piccadilly and walked toward the famed hotel.

"Welcome to The Ritz," said the door attendant as she saluted crisply and swung open the large door for them to pass through.

Bishop did not give another glance at the man, but Fida began to laugh uncontrollably. "What's so funny?" said Bishop, irked by her stupid behavior.

"Take a closer look at the chap on the door," she said pointing through the glass to the man ushering in another guest.

Bishop peered closely, but still could not see what was provoking Fida's laughter.

"It's Randy Burke, you dolt," she said. "What a loon he is."

Bishop pushed through the door and put his face closer to that of the doorkeeper. "Burke, is that you?" he asked, a bemused look sweeping his face.

"Mr. Bishop. How observant you are. Let's get out of here before they discover that I 'borrowed' this uniform from the regular man here. I gave him a few pounds to let me use it for a while. He's going to want it back soon."

Burke left to find a restroom to change back into his own clothes. He handed the uniform to the man waiting for it inside cubicle number two. The three of them then exited through the door of the hotel and flagged down a taxi to take them to Soho for an Italian meal.

As the candle on their table flickered, casting eerie shadows over Randy Burke's face, Arch Bishop looked at him as Burke studied the menu and said, "My friend, I wanted to see you again to talk to you about some information I have on the killers of your parents."

"You don't believe in small talk, do you Bishop?" said Burke as he looked up from the menu. "Still, it sounds like you have something important to tell me."

Just then the waiter arrived to take their order. At the next table was a well-dressed man who was intently listening to what was going on. It was Jeremy Brett-King, whom Burke had met with earlier.

Burke had told the British intelligence man then that he thought Rudeniah was beginning to crack and that she might be looking for a way out of the situation.

"Next time you go over to Prague, why don't you float the idea that she defect to us," said Brett-King, scenting a real coup for MI6. "I know you are due back there soon for the big meeting of *Operation Red Dagger* and that is when you must persuade her to leave.

"If we could get her here to London, we could pump her for some incredible information."

The waiter poured red wine for the three of them and then retreated to serve another table.

"Well, Archibald, you said you know who killed my parents," Burke said matter-of-factly, tentatively sipping the wine. "Who was it?"

Bishop paused for a moment, and then looked straight into Burke's eyes. "The Palestinians!" he said sharply.

The Ulsterman's eyes flickered for a moment and then he said with a grim, ironic smile. "Come off it, Bishop. It was a couple of guys from the Provos who did it. I've already taken care of them."

"Yes, that's as maybe," countered Bishop, nodding briefly, "but who was behind them? We all know that a Palestinian group is pushing your Provo colleagues into a situation where they are becoming dependent on them for money, arms and training.

"I now think I know who the person behind all of this is. If you really want to get revenge on the one responsible for the killing of your parents you should go after Reem Rudeniah."

Brett-King grimaced and nearly choked on his salad when he heard her name mentioned by the American journalist.

"I met her in Prague a few weeks back and I started to investigate her activities," Bishop continued as Burke exchanged a lightning glance with Brett-King. "She's definitely a psychopath who needs watching.

"Have you met her, Randy?" Bishop added as casually as he could.

"What makes you think that I have?" countered Burke, the lines around his mouth deepening.

"Because you're a snake who knows everybody," said Bishop. Taking the bottle of red wine on the table he refilled his own glass. "I happen to know she is involved deeply with your Irish friends and so I figure that you must know her." He added emphasis to his words by jabbing a finger at the Irishman.

"If I do know her, what interest is that to you?" asked Burke sharply. "And, anyway, I happen to know it wasn't she who murdered my parents."

"Maybe she didn't pull the trigger or plant the bomb, but she was certainly behind it," countered Bishop provocatively. "I would be willing to bet a day's supply of gin that she or one of her colleagues ordered the killing."

"Well, Mr. Bishop, what do you want me to say? Do you think I would tell a reporter like you the inside story of the link between Provos and Reem Rudeniah?"

"You're sure right, I do! You owe me more than one favor," blasted Bishop. "After all, I've given your cause a lot of free press in the past, and now I'm calling in my markers. I need you to get more information on Rudeniah. Are you in?"

Bishop paused briefly, and then added, "I am sure you want to know the complete truth about the death of your parents."

Burke looked at Fida who pouted at him and crooned at the Irishman, "Randy, I think you should help Mr. Bishop. Otherwise he will make my life a living hell. Working with him is already like playing Russian roulette with a loaded gun."

Arch continued to greedily gulp down the red plonk, followed by brandy that washed down the meal. He continued peppering Burke with questions, then, without warning, right in mid-sentence, Arch Bishop's eyes fluttered briefly and then he careened backwards, crashing to the floor.

The waiter helped Burke and the watching Englishman, revive Bishop, while Fida paid the bill and called for a mini-cab to take him back to his Barbican flat.

"I will need your help to get him from the taxi into his place," she told Burke. He nodded as they dragged Arch Bishop up to his apartment.

* * * * *

Brett-King found his temper burning on a short fuse the next morning as he waited for Randy Burke to meet him at the designated spot by the Serpentine in Hyde Park. November winds were gusting through the park as he swung his arms to keep warm.

"You would think they would set up a coffee stand here," he mumbled aloud as he again consulted his watch. It was 10:45 A.M. and Burke was already forty-five minutes late. Just as he was about to give up and return to his office, the Irishman ran up to him resplendent in a maroon jogging suit and white running shoes.

"Sorry, I'm late," he said, breathing heavily. "But I slept in after helping a damsel in distress. We had to put that stupid American to bed. As you noticed from your vantage point, he had a seizure. Something, I'm told he has regularly these days."

"Look, Mr. Burke, I believe the American could be of help to us," said Brett-King. "He's met Reem Rudeniah and so have you. Maybe, if Rudeniah does agree to defect, you could use Bishop to help bring her out. I can see that although his brain has been addled with years of drinking, he is still able to operate quite well while he's sober."

Burke bounced up and down as if still exercising. His breath popped in the freezing air. "I'm going back on December 19, for the final meeting for *Operation Red Dagger*. This is going to be a crucial meeting," he said.

"I am sure my silver tongue can persuade her to do the right thing."

Burke knew only to well that he was entering a shadowy world without boundaries. The question was, would Reem Rudeniah gravitate to the British plan like iron shavings to a magnet? Only time would tell, and time was fast running out.

19
A Funeral in Prague

The news wire clattered to life in the Fleet Street office of the *New York Tribune*. Arch Bishop's fuzzy mind normally paid scant attention to the infernal machine, but this morning he was waiting for an update on the bombing outrage by the Provos that had taken place in Portadown earlier in that day and had killed some seven people, including three school children and an off duty policeman. It had taken place as local children were making their way to school.

The machine spewed out the story and as the words zoomed across the paper, he leaned over to read the update of the bombing in the County Armagh town Portadown (which from the Irish language Port an Dúnáin means "port of the small stronghold.")

Bishop felt nauseated as he perused the story which also told of a police officer who had discovered the body of his mother in the rubble.

"The town was certainly not a stronghold today," he muttered to himself, after reading more details of how the huge car bomb that had "blown apart" those close to the blast.

The story ended with, *"The IRA today claimed responsibility for the bombing. A statement read by phone to our Belfast bureau, warned, 'We will continue our war in Northern Ireland against the occupying British forces.'"*

Bishop guessed he had probably met some of the bombers. He decided to phone Fida to get Randy Burke's hotel number to try to get more information on why they did it. Arch stopped dialing as Fida walked into the office, a red flush still on her face.

"Hey, Lady Tintagel. Thanks for showing up," he smoldered. "I know coming to work must interfere with friendship with half of the IRA."

Fida smoothed back her hair and said nothing.

Bishop was in no frame of mind for a continuing confrontation with her, so he violently ripped off the story and handed it to her.

"Read that," he said. "See what Burke, your lovely friend, and his comrades have been up to." With that he sat down heavily, a truculent expression on his face.

The color drained from Fida's face as she read the story. She had, of course, known of the bombing, but had not really taken it in. "I am sure Randy could not have done anything like this," she stammered. "He's too much of a gentleman."

"I seem to remember his gentlemanly behavior when he kidnapped and held a certain German industrialist," Bishop jibed. "He didn't seem much like a gent then; more like a sadist!"

Fida said nothing, deciding that she was not in the mood to cross swords again with Arch, who was battling the repercussions of his seizure on the previous evening.

"See if you can get that 'Irish killer' on the line," he ordered Fida. "Tell him I need to talk to him."

She obediently dialed the number of his Marble Arch hotel to discover that he was out. "Please tell him that Fida called and needs to talk to him urgently," she told the clerk.

"How do you spell that? Lady?"

"Spell it anyway you wish, daahling," she cooed, replacing the receiver.

* * * * *

"Well, Mr. Burke, what was your verdict? Is Ms. Rudeniah in the frame of mind to come over to us?" asked Brett-King who was standing shivering by the Serpentine Lake in Hyde Park. Randy Burke smiled at the MI6 officer.

"You don't beat about the bush, do you?" Burke said reproachfully, wearing a mask of bored innocence and jumping up and down to keep warm.

"I am sorry, Mr. Burke, but this is pretty important to Her Majesty's government," he said in a studiously cool manner, shaking his head and offering Burke a cigarette from his gold-plated container.

"No thank you," said Burke, sweating slightly, his breath rasping. "I have many vices, but smoking is not one of them. But to answer your question, I would say that she's right on the verge. She's about to crack."

"Was it the 'package' that did it?" asked Brett-King.

"That helped," said Burke, brooding on the question. "But I also believe the Almighty is on our side."

The Englishman was mystified, so Burke went on to explain. "During one long session talking with Reem in Prague, she came as close to breaking down as I've seen her. And she is a pretty tough cookie. I'm afraid I gave her too much vodka, and that seemed to loosen her tongue. She told me that Anatoly Rudeniah was her adopted father, and her real parents were killed by some of her Palestinians friends. She obviously felt some great guilt for that."

Burke's breath steamed in the cold air as he went on. "Reem was shaking when she told me how she had betrayed them and said she was constantly haunted by the face of her father and mother just before they were shot. She said that they constantly materialized before her in almost every dream she had.

"She even told me she had gone into a Prague church to be alone, and began to reestablish contact with God. I wondered though if it was to ask for forgiveness for all the people she had killed. If you ask me, she's a kook."

"She may well be a kook, Mr. Burke, but she's a very important kook. If we don't get her on our side, we may have a crisis on our hands that no Western government will ever recover from." The intelligence officer paused to allow his words to sink in, and then took a deep draw from his omnipresent cigarette.

"Do you believe this God business?" he asked casually. "Don't tell me that Reem Rudeniah has joined the Clean-Up-The-World Brigade."

"I wouldn't go that far," Burke chuckled, "but I would say that, 'God works in a mysterious way, His wonders to perform,' even with a killer like Reem Rudeniah."

Brett-Smith's face was now deadly serious. "We haven't got much time, Mr. Burke. The Vienna Summit is taking place on January 6 and so we have to get her here before then. The question is, "How are we going to do it, and when?"

* * * * *

Fida ducked as Arch Bishop's half-eaten pizza came whizzing across the office toward her. A plastic cup that spilled out Coke followed it as it flew through the air.

"You trollop," Bishop roared, red-eyed and visibly hung-over. "I ought to phone up Buckingham Palace and tell Queenie about your friendship with the IRA."

The pair had just returned to the office from a late lunch visit to the Stab and Fida had gleefully given the American a blow-by-blow account of the drinks she had enjoyed with Randy Burke after they had put him to bed.

Bishop hit back by delivering what he believed would be a blow to her ego. "I heard that no one in London takes an Irishman seriously unless the Irishman is armed," he chuckled.

Just then the office door was jerked open and Randy Burke peered around it, an enigmatic smile playing about his face.

"Is it safe to come in here?" he asked gingerly as he heard raised voices. It was not! Arch Bishop picked up a trash basket and threw it, yelling, with palpable hatred in his eyes, "You Irish murderer."

Burke reacted quickly, slamming shut the door. But he could hear from outside, as Bishop yelled, "Come here, you yellow-bellied Paddy."

The Irishman again opened the door slowly and responded. "Archibald, only if you stop throwing things at me. I'm afraid for my own safety around you. After all, I'm a young lad, totally unable to defend myself."

Bishop finally calmed down, unable to counter the Ulsterman's charm and, he pondered, why should he be upset about Fida and Burke?

"I promise to behave myself," Bishop said as Burke tip-toed in.

"Cross your heart, and hope to die?" asked Burke.

"Okay!" said Bishop.

Arch then handed Burke the Portadown story and asked for his comment. Burke scanned it then, looking directly at the American and said, "What do you want me to say?"

"I want the truth," Bishop said, pointing an accusing finger at the Irishman.

"The truth! What do you mean by that?" Burke countered, as he felt his jaw tighten. "I wouldn't think that was something you wouldn't know too much about."

Just then, the wire began printing out another story. Bishop walked over and looked at it, hoping it provided more information on the Ulster bombing. Instead it read:

DATE-TIME 06/10/94--03:15 P.M. COPY 01 OF 01 HUSDACK DEATH STORY.

+ NEWS FLASH + NEWS FLASH +

PRAGUE - The death has just been announced of the former Czech president George Husdack who, in December 1987, stepped down as Communist leader after ruling Czechoslovakia with an iron fist since 1969.

Husdack was 82 when he died. He had been replaced as Communist Party leader, by Milos Jacques, who oversaw the purge of nearly 500,000 Communist Party members after the Soviet-led invasion of August 1968, halted the liberalization begun by Alexander Dupkov, then party leader. Dupkov was finally removed from power eight months after the invasion and worked for a while as a Prague street cleaner.

Husdack had retained the largely ceremonial office of president.

"There will be a funeral in Prague within the next few days," said a Czech government representative. "We expect leaders from all over the world to arrive here to pay their last respects to our former president."

END OF FLASH

Randy Burke looked down at the story and an idea began to form in his mind. He turned to Arch Bishop and asked, "How would you like to have another world exclusive?"

"On what?" he hissed.

"I'm talking about a story with world-shattering implications. But you would need to come with me to Prague."

Bishop sat down and inquired with unsettling solicitude. "Tell me about this story and what it will cost me to get it."

Burke calculated, despite the friction over Fida, he had built up a good relationship with the American.

"Arch, why don't we talk alone about this," he said flashing a look at Fida that suggested she go for a walk. "The fewer people who know this bit of information, the better."

Fida huffily got the message, and left the room. As the door shut, Burke launched into his monologue.

"Archie-boy, you once mentioned the name of a lady called Reem Rudeniah."

Bishop nodded briefly as his eyes narrowed. "Sure did," he said opening the drawer of his cupboard, and pulling out a file with her name on it.

"The woman's a disgusting animal," he said. "She's also dangerous. I've been tracking his exploits and it seems like she can't stop killing people with religious beliefs."

Bishop then stopped. "But why do you bring up her name?"

"Before I tell you, I must have a written statement from you that nothing I now tell you is for publication. In fact, it is just for the two of us."

"You know me better than that," protested Bishop, a grim, ironic smile passing over his face. "You can trust me."

"I can," laughed Burke. "Since when?"

"Either you give me the written assurance, or I leave right now and you'll miss out on the biggest story you've ever been involved with."

Bishop reluctantly inserted a piece of New York Tribune paper into a nearby typewriter and typed out the required assurance for Randy Burke. He then handed it to the satisfied Irishman.

"Okay, now I want you and Fida to come with me to Prague," Burke said. "I will need your help Arch to get this woman Rudeniah."

Bishop immediately smelled a rat. "Why should you want Ms. Rudeniah to defect? After all, she's on your side."

Burke felt like smashing the American in the face. "Look, big-mouth, you have obviously drunk so much in the past few years that your brain is pickled," he said, throwing up his hands in exasperation. "My parents were murdered by the IRA. Even an idiot like you should be able to figure out whose side I'm on now."

With that, Randy Burke saw the light dawn in Arch Bishop's eyes. "Okay, Burke, let's talk some more," said Bishop, grinning weakly. "I think I get the picture."

20
The Border Wolf

The crackling fire cast ghostly dancing shadows around the room as the Provisional IRA War Council went into full session. The number-one item on the agenda was Randy Burke. Leading the attack against him was the sinister figure of Michael O'Hanlon, the Provo chief-of-staff. He sat menacingly at the head of the rough wooden farmhouse table in the very room where Burke had once held Klaus Wagner captive in a metal cage. O'Hanlon was a man in his early fifties, but his gray hair and well-lined face gave him the appearances of being much older. Burke anticipated trouble when he went missing for four days after returning from Prague.

"Where on earth were you?" growled the Provo leader vehemently in a heavy voice, his vizard looking even more fierce than usual because of a recently acquired green eye-patch. However, it actually only covered up a sty in his right eye. "We expected you back before now."

Burke glanced around the table at his fellow Irish killers. He tried not to betray the fact that his heart was thumping wildly and there was a queer feeling between his shoulder blades where a knife might easily be driven in. This inner circle of mayhem and murder, he conjectured, would not be the sort of men he would invite to a family picnic, if he still had a family.

Besides O'Hanlon, there was Belfast-Brigade leader Séamus

Muirghein, wearing dark glasses that concealed his cold brown eyes. This veteran of "war" had moved over from the original IRA late in 1969, when the big split took place. Next to him, a semi-permanent smirk on his face, was Sean McGrory, commander of the Armagh Brigade. His fiery red hair reflected his hot temper, which rose to the fore after he had consumed a belly-full of whiskey, which he did most nights. Seated at the far end of the room was Rory Mallon, his eyes bulging from behind steel-rimmed glasses. Mallon had planned the Enniskillen bombing and was the chief tactician for the Provos.

The final man in the War Council, which tightly controlled the activities of the Provos on both sides of the border, was Martin O'Connell, the public relations supremo and the only teetotaler of the assembly. O'Connell was bald with a tinge of gray hair around his head and had cut his teeth as the Provo publicist in the Bogside during the "Free Derry" episode.

Burke brooded for a moment, rose to his feet, and trembling slightly, started into his explanation: "Well, gentlemen" he said, his heart beating even faster, "can I begin by telling you about my visit to Prague? That went very well and everything is on track for the Vienna summit. The Red Dagger group has the necessary people in place in the various capitals to seize power when the strikes take place. As you know, my job is to 'take out' the British Prime Minister, Anthony Steele," he continued, now well launched into his own monologue.

"They consider him, and the American president, as the two most important 'hits.' They have a man to take out Lincoln Patrick and you will be interested to know that his name is Brent Fox, though I'm not so sure about him. He wore a diamond-stud earring in one ear and may be a queer."

O'Hanlon took a deep draw from his cigarette, sucked the smoke deep into his lungs, and then blew it out. A halo of gray smoke hung above O'Hanlon's head like a rain cloud over a tropical island. He allowed his visible left eye to narrow down to an ugly slit.

"That's all very entertaining, Mr. Burke," he pressed acidly on, a gruel predatory look on his face, "but we are still waiting to hear where you have been since you left Prague?"

O'Hanlon, like his colleagues, was not easily pacified. He folded his arms and opened his mouth revealing snaggled teeth that were yellow with nicotine.

Burke, lifted up his hands, feeling them tremble more than a little, and stammered, "I was going to get to that."

"Get on with it then," spat-out Mallon, a fierce scowling determination on his face.

Burke managed a watery smile. He knew he was treading on thin ice and had concocted a story he hoped they would swallow.

"Okay, okay," he bluffed, a flash of panic on his face. "I went to London. I found a man there in security who works at Number 10 and he gave me a briefing about where Hare will stay in Vienna and what arrangements they have made to provide him with protection."

The room was by now ominously silent and charged like the atmosphere of an electric storm. "This man - Bert Peters - is trusted by Hare and has been in on the planning for the summit," Burke continued. "I got his name from Reem Rudeniah in Prague and she suggested I go straight to see him.

"Peters lives in Lewisham, and I found him in the 'Bird in the Hand' pub on the High Street. I had to act quickly because time is running out for us. This is the most important project we've ever been involved in and I knew you wouldn't want me to waste any time."

Burke shot a knowing glance at O'Hanlon, adding what he hoped would be the clincher. "The information Peters gave me was pure gold. He even said I could take his place in the Vienna hotel as part of the British security team. As you all know, I happen to be quite good at disguises." Even as he spoke, his legs felt hollow, and a prickly heat - like a thousand tiny needles - jabbed at his chest and shoulders.

"But why would he cooperate with us?" asked a puzzled O'Connell, voicing the lingering doubts of the war council.

"That's simple," Burke replied, his voice rising strong and clear over them. "Peters is a convinced Marxist and was in the pay of the KGB and is now taking money from Red Dagger. He considers the elimination of James Hare to be a devastating blow to Western imperialism."

With that Randy Burke, anxiety gnawing at his inside, rested his case. He was acutely conscious that he was under observation from hostile eyes and his mouth was sour from the confrontation.

O'Connell's lip curled into a sneer, and indicated he still could not accept Burke's explanation. "Do you have any proof that this information is on the level?" he asked doubtfully.

Burke calmly took out his wallet and extracted a piece of crumpled paper and handed it to O'Connell. "You will see on this sketch the layout of the hotel where Hare will be staying. The arrow indicates which room he will make his headquarters and where his security men will be stationed. I will be with these men for the **final kill**. And, gentlemen, I will have the privilege of pulling the trigger."

Burke paused briefly for breath, and then pressed on. "I am well aware this will be a suicide mission, but like all of us here, I am prepared to die for the **cause!**"

A hushed silence greeted Burke's words.

"Very good," said O'Hanlon, grinding his cigarette into an ashtray that he had lifted from the Dublin Hilton. "I think we accept your explanation." With that, Randy Burke's chest momentarily lightened.

O'Hanlon looked down at his typed agenda and added sardonically, "Right, gentlemen, let's move on to item two, Mick Moynihan, alias *The Border Wolf.*"

A shiver ran down Randy Burke's spine as he thought about Moynihan, a psychopath who was once the leader of the Falls Road cell of the Provos before he had left to form the even more vicious International Army of Irish Patriots (IAIP), which wanted an old-time Albanian-style Marxist-Leninism in a united Ireland. When they had first met during a planning session in West Belfast, Burke was chilled to the bone by the man's cold eyes. It was a case of hate at first sight for Randy Burke. He knew Moynihan would stop at nothing to achieve his goals.

"We need a volunteer to eliminate this cocky man," said O'Hanlon slyly. "He's going around with his gang of thugs picking off our people and then leaving the logo **EH** on their bodies." (The logo in question was the initials of his hero, Enver Hoxha, the late Stalinist leader of Albania, a country that proudly had declared it to be the "world's first atheist nation.)

"We are becoming a laughing stock among our own people. If we don't crush Moynihan quickly and completely now, he will continue to get popular support from the people, and we just can't have that. There is only one Army that can represent the aspirations of our Irish people." His voice dripped contempt for the debased times he had lived to see.

The chief-of-staff gave a speculative gaze around the table hoping for support in favor of his statement. He was pleased when the others loyally nodded in agreement. Burke had found himself caught up in a raw power-struggle between the old and new guard. "Now, do we have someone to take care of this Wolf?" he asked, a name Moynihan had been given by the Irish police because of his cross-border activities.

"What about you, Burke?" asked O'Hanlon, posing the murderously perfect question and turning his piercing one-eye on Randy. "You've said you are willing to die for the **cause**. This could be the penultimate feather in your cap before the big one!"

Burke looked nervously around the table. He knew he was cornered and felt a wave of anxiety wash over him. The room made him feel quite claustrophobic. He took a deep breath and let it out slowly.

"Of course, sir," he said, struggling to keep his voice from rising. "I'd be honored to get rid of this piece of vermin. The world would be a better place without rubbish like him." Burke pretended to be sanguine about what he knew would be a deadly mission.

O'Connell voiced the gratitude of the others, but warned, "Burke, you'd better be careful with Moynihan. He's so cold; he'd kill his own mother if the urge took him. I was with him when he was in charge of the Falls Road. He'd put a bullet in your head, no questions asked, then eat the ham and cheese sandwiches you had in your pocket."

"Yes," interjected Mallon, smiling broadly, his glasses by now halfway down his nose, "he used a hammer and chisel to chop off part of the fingers of that Dublin doctor he kidnapped in his surgery and held for the 200,000-Euro ransom.

"Then he mailed the fingers to the doctor's wife with the message, 'It will be his right foot next if we don't get the money by next Sunday.' She raised the money and got him, and his foot, back."

A smile darted, lizard-like across Mallon's lips, and snickers rang around the room, but Burke was not smiling. He knew the incredible danger of his mission.

"Do you know," said McConnell, "one of our men tailed him to a fish and chip shop in the north of Dublin where he watched him, and his wife, Eileen, go inside and then come out. They had an argument, and Moynihan pulled out a gun and shot her in the thigh."

"Why?" asked Burke, a puzzled look on his ashen face.

"Well, he was heard to say to her, 'I told you I wanted two portions of cod, not one.' After shooting her he put the pistol back in his green parka and walked to his car, leaving her writhing on the floor."

"The man's an animal!" snarled McGrory, his strong-featured, freckled face coloring red.

"That's quite a statement coming from you," commented the public relations man, giving a short, mirthless laugh.

"Well, now we have a 'volunteer,' I believe tomorrow will be just fine for the assassination to take place," said O'Hanlon. We have information that he is going to try to rob the Farmers Bank in Enniskillen High Street at 11:20 A.M.

"Be there, Mr. Burke, and blow him away. But first let him get the money and then, after killing him, take custody of it for us."

* * * * *

Randy Burke found his nerves wound up so tight they were ready to snap. In an escalating, dreamlike sense of terror, he almost decided not to go ahead with he hit.

"Why can't I live a normal life like most decent people?" he asked himself as he strapped on his bullet-proof vest in his car on the outskirts of town just ten miles from the Republic's border. He knew that once he got close to the bank, he would have to stay in his car until the last moment. The town had a control zone and, if a car was left empty or unattended, a warning siren was given and the town center cleared. If the driver was found, he received a hefty fine; if no one claimed the vehicle, the Bomb Squad moved in and it could soon be blown to pieces.

With the protection in place, Burke checked his watch. It was 11:30 AM. He then made sure his AK-47 was well hidden in a special compartment under the back seat. The assassin knew he would have to go through the Army checkpoint on the edge of town and he soon came to it.

"Open yer boot?" ordered one of the six young British soldiers at the barrier.

"Certainly, sir," said Burke, carefully getting out of the driver's seat and inserting a key in the trunk. A cursory check by the young soldier revealed nothing untoward and Burke was told, "Close it up and get on yer way."

Burke licked his dry lips. Another wave of nausea enveloped him, but still he forced himself to press on. He had become accustomed to the sleepy face of bankruptcy of such towns in the North and did not give a second glance at the Royal Ulster Constabulary police station cowering behind elaborate gates and high barbed wire, tented with steel mesh to guard against homemade bombs being lobbed over the walls. He drove past a weary cluster of cottages, in need of a lick of paint, onto Church Street, past a series of bombed-out buildings that had once been the nicer part of the street and onto High Street. Burke parked across from the bank, by a sign that read, **PEACE THROUGH SUPERIOR FIREPOWER**.

It was now five minutes before the scheduled robbery was to take place. Burke leaned over to the back seat and pried free his firepower that he hoped would *not* bring peace to Mick Moynihan. No one noticed his action, so he slipped the weapon onto his knee, covering it with his heavy raincoat.

Burke turned on the radio hoping it would calm his near-shattered nerves. He allowed a jittery smile to cross his face as Jimmy Young's chirpy West of England voice from London coming over the airwaves of BBC Radio Two, stated he would be "spinning" his one-time hit, "Unchained Melody."

As the song began playing, Burke spotted a blue Ford Escort glide toward the bank. There were two figures in it; one was definitely Moynihan, though he did not recognize the other. In a blur of movement, Moynihan, pulled a ski mask over his face, withdrew a sawed-off shotgun from under his parka, and dashed into the bank.

Randy Burke, his heart hammering in his chest, started his car and hung a U-turn, ending up a few yards behind the getaway vehicle. He did not switch off the engine, as the driver had not noticed him. The concentration of the accomplice was aimed at the front door of the bank as he nervously revved the engine.

In seconds, the jangling bank alarm went off and Moynihan came dashing out carrying a briefcase bulging with money.

As he did, Burke stepped out of his car and, in a heavy, husky voice, shouted, "Hey Moynihan, over here!" The "Wolf-Man" hesitated for a moment, and stared at him in an almost hypnotic state. That was long enough for Randy Burke to whip out the AK-47 rifle and squeeze the trigger, blasting the bank robber with a hail of bullets. Moynihan lay crumpled on the sidewalk in an ever-increasing pool of blood. Burke then turned his weapon on the driver. Blue fire roared from the barrel into the open side window, blowing the back of his head off and leaving him slumped over his wheel, blood pouring from terrible head wounds.

With both men dealt with, Burke snatched up the briefcase from the sidewalk and shouted to the dying Moynihan, "Hey, 'Wolf-Man,' you lived like an animal and now you can die like one." He guessed the man could not really hear him, but still the words gave him a savage satisfaction. He laughed aloud and punched the air in triumph.

Burke jumped back in his car, slammed the stick-shift into reverse, backed a few yards, and jammed it into first gear and flew forward, turning right at the corner, disappearing down a side alley. His head was thudding so much that he did not notice the crowd that was beginning to assemble around the two blood-sodden scene.

He guessed there would be many happy people in Ireland today. But none was happier than he!

21
A View From the Mirror

Randy Burke's face broke into a grin of satisfaction as he spotted the unmistakable figure of Reem Rudeniah waiting for him as he came through to the barrier by the baggage carousel at Prague International Airport after collecting his suitcase from his Dublin flight. She was clad in an expensive brown fur-coat and a fur hat was perched firmly on her head.

"Ms. Rudeniah, I feel honored," Burke responded warmly as an aide took Burke's suitcase and guided them out to the waiting Mercedes limousine. Its engine gently idling, heat flowed cozily through ventilators into the plush interior of the beautiful limo. The car seemed, to Randy Burke, to be like a luxurious living room on wheels.

"I didn't realize I was such a VIP," Burke chortled as he sank comfortably into the back seat and unwound the plaid scarf around his neck.

"Believe me, you are!" Reem remarked affably, deliberately closing up the window between herself and the driver.

"You are the first to arrive for our little tête-à-tête and I wanted to make sure you were properly welcomed."

Burke knew Reem must have read the message that had been slipped under the door of her Prague apartment by a "janitor," who was actually a staff member of the British Embassy. It read, "Will arrive flight 101, Aer Lingus, 3.00 P.M. for meeting. R.B." The scrawled handwriting added, "Destroy this note."

As it had dissolved in the crackling flames of Reem Rudeniah's fireplace, the message set her mind frantically thinking about Randy Burke. The Irishman claimed to represent the Provisional Wing of the IRA, yet something about him did not ring true. He was too freewheeling. Did he actually represent a Western intelligence agency and, if so, which one?

It was late afternoon and the last weak rays of November sunlight were fading into the Prague gloom, as the car swept through massive gates into the Hradcany Castle complex, which encloses the Cathedral of St. Vitus and the 14th-century chapel of St. Wenceslas. The brakes squealed as it drew up at the side of the ancient castle. The high walls of the castle perched on the left bank of the Vlatava River looked positively medieval to the Irishman.

Burke noticed six men posted at the main entrance to the castle, who he guessed were private security guards she must have hired under the auspices of the "Middle East-West Friendship Association," the name she had used to book part of the Castle. Under the gaze of their austere eyes, the pair got out of the car.

"They obviously enjoy their work," remarked Burke brightly, inclining his head toward the shivering men. "You can tell by the permanent smiles on their faces."

Reem did not appear to hear; she was wrapped up in her own thoughts. She had to somehow discover if Burke had a hidden-agenda and if so, for whom?

"Would you like to join me for dinner?" she asked casually, as they reached Burke's room in the castle. "I know a pleasant little Hungarian restaurant just a few minutes brisk walk from here."

Burke said that would be "very nice" and walked through the door that Reem had opened for him. It was the same neatly furnished quarters he had been billeted in a few weeks earlier. A settee was at the far side of the room, along with a fancy twin bedBurke went over to the wash basin and began splashing water over his face.

"Let's meet downstairs at the main entrance in half an hour," suggested Reem tentatively. "That will give you time to freshen up."

* * * * *

Reem Rudeniah was irritated with the Gypsy violinist who would not move to another table, but kept scraping away at the cat-gut with his rendition of the Hungarian Rhapsody. It finally dawned on Reem that the man was waiting for a tip.

She reluctantly reached into her purse and thumbed through it. She pulled out a $20 bill and stuffed it into the man's top pocket, expecting a grateful "Thank you, ma'am." Instead, all she was rewarded with was a scowl, which indicated he would have much preferred a little more. But, at least, the "tip" had the desired result. The infernal fiddler moved to another part of the restaurant, which was unusually full for the time of year.

"Husdack's funeral has brought a lot more people than normal to Prague," explained Reem.

Eventually two plates of goulash were laid in front of the pair and they began eating.

"Mr. Burke, you may have noticed that I am a direct person. I don't, how do you say it? Beat about the bush."

"I had noticed," chirped Burke while taking a mouthful of goulash. "When we first met, I realized you had not read Dale Carnegie book on 'How to win friends...' although I must admit you do have your own way to 'influence people.'"

Reem ignored the barbed comments. "Mr. Burke, I have reason to believe you are not all you say you are," she continued pointedly, her brow darkening. "You appear to be playing both sides of the fence."

Burke chewed on the well-cooked meat, wondering what was coming next. He listened intently as Reem pressed on.

"In fact, my guess is you are working for MI6. You are much too smooth to be just a part of that moronic Irish group."

Burke paused reflectively, smiled and responded innocently, "Ms. Rudeniah, how could you say such a thing about my wonderful Provo colleagues? They are truly kindly people who only want to help their downtrodden Irish compatriots."

He wiped his mouth with his starched white napkin and declared ironically, "I guess they are about as kindly as the security men shivering outside the castle. They love their mothers and treat their children kindly.

"Well," said Reem as she continued undeterred, "I'm waiting for an answer to my question. Just whom do you represent?"

Burke paused briefly, and then replied, "If I do work for someone else, why do you want to know? Is there a special service 'we' could perform for you?"

The Palestinian tried to remain calm, as she began to see her chance at escape from this mess. Then she decided to throw caution to the wind. "Yes, you can get me out of this impossible situation," she blurted out. She was caught in a straight jacket and needed the Irishman's help to get unstrapped from it.

Burke kept his gaze firmly on the Reem Rudeniah's classic face. "Randy - I can call you Randy? - I recently took a long look at my life and I didn't like where I was headed. I need to get out...now!

"I have gone through a change in my life," she said tentatively. "I met this man called Beckett and he was so incredibly brave and remained firm to his beliefs, that he got me to think about what I was doing with my life."

Burke looked intently at her. "And what conclusion did you come to?" he asked, keeping his eyes locked on hers.

"I came to the conclusion that there is a spiritual dimension to life and I have been exploring that. I have decided that this is the path I must now take now.

"But that now causes me a serious problem. I can't go through with the project. But I don't know where to go to escape from this dreadful situation."

The Irishman knew Reem was no longer hiding behind her normally stiff mask. Although Burke could tell the woman was still just in control, she had become vulnerable. Still, Burke guessed the steel that had been put into her character through years of training, would carry her through her ordeal.

"Mr. Burke," she went on, her face hot and burning, "I know you lost your parents in Belfast, so you will understand my feelings about my own mother and father.

"I got brain-washed so badly that I betrayed them," she said, as the words tumbled out, unmasking her deeply held feelings. "They both died a terrible death, and I am to blame! How can I ever forgive myself?

"We must act fast if we are going to stop the 'plan' that is about to be put in motion. I must get out and warn the West about what's going to happen. If I don't, we'll have a massive problem on our hands.

"To sum it up, I guess what I'm saying, Mr. Burke, is that I suspect that you are the only person in Prague who can help me."

Burke pondered for a moment, and then broke his silence. "Reem, I might be able to help you. In fact, because of Husdack's funeral, this is a good time for you to escape.

"I believe I can set up a situation which will make people feel you are leaving one way, and then you can slip out, completely unnoticed."

For the first time for weeks, Reem Rudeniah's face relaxed, and an expression of almost indescribable relief flowed across it. Her need for a way out was beginning to become a possibility.

* * * * *

When Randy Burke returned to his room at the castle, he took out his pocket radio and turned up the sound. He was surprised to hear Johnny Cash's "A Boy Named Sue" coming in loud and clear through the speaker. He opened his bulging briefcase and brought out a lightweight radio-transmitter hidden in his shaving bag and slipped it into an inside pocket.

He again headed out of the front entrance of the castle, and ducked into a nearby alley where he switched it on and spoke into his wallet pocket.

"This is one, is that you two?" he asked into the microphone as quietly he could. After a brief silence, the answer "affirmative" came back.

"Plan one is go for tomorrow afternoon. I said go. Understood?"

"Affirmative!"

With that Burke switched it off and walked back to the castle.

* * * * *

Arch Bishop heard a faint ringing in his ears and as he stood by the door, then felt an unexpected wave of vertigo. Fida was able to grab him and stop him from falling over.

"Here, open the door," he slurred, groping in his pocket for the room key and handing it to the photographer. Bishop's hands shook uncontrollably as she took it and inserted it into the lock. Fida was becoming increasingly worried about Arch. He was losing weight at a frightening rate and looked malnourished, the result she thought of giving up most forms of food except coffee, sugar and, of course, alcohol.

"Arch, you've got to slow down on the booze," lectured Fida as she led him across the room and laid him out, fully clothed, on his bed. "Otherwise, you'll kill yourself."

The American heard what she had said, but his mind was numb from another epileptic fit brought on by alcohol. It would be hours before he would feel himself again, but he would have no recollection of what had happened the previous night. Bishop was past the state of retching nervous spasms, sweaty and sleepless nights; dehydration, matched with moments of terrifying panic. He was actually getting a little better; his attacks were down to one or two a week.

He needed to have a crystal-clear mind to cope with the events about to occur. The question was, would he?

* * * * *

William Franklin was turning in for the night in room 861, on the floor above the Arch Bishop. It had been an interesting day for the preacher. After attending the Husdack funeral along with an array of world leaders that included British Prime Minister, Anthony Steele and German Chancellor Gertrud Schmeling, he had conducted discussions with top brass at the Czech Ministry of Religious Affairs about his proposed crusade in Prague.

"I thought it went well," he told Grady McKeown, his loyal advance man. "It still amazes me they would allow a country-boy like me from the ol' U.S. of A. to preach the Gospel in a former communist state."

"You shouldn't be amazed, sir," said McKeown respectfully. "After all, think of all the publicity value it is to them. It isn't really a high price to be able to share your life-changing message with the people of the Czech Republic."

McKeown turned to look at his leader who possessed the looks of a film star and said softly, "There will be some criticism," he added, "but still I guess that won't stop you. Being able to address a nation and talk face-to-face with its leaders is quite a coup. You're probably the only preacher in the world they will listen to."

As Franklin took off his purple silk robe and climbed into bed, he opened his large leather Bible and began reading out loud, Matthew 7, verse 7, "Ask, and it will be given you; seek, and you will find; knock, and it will be opened to you." He closed his Bible and said to McKeown, "We've asked and knocked on the door and now they've opened the door for us."

McKeown nodded his head in agreement. He found it paid to always agree with his leader. The generous salary he received made him pliable.

Before retiring to bed, and McKeown moving to his room next door, Franklin asked McKeown seriously, "Why am I returning to Vienna by bus?"

"Because there are no flights tomorrow that would get you into Vienna in time for tomorrow night's crusade meeting. The bus leaves at midday and arrives in Vienna at 5:00 P.M. That'll still give you time to freshen up before you preach."

Franklin was satisfied. He would use the bus ride to prepare his sermon.

22
A Bus Ride to the Border

The final planning meeting of *Operation Red Dagger* was called to order by Reem Rudeniah with a bang of the gavel on the heavy oak table. It was 10:00 A.M. and, outside the double-paned windows, snowflakes began to dance out of the gray, curtained heavens.

Among those sitting around the table in the special conference room at the Castle was Brent Fox of the American Weather Underground, Randy Burke of the Provo's, Pierre Rowlands of the French Black October group, Guiseppi Pacino of the Italian Red Fist, as well as Carlos Rodrigues of the Basque Separatists and George Markos of the Greek Liberation Organization (GLO).

"I'm afraid Heinz Borman missed his flight from Bonn, but he'll be here later in the day," Reem reported matter-of-factly. "I thought we could make a start. I trust you are all in agreement."

They all nodded and so Reem handed out the agenda to each of the killers sitting around the table.

"While you are looking at this, let me thank you on behalf of my friends in Gaza City for coming to Prague," she said, a false warmness in her voice. "This is an historic meeting which could see the destiny of the world turn in a new direction."

No one spoke, so she continued. "Maybe we could start with each of you bringing us up to date on your plans for the Vienna summit," continued Reem, whose mind was far from the Austrian capital.

"Let's start with you Mr. Fox. I think we'd all be interested to know how you plan to eliminate your president."

Fox played with the diamond-studded earring in his left earlobe and went over to the blackboard set up at the top of the table.

"Patrick hasn't got a hope," he began, a deep hatred flashing in his eyes. As the American outlined how he had been able to bribe a member of the hotel staff to become a room-service waiter during the summit, Reem allowed her mind to drift back to his breakfast meeting with Burke a couple of hours earlier.

They had found a quiet corner in a large room that had been set up at a restaurant for the group, where they took their coffee and Danish pastries. "Well, Mr. Burke, were you able to talk with your people about what we discussed last night?" she asked as Fox walked into the room.

Reem acknowledged Fox with a wave, but gave him a look which indicated that they did not want to be disturbed. The American took the hint and poured himself some coffee and sat down with Rowlands.

Burke sipped his coffee and eyed the Palestinian beauty. "Now, I have to ask you one question before I answer yours."

"Go ahead," said Reem quietly.

"The people I have spoken with want to be assured that you are not setting them up. They want to know if they help get you out, that you are going to tell them all you know about the people behind Red Dagger."

"I understand their concern," said Reem. "I would ask the same question if I were in their place. Mr. Burke, I am deadly serious. I have to get out and I will totally cooperate with them.

"But," she added, "do not waste anymore time."

Burke could see the stress in Reem's face and felt, for once, she was telling the truth.

"Okay," said Burke, a slight cynical smile playing on the edge of his mouth, "I know you have acquired a deep interest in religion, so we have arranged for you to become an Archbishop of the Greek Orthodox Church. During this morning's opening session you will have to feign an illness and I will help you to the room you have reserved for yourself during this meeting. I'll tell them we will try and meet later in the day and you will then put on a servant's disguise I'll give you to get out of the Castle.

"Turn left and keep going to The Loretto restaurant where you will be met by one of our people who will pull up in a green Fiat. Get into his car and he will take you to a place where you will change into your priestly robes, and he will give you a Greek passport."

Reem listened attentively. "But what about you, Mr. Burke? What will happen to you?"

"I will be taking a bus journey to the Austrian border with an American evangelist," he chuckled. "When we get near to the crossing-point, a tip-off will go to 'your people' that you are also on the bus. That will create a diversion, while you leave via the airport."

A wave of apprehension swept over Reem's face. "But isn't that going to put you in great danger?"

"Of course," replied Burke. "But that's the name of the game. If this plan is to succeed, there's going to be risks for all of us."

* * * * *

Fox was obviously enjoying having the floor among this room full of professional murderers. After half an hour of droning on, he concluded his presentation with, "Ms. Rudeniah, I wish to thank you for the great privilege of being able to do away with Johnston. During my many years in prison I dreamed of striking such a blow against our ludicrous leader."

With that, Fox brandished his fist in the air and shouted, "Power to the people."

All those around the table shouted the words in unison. Reem shivered briefly as she looked at Fox. It seemed the man had liquid oxygen in his veins.

Burke then began his presentation. "We, in Ireland, are glad to join with you all in this unique 'restructuring' plan," he said in his soft Ulster brogue. Burke stood by the blackboard chalking up the floor plan of the Vienna hotel where James Hare was to stay. Suddenly, Reem began moaning loudly and toppled backward off her chair and onto the floor.

Perspiration beaded her forehead and her eyes fluttered wildly, as if she was having a fit. Burke dashed over to where Reem lay and knelt down beside her and mopped her perspiring brow. Pierre Rowlands joined him.

Burke felt Reem's pulse and remarked, "It's still there, but we better get her to her room and let her rest for a while. I guess she's been overdoing it lately."

Reem's eyes opened momentarily and Burke inclined himself close to her. "Reem, are you all right?" he inquired with unsettling solicitude.

Reem attempted to speak, but was not able to form any words.

"Okay, Pierre, let's get her to her room and postpone the meeting for a while until she is feeling better," suggested Burke.

Both men lifted the Palestinian woman to her feet and, as she groaned, she put his arms around their shoulders. Breathing heavily, Reem allowed herself to be guided slowly down the corridor to her room. There they lay her on her bed.

"Do you want me to get a doctor, Reem?" Burke asked warily.

Reem shook her head weakly. "No, let me just lie here. I'll be fine," she whispered.

With that Randy Burke signaled to Rowlands that they should leave and let Reem take a rest. "I think I'll take forty winks myself," said Burke. "I'm really bushed. What about you, Pierre? Why don't we all take a break as well?"

Rowlands agreed that that was a good idea and returned to inform the others and then went to his room. When Burke felt the coast was clear, he returned to Reem's room with the costume, then back in his own room, put on his overcoat, picked up his briefcase, and headed for the main entrance.

The shivering guards standing there saluted crisply, making no attempt to stop him, believing he was just leaving for a few minutes.

* * * * *

The Vienna bus was about to pull out from the Prague bus terminal when Randy Burke banged on the door.

"Hey, let me on board," he yelled breathlessly.

Arch Bishop spotted the frantic Irishman and shouted to the driver, "Hey, guy, let him on board. He's with me."

The driver heard and pulled the lever that operated the door and Burke leaped on board.

"Where have you been?" Bishop called out loudly, as Burke made his way down the aisle.

"Sorry, but I've been busy," responded the Irishman. Gasping for breath, Randy Burke walked toward the empty seat across from Bishop and Fida.

As he took his seat, he had not noticed the American evangelist, who occupied the seat behind him and Fida and was deeply engrossed in his Bible.

"Hi, Mr. Preacher," shouted Bishop over his shoulder. "Hey, you're slumming it a bit, aren't you? No QE2 this time?"

Fida slapped him on the arm. "Arch, you're an uncouth slob. Don't drag everyone else down to your gutter level."

The Irishman looked across at Bishop, who had not shaven and had well-defined black circles under his eyes. "Arch, baby, you look terrible."

"I feel terrible," Bishop responded gloomily.

"Did you bring the garment bag I gave you?" Burke cut in urgently as the crowded bus began to pull out of the terminal and make its way through the snow-covered streets of Prague.

"Yes, it's up there," replied Bishop, eyeing the luggage rack above his head.

Burke smiled with satisfaction. "It looks like we're in for an exciting trip."

* * * * *

The telephone pinged at the border post and Jan Novac, the head honcho, quickly snatched it up.

"Yes," he snapped curtly.

"Jan, this is Prague. Vlad speaking."

"Hi, Vlad, how's the wife keeping?"

"Look, Jan," said the official standing at his desk and ignoring the question from his former schoolmate, "we've got an emergency on our hands. There's a tourist bus heading your way and we have reason to believe a dangerous Palestinian lady is on board. Her name is Reem Rudeniah.

"Make sure she doesn't get away. At all costs, don't let that bus through until you have picked her up. I can't tell you anymore."

Jan looked down at the receiver as the line went dead. He got on the loudspeaker and asked all guards to report to his office.

As ten armed men stood before him in their heavy gray greatcoats, he told them that the bus had to be searched thoroughly and Reem had to be found.

Meanwhile, on the bus, Burke looked with squinted eyes at the snow-covered landscape and guessed they were getting close to the Austrian border. There were fewer houses and the fields were getting increasingly bare. Soon the lumbering bus pulled up to the crossing point, and a young guard ordered everyone to disembark.

The Irishman told Bishop they should let most of the people get off the bus before they made their move. The driver had already alighted and was helping passengers onto the icy pavement, when Franklin began to walk down the aisle.

Suddenly Burke made his move. He pulled down the garment bag, unzipped it and drew out a Kalashnikov rifle. He came up behind the American evangelist and pointed it at his head. "Don't move Mr. Preacher and you'll be okay," he said ominously. "We need your body to get us out of this place."

Bishop then grabbed a rifle from the bag and another for Fida, which he threw to her. He then moved to the front of the bus and into the driver's seat. In a split second he pulled the lever and slammed the door.

"Hey, open the door," yelled one of the guards angrily. "Open up, or we shoot."

Burke pointed the firearm at Franklin's head. "You shoot and he's dead," he yelled loudly at the guards so they could hear him.

Turning to Arch Bishop, Burke shouted, "Get this bus out of here." The reporter turned the ignition key and pressed the gas pedal to the floor. The bus began to slew wildly in the slush and struck a guard standing nearby sending him spilling to the floor.

Other guards responded by opening fire and bullets rained through the windows. The bus continued to skid toward the red and white border pike, and Burke shouted to Fida, "Get Arch's weapon and use it."

Without questioning the order, Fida took the weapon. She slipped open a window and picked off a guard who was running madly after the bus. All he felt was a cold circle at the base of his skull. He died without knowing how or why.

Bishop felt a surge of adrenaline in his bloodstream as he crashed through the first pike. A hail of gunfire followed the bus. Again the vehicle skidded crazily and William Franklin slipped awkwardly to the floor.

Fida, who was not experienced with a rifle, also began to stumble. As she fell, the weapon went off, hitting the preacher in the arm. He crashed heavily to the floor, hitting his head violently on the metal step by the seat. Franklin lay in the aisle with blood pouring from the wound, spoiling his neatly starched white shirt. He was all twisted up like a rag doll.

"My God, I've shot the evangelist!" she screamed.

With that she dropped the rifle and sank beside him joined by a panic-stricken Grady McKeown. Franklin was already unconscious. He would miss that night's crusade rally.

Bishop whooped with frenzied excitement as he crashed through the second border pike and arrived in Austrian territory. He kept going through the Austrian border until he was well into the new country, and then put his foot heavily down on the brakes.

"Wow," he screamed, "I haven't had so much fun since I went on the roller coaster at Coney Island when I was a kid."

With that, William Franklin continued to struggle for life and Arch Bishop came alive.

The bus came to a screeching halt when Bishop spotted a helicopter put down a few yards in front of him.

"Go for it," shouted Burke. "These are my friends."

Burke, Bishop and Fida exited the bus and ran toward the waiting helicopter, leaving the evangelist and his aide still on board.

Soon they were soaring heavenwards and, as they looked down they could see a cluster of Austrian border guards running toward the bus. "I hope they can do something for the preacher," said Fida.

Bishop said nothing. He was still thinking about his bus ride over the border.

23
The Cross is Victorious

It had been a long day for George Hus at Prague's international airport at Ruzyne. He checked his watch. It was 3:45 P.M. and there were just fifteen minutes to go and then he could get off and be able to have a drink. Hus vainly tried to suppress a yawn as the bearded face of "Archbishop Petra Makarias" appeared below his immigration desk.

Wearing the black armband all officials had been given, Hus dutifully ruffled through the pages of the Greek cleric's passport and compared the photograph in it with the "Man of God" standing there. They looked similar, but to Hus's jaundiced eyes, all Greek Orthodox ecclesiastics looked the same.

The Czech official then checked over the list of VIP's who had come to the capital for the Husdack funeral. The Archbishop's name was there and so he sharply checked it off as "departed."

"You were here for the funeral then, sir?" Hus asked wearily as he stamped the passport and returned it to the "Archbishop."

"Yes," "he" replied nodding "his" head. "It was a very moving occasion for all of us who had the privilege of attending. Mr. Husdack was a great leader. He will be sorely missed."

"Not by me," Hus was tempted to mutter, but he managed to restrain himself.

The "Archbishop" appeared calm as "he" headed through to the security check, but "he" had an uneasy feeling of possible failure. Had "he" been betrayed? Was "he" heading into a trap? The paranoia, however, was unjustified, for the security man waved "him" through and soon "he" was boarding Olympic Airlines, Flight 6, to Athens. The glue holding the heavy beard in place itched terribly and "his" heart pounded unmercifully as "he" found "his" seat in the first-class compartment.

The steward tried to engage him in conversation, but the "Archbishop" smiled and said nothing. What could "he" say? "His" command of the Greek language was almost nil!

Within a few minutes, the Boeing 707 swept down the runway and rose rapidly into the clouds. No one was seated next to "him" and "he" closed "his" eyes, experiencing a curious mixture of relief and dread. "The Archbishop" pretended to go to sleep, but smiled, realizing the severe repercussions for the former associates still at the Castle. However, there was no going back now! The vigil of waiting was over.

* * * * *

Jeremy Brett-King was waiting nervously at the Athens barrier, a red rose resplendent in his buttonhole. He proffered his hand to the fake Archbishop as "he" appeared and said, "Welcome, 'sir.' We are glad you were able to make it. We have an RAF plane standing by to take you to London. First you will need to get out of your theatrical outfit."

Like a person emerging from a deep fever, Reem was guided to a reserved room, where Brett-King handed her a well-cut two-piece dark suit and other items of feminine apparel. The elegant Palestinian gingerly pulled off the beard and gladly discarded her garb, which Brett-King stuffed into a suitcase.

She then went into the bathroom and splashed cold water over her perspiring face. She was still in a daze. Things had moved so quickly, but she did not regret what she had done. Yet....

Some ninety minutes later, as the Royal Air Force plane hovered in the darkness above Northolt Airport, Reem could see from her window the lights of a steady stream of cars heading like lemmings out of London on the A40.

"We are landing just to the west of London," explained Brett-King. "Once we are down, we will go to a house we have reserved for you where we can talk. I am sure you have a lot to share with us."

Reem said nothing and kept her gaze on the bumper-to-bumper traffic below. She guessed by now there would be panic at the castle and the men would be fleeing to the airport to catch flights out of Prague. She opened her purse and silently handed a handwritten note to Brett-King. It contained a full list of all those who had attended the terrorist summit.

Brett-King studied the names and smiled grimly. "Thank you, Ms. Rudeniah. There are some surprises here. We'll alert the airports to watch out for these men."

A black Daimler drew silently up to the jet after it had taxied to the spot where it was due to unload its important passengers. As soon as the stairs were propped up to the exit, Brett-King stepped out of the plane and led the way into the blustery evening. The gray-clad chauffeur held open the back door of the car for the pair to climb in and the magnificent machine then began to glide out of the airport and across the countryside for a thirty-minute drive to Old Windsor, where the hideaway was located in a mock Tudor house at the end of a long drive.

Reem noted two men armed with automatic rifles standing at the entrance to the property and she cast a quizzical glance at the

Englishman.

"They are here for your protection," explained Brett-King. "After all, you're now a hot property. Your friends in Gaza will not be at all pleased that you have defected."

Reem laughed sardonically, knowing that these two men would provide sparse protection against the "sleeper" groups already in place in London. She knew they would soon be instructed to find and destroy her.

The Palestinian was ushered into the house and taken into the dining room, where three men were already seated. They rose in unison to greet her.

"These are 'friends' from the same organization I belong to," explained Brett-King. "They speak fluent Arabic and will join us for our meal and conversation."

The trio extended their hands and Reem shook them and sat down at the seat offered her by Brett-King. "I hope you like roast beef and Yorkshire pudding, Ms. Rudeniah," he said warmly. "It's one of our few national dishes."

A video camera set up in the far corner of the room had been recording from the moment that Reem entered. The Palestinian did not express surprise; she would have done the same if he had been in Brett-King's position.

A surreal feeling swept over Reem as Brett-King produced a chilled bottle of red wine and was about to pour some of it into a glass and was surprised when she refused it. "I have given up drinking," she explained.

Brett-King then told the waiter that the meal should be served. The Palestinian tried to clear her head. Just a few hours earlier, she had been chairing a meeting of terrorists in Prague, now here she was in the south of England, with a group of Englishmen she had never met before, all wanting to extract the critical knowledge that she possessed.

Reem took a tentative sip of a glass of water that had just been poured for her and then waited for the questioning to begin.

Brett King peppered her with questions about Red Dagger and other terrorist groups that had similar aims of driving the Israelis into the sea. She answered each one as honestly as she could.

Reem then picked up her knife and fork and began cutting up the meat on the plate. She was about to put a portion in her mouth when the door opened and the large figure of a man walked into the room.

Reem felt a chill criss-cross her body and she dropped her fork onto the table. It was Anatoly Rudeniah, who said quietly, "Hello, my dear. I expect you are surprised to see me here."

The younger Rudeniah was speechless. Her lower jaw was locked with shock and hung almost to the carpeted floor. It took a full minute before she could speak. "What...what are you doing here?" he finally asked.

Her stepfather went to her side and put his arm gently on Reem's shoulder, but she froze. He realized that she must know more than he had hoped.

"Reem, I don't know what you've heard about me, and I know I have been living a double-life for years," he said. "But I've been no different to our so-called brothers in arms. They have said all the right things, but have stolen blind from the people.

"The whole thing has been a terrible farce, but we all played the game to survive."

Reem still did not utter a word, so he kept on speaking. "I've known for a long time that our system was evil and wrong. I realized I am no longer a Palestinian in spirit, and I can no longer defend our position while pretending to act objectively. I had become a robot to a cruel master, and I had to put an end to my mental double life.

"I began working for Western agencies some three years ago and, when I learned you were going to defect, I took the same decision. I wanted to be near you at this time."

"But what about Mother?" interjected Rudeniah, who had listened in silence. "Where is she?"

The older man looked sadly at his protégé. "I'm afraid she's still in Gaza. She would not come with me. She considers me a traitor, someone who has betrayed the cause. She believes traitors should be shot and she would now willingly pull the trigger on me. We haven't really loved each other for many years. We were just going through the pretense of being husband and wife for the sake of my career."

Reem stood up unsteadily and walked toward her stepfather. "Papa," she sobbed, "I can't believe how all of us have been involved in one huge charade. And, so many have died because of us. I don't know if I can ever love you again, but I'll try to forgive you."

The funeral in Prague had brought the pair back to life again. They had emerged from a dark shadowy world without defined boundaries, to face an uncertain future as unpersons.

* * * * *

Arch Bishop pulled up the barstool in the Stab and ordered up a "g" & "t" and lit another cigarette. A week had passed since the escape from Prague. Reem's sensational story had run as the Tribune's lead story for days.

"Hey, Bishop, I understand you're a national hero in Small Town, USA," said Frank Bramble. "If you're buying, I'll have a pint of Watneys bitter."

Suddenly Bramble's eyes were drawn to the bar TV, perched above the drinking area, as Reem Rudeniah's figure appeared on the screen.

"Hey, isn't that your Palestinian friend," he yelled to Bishop. "Turn up the sound, George."

Bishop watched Reem being interviewed on the early evening news by Sir Robert Knight, the veteran interviewer of everyone who was anyone.

"Aren't you afraid for your life?" Knight asked Reem, who looked decidedly uncomfortable.

"Why should I be?" she retorted.

"Because I have just received news that the leaders of all of the West's terrorists groups have been arrested at airports all over the world," he said. "I understand the sweep took place as a result of your information."

Reem's face twitched slightly. "Well, I guess that's the price I will have to pay. I've signed my own death warrant and I will be on the run for the rest of my life.

"Still, even if I die, hundreds of millions will live because of my actions."

Bishop's eyes were glued to the screen. He was watching a woman whom he had so despised, a sadist, a traitor to her country, yet a person who, in the end, had finally done something worthwhile with her life.

He eyed his glass with the "g & t" still fizzing in it. He did not feel like getting drunk tonight, not yet at least. Maybe there was more to life than booze. Because of that funeral in Prague, the old Arch Bishop had begun to die. The question he had to answer was, "Would there be a resurrection?"

Two weeks later, Arch Bishop nervously stood in front of a circle of fifteen men and said firmly, "Hi, my name is Arch, and

I'm a recovering alcoholic." A ripple of applause broke out; the loudest came from Lady Philda Tintagel, who had talked him into joining Alcoholics Anonymous. "After years of trying to kill myself, I've finally gotten smart and decided to go on the wagon."

The American told his story to the others saying, "I drank so much that even among the other reporters, I stood out like W.C. Fields at a temperance meeting. And that's saying something!

"Now, with your help and support, I'll stay off the booze. I'll take it one day at a time."

When he finished, Bishop sat down, struggling to hold back the tears. Lady Tintagel gave him a thumbs-up sign and he nodded back in response.

"I'm proud of you," she mouthed. "Very proud!"

* * * * *

Randy Burke smiled to himself and instructed Brendan Murphy, a Dublin taxi driver for five years, to "pull in by the British Airways sign." Murphy touched his cloth cap and checked his rear window mirror. When he saw it was safe, he flicked on the indicator and pulled his cab to the left.

For the umpteenth time, Burke nervously pulled out his travel wallet containing tickets to Tortola in the British Virgin Islands, via St. Thomas, and his new British passport under the name of George Scott. In just a few hours, he would start a new life in the sun. There would be no more intrigue or danger; just lots of sun and lying on golden beaches.

Murphy opened the trunk of his cab and swung out the heavy suitcase. As Burke handed him a five-Euro note, Murphy tipped his cap and, in a broad Dublin accent, said, "Tank you sirrrr." The words froze in his gullet as he saw two hooded men jump out of blue Ford Escort that had pulled in behind his.

"My God," he shouted with a reflex jolt of panic. "Don't shoot me. I'm a married man with two small children."

"Shut up, you idiot," one of the men thundered. "It's not you we're after."

"Mr. Burke, it's time to go," said Sean McGrory hoarsely, pointing his Kalashnikov machine-gun at him and squeezing the trigger. Six 7.62 mm rounds from the Kalashnikov tore into his chest. Burke made a very short glottal sound of surprise as his eyes bulged and blue fire continued to pour out of the barrel and into the Irishman's body, ripping scores of bloody holes in it.

Covered in blood, Randy Burke slumped to the sidewalk. Behind him was a sign that read, "Cead Mile Failte," meaning, "A hundred thousand welcomes to Ireland."

His world went gray, then black. He could do no more - BUT DIE! There would be one more funeral in Belfast, and he would be the guest of honor. For Randy Burke "the troubles" were, at last, over.

* * * * *

Reem Rudeniah was startled at who her guard, George Jones, had discovered at the front door of her "secret" hideout in Chelsea. "It's a Yank," he shouted to her. She went to the door to find Bill Ehrlich standing there. She had been set up by MI6 at a house just off the Kings Road and had been given a new identity and a British passport.

"Mr. Ehrlich," she said, as he stood there, smiling, "please come in. What can I do for you?"

The CIA operative followed her into the living room of the beautifully appointed house. His eye caught the sight of a print of

William Holman Hunt's famous picture Christ holding a lamp and called "The Light of the World" hanging on the wall.

"Beautiful, quite beautiful," he muttered.

"I am sure you didn't come here to admire my picture," said Reem.

Ehrlich allowed himself the pleasure of a smile. "Yes, you're right, honey. I've come to offer you the chance to fly with me to Jerusalem. I want you to see the city that you have so wanted to destroy."

Reem was shocked with the invitation. She never dreamed of ever being able to visit to Israel again.

"Don't worry about the danger," he said. "We will employ a man who is a master of disguises to help you, so you will not be recognized. And, anyway, all of your former colleagues in Red Dagger are now safely under lock and key."

* * * * *

Before the half-asleep security man could stop her, Reem quickly clambered over the fence surrounding the olive trees in the Garden of Gethsemane. She then stood by one of these ancient trees and was transfixed as she remembered the last night of Jesus and what He was about to do for her and all of mankind. She recalled from her childhood of reading how Jesus was under severe pressure in this very place while he struggled in prayer - releasing his burden to the Father's will: "if possible, let this cup pass... yet not my will, but Thine be done."

Reem knew that also she had to release her burden. She knew that the killings had to stop and she allowed her mind to summon up the times her parents had read the Bible to her in their cramped apartment in Gaza City. How, she wondered, had she allowed herself to become such a monster.

By now, the guard had noticed her and yelled, "Hey, lady, you shouldn't be in there."

"I know," she smiled. "But I couldn't help myself."

She then climbed back over the fence and moved into the Basilica of the Agony church at the side of the garden and knelt before a cross at the front of the sanctuary and began to pray. "Jesus, I want to repent of all the damage I have done to Your Kingdom. But I need to know if I can be forgiven for all the terrible things I have done. Please show me if your cross truly is victorious."

Suddenly, an overpowering joy rushed into her mind. She felt clean for the first time in many years. She then rose to her feet a huge smile enveloping her face.

She did not notice a priest who silently watched her. He smiled as if understanding what she was doing. He was right, for shortly afterwards, she found the faith she had been so long been looking for.

He went up to her and asked, "What is your name?"

"Reem Salameh," she said firmly, emphasizing the surname of the family she had long ago denied. "Yes, my name is Reem Salameh." She had finally been re-born - twice! But now she knew that the cost of this re-birth could be very high. Reem Salameh would be hunted for the rest of her life.